Don't Poke the ⊔⊔⊔ ⊥⊥

by

Ted Dunphy

Canaan-Star Publishing

First published by Canaan-Star Publishing, United Kingdom.

www.canaan-star.co.uk

A Catalogue record for this book is available from the British Library.

ISBN: 978-1-909484-22-1

Book cover design © Kerry Miller and Eugene Rijn R. Saratorio.

Printed and bound in United Kingdom by Lightning Source, (UK) Ltd.

Dedication

To Sorcha, Zack, Killian and Neve
My four 'little monkeys'.

You showed me the delight of
'telling stories from my mouth'.

The Fire

Sunday 4th January 2015 – Rowan Moon

I fell into the open fireplace on my birthday. The others said I was lucky the fire wasn't lit. I needed two showers to wash the ashes out of my hair, excessive for a man who showers only once a week. The taste of ashes was in my mouth for days. No one believed it was the uneven stone floor of the pub that brought me down.

Cyril the Anglican Druid said my tumble was like a spiritual birth and I was raised from the ashes a new man. His twinned religions make him come out with stuff like that. Cyril suggested once that we should spit-roast an ox in that open fireplace to celebrate some druid festival. We might roast a small pig, but not an ox. Why would we roast anything when Basher Brannigan serves mass-produced 'home-made food' behind the bar?

Basher glowers at us when we arrive each Sunday night. He glowers at everyone, a skill acquired over many years as a member of Her Majesty's Constabulary before he had to abruptly leave the police. He still regards himself as part of the long arm of the law reaching out to smash criminals. His belief in the effectiveness of brutal interrogation has not left him. It shows itself in his disdain for the public who are now his customers.

The pub reflects the owner's hostile attitude. Genuine plastic oak beams are pitched low enough to assault customers over the height of 5′11″. The uneven nature of the stone-flagged floor is a trap for those who are balance-challenged after a night of heavy drinking.

There are rules. Basher hides the poker before we arrive each Sunday night. By the time we reach the pub, the fire is a mesmerising mound of redness with small blue flames licking around the edges. We are forbidden to touch the fire. Rule number one is don't poke the fire.

Disagreeing with Basher is banned under his second rule. Like all authority, he has his opinions and allows no others. When we suggest facts that challenge his views, he resorts to personal abuse, which is always more telling than logic.

Rule number three: drunkenness is not tolerated if it involves embracing drinkers not known personally to us. As a result of some unfortunate experiences during his time in uniform, he dislikes strangers finding common cause. Two pints each, the sum total of our Sunday-night drinking, is insufficient to cause inebriation. I learned at my retirement party last year that it is the drink poured into you beforehand that causes the damage. The group kettled me in a corner by the fire so that I kept my embraces to myself and avoided Basher's wrath.

The fire compensates for the disadvantages of the pub. It is the focus of our fascination, a dream world peopled by our imaginations as we gaze into the pulsing glow. Two benches stretch out from either side of our fire, like harbour walls reaching out, offering a safe haven from the storms of life. The fire and its benches draw the five of us together each Sunday night. Between the benches we find calmness and the certain knowledge that those invited to steer into this harbour are on our side, even if they crowd our anchorage sometimes.

Uninvited docking alongside our fire is as welcome as a Spanish trawler anchoring among the British fishing fleet off the coast of Scotland. Strangers intruding into our space are fended off as if they were marauding pirates.

The fire is more than the centrepiece of the pub to Cyril our Anglican vicar. As a practising druid, the proper balance of fire, earth, air and water are important in his version of the cosmos.

The Commander (RN Rtd) says the fire is confirmation that he has sentenced to be ashore. The Navy has little truck with open fireplaces, especially aboard nuclear submarines, where the Commander spent most of his service. When they decommissioned his boat, he said, they marooned him ashore, washing him up on a desk, a castaway on the desert island of paperwork. He stares into the fire, reliving the feelings of power he had when his finger on a button could have sent China cartwheeling into space and nuclear oblivion.

Pete the Gristle squats on a low stool in front of the fire. It reminds him of sitting by his campfire when his father made him live for a year in the woods at the back of their house. During that year he learned to fend for himself. The experience also bred in him a disregard for washing, disrespect for private property and a disdain for the practices of normal society.

Card Index Hathersage regards the fire as his personal bum warmer. Stretching up and down on his toes, with his bottom to the fire, gives him an edge when it comes to pontificating and talking through his arse. Much of the time we let him gabble on.

They call me Green Goalie, GG for short. I hide in the shelter of the company gathered around the fire. I prefer the smell of a turf fire, with the sea murmuring in the background, but exiled and hunted fugitives can't be choosy.

By late Sunday night, we expect that the early diners will have left for a bed, or to have sex. We treat late departures with the same resentment residents of seaside towns show day trippers loitering in their town before going home.

The pub is our meeting place. The space in front of the fire is our conference area. It is the birthplace of the

Venerables Ninja Retribution Front (VNRF). As the founding members of the Front, the five of us lead the opposition to the discriminatory treatment of retired people, or Venerables as we prefer to call them

When we formed the Front we underestimated what we were creating. Who would have thought our efforts would escalate so quickly to a touch of law-breaking, the occasional act of violence and a threat to national security? Well, actually, our efforts grew to be a smidgen more than the occasional act of violence. To condemn us for law-breaking would be harsh. Readjusting the scales of justice is a more accurate and benign description of our activities. We never intended to pose a threat to national security. But then, I never meant to fall into the fireplace. Shit happens, as Gristle was fond of saying, even when it is not planned.

My task is to keep a record of our activities. The Commander says 'the Captain's Log' is vital in any operation. Card Index agrees. He has an obsessive need to gather and tabulate information if he is to function properly. Gristle doesn't care what I record as long as I don't describe him as a nice person. He has worked hard to create a piss-poor public image that any miscreant would be proud to own. Cyril the Druid requests I use star signs and phases of the moon to record the 'time path' of our movement. He gave me a two-year-old *Moonwise* calendar to help me with this task. Only Cyril would think an out-of-date calendar would be of useful.

I was appointed as 'the Keeper of the Cosmic Log', as Cyril calls me, because on my last tax return, looking for a different occupation to add this time, I opted for 'writer, author,' hoping it would mislead the Revenue into accepting the piddling amount I falsely listed under earnings. Being the chronicler of our group is my punishment for lying. I will suffer even more if the supermarket bosses, or Basher, or the dangerous characters who run our country catch us.

Our smouldering fire is a sharp reminder of where I may eventually finish up.

The Supermarkets' Indifference

Sunday 11th January 2015 – Rowan Moon

Bottle Blonde and Skinny Slug, her husband, were still in the bar when we arrived at the pub tonight.

You could describe Bottle Blonde as brassy, big-busted, braying, bouffanted, in your face and vulgar; not a woman to invite for a quiet drink on a Sunday night. Hearing that woman up close could be used as mitigating circumstances in your murder trial if you killed her. Being in the vicinity of that mouth in full flow is like feeling the air-shaking approach of a train at an underground tube station.

Skinny Slug trails after her, eyes scanning the ground, head bowed and tilted slightly to the side, as if listening for any word of wisdom blasting out of that mouth of booming sound.

Each Sunday night, Bottle lingers long over her raucous goodbyes to Basher, all the way from the corner of the bar, where she parks one of her breasts while drinking a pint, until the door closes behind her. The sound of her voice diminishes as she crosses the car park, like the fading roar of a jet taking off into a night sky.

Tonight, she bumped into the Commander as he was on his way in and she was leaving. He checked his condition to make sure he was not holed below the waterline, corrected his course, took a deep breath and sailed towards the safe harbour of our fireplace. A frailer man without the Commander's experience of a lifetime at sea, with his thumb on the nuclear button ready to destroy the world, would have foundered like a holed trawler sinking in a Force 10 gale off Iceland. He said their collision was similar to the lurching feeling of a docking ship glancing off a quay.

The Commander once deliberately bumped a Russian nuclear sub in the Barents Sea in a naval exercise to demonstrate the superiority of the Royal Navy. Listening to the Commander, you would believe he pulled back the Iron Curtain and dismantled the USSR single-handed. Being bumped by Bottle Blonde, feeling her soft flesh wrapping around his fenders, was much scarier than bouncing off the steel hull of an enemy nuclear sub, he told us.

Apart from Cyril the Druid, none of us wanted any detail of how it felt to be bumped by Bottle Blonde. Such information was too delicate to be voiced to a group of retired men in a pub on a Sunday night.

Gristle proposed lodging a formal complaint and a request that Basher bar Bottle Blonde on Sunday nights. Cyril the Druid opposed the motion, expressing a strong desire to physically encounter the soft, yielding protrusions of the big-busted woman. Card Index put forward a compromise motion that Cyril the Druid should act as a buffer between Bottle Blonde and the Commander. I protested that each of us would welcome the services of Cyril as a buffer, not just the Commander.

My motion was carried, to the delight of Cyril the Druid. He promised to commit himself, even to the point of martyrdom, to thrusting his body between Bottle Blonde and each of us on Sunday nights. He would be our body-buffer, he said, fending off her large bust, like a tyre protecting a quayside against a poorly piloted docking ship. I imagined it in more in terms of Cyril throwing himself against the walls of a bouncy castle.

Cautioning restraint in matters of sexuality and physical contact is wasted on Cyril. Sexual activity with women as a way of being at one with Mother Earth was a major attraction that led him to be a druid, as well as being our local Anglican vicar. His 'God's Nature Church', as he calls it, looks less like a congregation and more like a harem. Not knowing any druid theology, we are unable to dispute the link he claims between religion, Mother Earth and women cavorting with him.

His crusade to convert women to his conjoined faiths has borne fruit in the increasing number of female followers in his Anglican congregation. Even when he was in hospital last summer for a hernia operation, he recruited the ward sister to his church and 'inducted her', as he calls it, in his screened-off bed in the pre-op section. He was in the Day Unit for the operation, without the luxury of time on his side. We exercise little influence over his practices other than to advise caution and a degree of restraint, at least in recognition of his age.

The comfort of the fire eased the turbulence caused by Bottle Blonde and her frontal assault on the Commander. Fire is like that, soothing and relaxing as the heat works its way through clothes and the skin, easing its way deep into bones and seeping inside minds. Soporific and sated, we were content to sit and stare into the fire, enjoying this retreat from the world.

Gristle brought us back to earth. He told us of the recce of the biggest of the local supermarkets by himself and Card Index. The staff were hostile and the store was not a good environment for Venerables. Both facts make the store a likely target for the Venerables Ninja Retribution Front.

Gristle is our forager and intelligence gatherer, the Commander is our strategist and Card Index is in charge of logistics. Cyril, because of his two religious affiliations, is the public face of our campaign to protect Venerables. His role would be more effective had he been Nigerian and a bishop, along the lines of Bishop Sentamu in York or Desmond Tutu in South Africa. Their way of talking makes them sound sincere and the red and scarlet of their robes contrasts well with their dark skin. Cyril's wild hair and staring eyes do little to inspire confidence, but they win over women who think they can tame him.

Gristle reminded us that we already knew about the supermarket's tricks of putting cheaper items on high or low shelves out of the reach of the elderly. Ambushing shop assistants to ask where they have hidden common items is tiring. They mutter through the pen grasped between their teeth, 'try aisle 5, if not there it might be in aisle 11, 2, 14 or 7, or it could be out the back, or out of stock'. Or they offer to guide, move off too quickly, leaving those on shaking legs unable to keep up. They take the enquirer around the store, back to their starting point and leave the Venerable in a heap and not a seat in sight.

Gristle expanded on the seat issue. 'Hardly a seat in the place,' he said. 'If you need a rest you have to wait until you pass through the checkout. Then you can sit on the low windowsills, but often those are full of empty boxes. I did a survey of the Venerables who were in the store—'

'How many?' Cyril asked.

'Three. An old couple were pushing a *very old* woman in a wheelchair. I spoke to them, not the one in the wheelchair because she was unconscious or maybe asleep. When they need to rest they lift the old lady out of the chair, lay her on the floor in the corner by the cider display and they take it in turns to sit in her chair.'

Card Index butted in at that point. 'While Gristle was talking to the old couple, I spotted the store manager, except it wasn't him. They use a lookalike person to walk around the store because customers attack anyone wearing a 'manager' badge. The real one hides in an office upstairs. You only see him if you pee in your pants in the dairy section, take off all your clothes or shout you are a shoplifter as you run out of the place.'

'Did you meet him?' the Commander asked.

Card Index nodded. 'I sent a message telling him I had compromising photos of his wife and would publish them.'

'A lie like that could have backfired,' I said.

'It wasn't a lie,' Card Index said. 'Cyril gave me the photos. She is one of his lot. You remember her, the one on that trapeze bar thing, the blonde one, wearing only high heels and a bandanna.'

Cyril smiled at the image. 'Gretchen, he means.'

'Her,' Card Index confirmed. 'The manager met us and demanded the photographs. There are plenty more on my computer. He refused to listen to our grievances and suggestions for what the Venerables need. He had both of us thrown out. That security bloke, the one growing out of his shirt and uniform, with the short hair and the bad breath, he bundled us out without any regard for our dignity.'

We sat staring into the fire, picking over the scene Card Index and Gristle had painted. The Commander was the first to speak. 'He had his chance. Ignore a shot across your bow and you take the consequences of the next salvo.' He gritted his teeth and pursed his lips after he said it. He does that with his teeth and lips when he wants to show he is serious. I bet he looked like that the time he was about to annihilate China. The Venerables Ninja Retribution Front was on a war footing.

Death Threat

Sunday 18th January 2015 – Rowan Moon

A voice from the bushes by the car park hissed my name as I approached the door of the pub. The Commander shushed me to silence when I pointed out he could just as easily use the toilets in the pub.

'It's not that. I don't want that woman to see me,' the Commander whispered.

'Which one?'

'Bottle Blonde.'

'You're hiding from her?' I asked. This was the man who had sailed rings around the Russian Navy in the Barents Sea, won several war games against the American Seventh Fleet Submarine Force and had saved the world from nuclear disaster when he couldn't open the safe holding the launch code to blow up China because he had left the key in his cabin. Fortunately, the communications hitch with London had been ironed out before he returned to his command post with the key. China was spared for another day.

He looked down his nose at me. 'I'm going to kill her.'

Even from the Commander, this was unexpected. 'You can't,' I said.

He grunted before shifting his attention back to the pub door. 'Why not?'

'Not in the car park. The police will cordon off the pub for weeks. We won't be able to buy a drink. Every fox and every dog in the area will be licking up her blood in the car park for months. Think of all the shit they will leave. Basher will go mental. He will bar you and the rest of us.'

'I don't mean kill her here. This is a surveillance point.'

'Oh,' I said. 'That makes sense.' I waited with him,

11

watching for any sign that his prey was coming out. I saw Card Index walking up the road and stood up to wave him over to us.

He took in the Commander and me huddled in the bushes. 'Have you two got women in there? That's Cyril's game.'

'He's going to kill Bottle Blonde,' I said, in what I thought was a conspiratorial tone.

'Good, about time someone did.' He crouched down with us, staring at the pub door. 'What about Skinny Slug? You snuffing him as well?'

The Commander breathed evenly and waited a while before answering. 'I think not. He hardly talks. You have to give the man credit for that.'

'Why do you want to kill her?' I asked.

'Her mouth could cause the death of a hundred and thirty-five men on a Vanguard submarine,' he answered.

That was a good reason to kill her if all those men would be saved from a terrible death. I thought of the glowing fire and our pints waiting for us in the pub. 'Should we go in now?' I suggested in a quiet sort of way, not wanting to lessen the Commander's bloodlust.

'Give it a few more minutes,' he said.

Card Index shuffled around to get a view through the window of what was going on in the pub. 'How would her mouth kill all those chaps?' he said. 'She might deafen them. That's not the same as killing them.'

I could feel the Commander stiffen beside me. He looked like he was struggling to find words. Eventually, he answered. 'Once,' he paused and took a shuddering deep breath, 'once, we were on manoeuvres in the Pacific with the Yanks and were challenged by their top sub to a game of seek and destroy. Silent running, the winner was the one who manoeuvred behind the other with a clear kill shot.

Best of three. Score was one each. Decider being played. We were almost there and…' He stopped.

Whatever happened had brought disaster. I could tell by the way he caught his breath and stopped talking. Dear God, I thought, there was never any mention on the news of a submarine loss when the Commander was captaining a Royal Navy nuclear sub. But the powers that be would hardly announce the destruction of one of their subs with all hands lost.

The door of the pub opened and a booming burst of sound shook the air and rushed towards us like the front edge of a rainstorm howling across the sea. Bottle Blonde, followed by Skinny Slug, was on her way out. The wave of sound washed over us. Bottle and Skinny scrambled up into their G-Class Mercedes, slammed the doors, cutting off her noise, before roaring out of the car park.

Inside the pub, a dejected Cyril the Druid greeted us. 'Where have you lot been? I was ready to throw myself in front of Bottle Blonde to protect you. I kept her talking as long as I could but she had to go. Skinny Slug has to check out his massage parlours before it gets too late. What kept you?'

'Thinking about killing someone,' Card Index told him.

'Oh, ok. Go and sit down,' Cyril said to him. 'I'll bring over your drinks. Gristle will be here in two minutes. You two can tell us what you found in the supermarkets since last Sunday.'

Gristle bustled in on time, settled himself with his pint before Card Index started their report on their latest reconnaissance of the enemy store. 'It took us all week to get this information, but our evidence base is secure and our judgements are sound.' He speaks like that. He used to be an Ofsted school inspector. That experience also accounted for his preoccupation with tabulating information on a portable card index system, until we persuaded him to buy an app for his computer and phone that would do the trick much better.

He started his balancing act of stretching up and down on his toes, his bum to the fire. 'Most Venerables shop on a Wednesday, hundreds of them clogging up the store. Gristle and I found there are no special offers in the store on a Wednesday, other than 2for1 deals that are no use to Venerables; own-brand item shelves are emptied and there are fewer staff on duty to give the useless help you expect in these places. As a result, Venerables pay more for their shopping than the young 'uns shopping the rest of the week.'

'The Venerables should switch days to beat the system,' the Commander said. Always the strategist; you look for that in a hunter-killer submarine commander.

'Not that easy,' Gristle took up the story. 'The store puts on special free buses to collect Venerables from the care homes – only on a *Wednesday*. For those living by themselves, *Wednesday* is the day most of them collect their pension. They need to spend it quickly before their home help and family members steal it from them.'

Gristle nodded to Card Index to continue. 'The store knows Wednesday is the day the Venerables are funnelled into doing their shopping. They take advantage of it by removing anything that will save money for the Venerables. That way they boost the profits of the store.'

'What Card Index didn't say,' Gristle added, 'is that he was assaulted by one of the staff, who dragged him away from some Venerables he was interviewing. He was taking notes but that does not justify being manhandled. Then that security brute, Bad Breath Bailey, dragged him to the entrance and threw him out with everyone watching.'

'It's not the first time,' Card added.

Gristle took over again. 'Some Venerables tried to interfere, only Bad Breath pushed them out also, shouting they were not wanted. There was a lot of booing and shouting. Shoppers were upset at seeing Venerables being treated so badly. No one could do much because Bad Breath is too big. Most of them rushed back to their shopping, or the bus laid on for them would have left without them if they were late. They have no way of getting back to the care homes by themselves.'

The comforting warmth of the fire took a long time to work its relaxing ways with us as we listened to this account of infamy and dastardly actions that took advantage of vulnerable Venerables.

We waited on our orders from the Commander. The Venerables Ninja Retribution Force was about to leap into full-frontal assault on the forces of mammon, supermarkets and Bad Breath Bailey. We were on that level of alert the Commander knew from his days of going periscope to periscope with the Russians in the Barents Sea. Stealth would be our hallmark, the Commander told us, as he outlined his plans for retaliation. Even we were surprised at the richness and the swiftness of the responses he proposed. With a brain like his on our side, it was no wonder we won the Cold War.

Later, when I was walking with the Commander across the car park, I plucked up courage to go back to the conversation with him earlier in the evening, anxious about the terrible tale of slaughter I expected to hear. 'What happened with the Yank?'

'When?'

'The time you were about to beat him at the game of seek and kill subs.'

He took a deep breath and released it in a loud sigh.

'We were within feet of lining up a killer shot, the winning shot, when my Logistics Officer passed wind, loudly.'

'He farted?' I said.

The Commander nodded. 'Noise travelling through the hull and water is like a hammer hitting pipes. The Yank was alerted, dived and came around behind us. We had to concede defeat. They won 2:1. We were ridiculed every time we met them after that.'

'What about the bloke who broke wind?'

'I court-marshalled him. I put him ashore in chains on the supply ship two weeks later. He never sailed in a sub again. Acting irresponsibly in a conflict zone leads to the death of all aboard. That woman reminds me of that fart every time I hear her.'

Disruption at the Store

Sunday 25th January 2015 – Ash Moon

Cyril was late tonight. He looked peaky when he hurried in, muttering about a heavy workload of church services, preparing for new moons and welcoming some Brigid goddess in his Druid religion. In just over a week, he will be up to his eyes, to mention just two of the body parts that will be active, as he celebrates the start of spring with his harem. He rambled on about cross-quarter days and the symbolism of Imbolc dark moons. I asked him if it would be easier to avoid the Customs and Excise men on dark-moon nights, until the others told us to shut up. They have no need to watch for the Excise men. If there is such a thing as a dark moon, it might be possible to dig up the container load of illegal Romanian whiskey buried in Matty McGrath's pasture.

Cyril was disappointed to discover his service as a Bottle-Blonde-blocker would not have been needed, even if he had been on time. She had left early with Skinny Slug to sort out a fracas at one of Skinny's massage parlours. A bloke from Dudley had kicked off because he genuinely wanted something done about his bad back, not realising it was the sort of massage parlour where your back was the last thing they handled.

We turned our attention to a couple who were sitting on our seat in front of the fire. In spite of a few not so subtle hints, they had not moved. Their obduracy offended Cyril and increased his irritation at having missed the chance to throw himself at Bottle Blonde's ample bosom.

Gristle advised patience. 'Look at the sweet and sensitive way they are gazing into each other's eyes and holding hands. Obviously they are in love. Isn't it delightful? Give them a few more minutes and that bloke will drag her out to his car and shag her silly.' He turns to crude comments when he is trying to be sensitive.

The suggestion that sexual activity would take place without involving Cyril increased his agitation even more. 'We have a right to those seats. It is our fire,' he hissed.

'It's my fire,' Basher said across the bar where we were standing glaring at the couple. 'They can stay if they want. You lot can share the fire for once.' He turned to me. 'It's your turn to pay tonight. Don't give me one of your dodgy credit cards or you will be banned again.'

I bridled at such insulting charges uttered aloud but handed over one of my genuine cards. It doesn't do to antagonise Basher. His years as a police inspector, before his abrupt early retirement, had given him a nose for dodgy dealing and make him as unpredictable as a trapped cat.

Cyril could stand it no longer. He crowded onto the bench alongside the cooing couple, like a crow alighting next to two doves on a telegraph wire. I sat opposite them, beside the Commander. Card Index stood with his bottom to the fire groaning with pleasure as he massaged the heat into his bum, like an athlete applying deep-heat treatment. Gristle crouched in his usual position on the low stool to the side of the fire, his knees touching the woman's legs. He smiled and nodded a greeting when she turned to glare at him. Turning her back on him, she found herself looking over her companion's shoulder into Cyril's eyes.

'Are you God-fearing?' Cyril asked.

The man turned around to Cyril. 'Excuse me?'

'God,' Cyril said. 'Bit of an Anglican thing I do. I'm the Vicar. Expected of me to bring up God at unusual times. You must have heard of God. Almighty Being. Creator. Omnipotent. All-seeing. Slayer of fornicators, adulterers, sodomites and rapists. Him. He sees what's in everyone's mind.' He leaned towards the man. 'Right now, he sees what's in your mind, in every detail. The lady woman knows what you have in your mind, so it isn't hard for God to see it as well.'

The man stared at him and then took in the rest of us looking at him.

'Evening,' we muttered in turn, smiling, with looks suggesting we were out on day release and were waiting for our minders to bundle us into the van and take us away.

'Druids, on the other hand, are more relaxed about sex and religion,' Cyril continued. 'It is a wonderful fusion of the sublime and being horny. We do it in the woods a lot, or in Lloyd Sissibutt's barn, if it's raining or too cold. We feel the fusion better outdoors. We do big-time fusion. Get a lot of practice. Have you done much fusion in the woods? It's common around here. Blokes pass out exhausted with so much of it. Would you like to sign up? I'm a boss man, you know, a druid priest chap. I'm in charge of ceremonial knives, flaying with birch twigs, leaping over fires, dancing naked, dripping warm oil on naked bodies. I lead the rituals. Not that I wear vestments when I do. I keep them for the church stuff. I divest myself of them in the woods, if you see what I mean. Are you interested? You can have a trial period if you like.'

Gristle, the leering gnome on the low stool, put his hand on the woman's knee. 'I help him. Main assistant.'

'Acolyte,' Cyril corrected.

We waited for a few seconds as the couple scurried out of the door leaving their drinks unfinished behind them.

The Commander started the meeting. 'Crew, come to order. Tuesday raiders, report in on foray number 1. Use the proper code names for targets. Careless talk costs lives.'

He likes saying stuff like that. It reminds him of the days on his nuclear sub when he was dropping off

19

commandos or picking up SAS assault gangs after their blowing-things-up raids and assassinations. He is proud that he has delivered or picked up legalised killers in each of the oceans and most of the seas of the world. Sometimes I worry that his bouts of sombre silence are to do with him withdrawing more and more into himself as he realises those days are over. He is a castaway now without power or significance. He might as well be on a desert island. Just like everyone else who is forcibly retired without their permission.

I took the lead. 'With my fellow operative I drove to the Tango Echo store on Tuesday and reached our objective at 0930 hours, as planned. Having parked in a secure place, we had breached the perimeter through the front door and were deployed safely among the aisles by 0935.'

Gristle took over the report. 'Our initial reconnaissance showed little evidence of enemy defensive activity. There were no signs of Bad Breath Bailey and none of the security platoon were patrolling the perimeter.'

Talking in military lingo goes down a treat with the Commander, and Gristle can talk the battle jargon as good as anyone. We got the hang of it from listening to the Commander.

At a nod from the Commander I went on, 'I split from my fellow operative, as per our operational plan and began spreading the rumour, speaking quietly and in a conspiratorial manner to give substance to the misinformation we were spreading among the population. Agitation soon ran rife.'

The Commander smiled in approval. He loves phrases like that one.

'People scurried, each eager to spread the story with many additions being made, as per our expectations. Knots of shoppers bumped each other with trolleys like the riders in the peloton in a *Tour de France*.'

Card Index cut in. He can't stand too much hesitation, deviation or repetition. It was bred out of him in his report writing days with Ofsted. 'Stop rabbiting on. What happened? Did you succeed?' He could be quite curt and officious in his conversation. Another trick picked up from his Ofsted days.

'We spread the story and then left the store,' I told him. 'The tension in there was rising. Agitated shoppers were heaving around in swirling groups at the ends of the aisles, like a river penned back by a dam. Each one wanted the best start for a sudden dash to the checkouts.'

'The aisles were soon bulging, but with no customers at the tills,' Gristle said. 'Cashiers wondered why the shoppers were holding back. Each shopper was calculating who would be the lucky 10,000th shopper. One woman said she would kill herself if she was the one at the checkout just before or immediately behind the winner.'

'Anyone ask you to prove what you told them about the lucky 10,000[th] winner?'

I shook my head in answer to Cyril's question.

'Response from the enemy forces?' the Commander asked, back in his Horatio Nelson mode again.

'Staff saw the crowd building up but thought it was a fight among the women over a bloke they didn't want to share. They get a lot of bloke sharing in that Tango Echo store. The staff left them to it,' Gristle said. 'By the time they realised it wasn't a fight, the crowd had grown unmanageable.'

'On our way out,' I said, 'we spread the word about the prize to shoppers who were on their way in. People ran across the car park, shouting down their mobiles for their families to get down there immediately. Shortly afterwards we heard a newsflash on Radio Hereford and Worcester that all the roads in the area were jammed, with access to Tango Echo store impossible.'

I felt a warm glow as I recalled the details of our first successful foray against the retail giant. At the same time, I knew that the burning logs on the fire in front of us caused much of my glow. Fires are as seductive, as sensuous and as eager to please, as a welcoming woman. Men sit for hours around that red glow with smiling faces, fat with feeling, convinced they can now master the whole world. I stretched out my legs towards the fire and gave a long and satisfied sigh. 'We struck a successful blow for all Venerables. A blow that will be talked about wherever men gather around fires to discuss their exploits.'

Nodding heads signalled agreement with my judgement.

'The outcome of the mission?' the Commander asked. In his imagination, he was probably back on the conning tower of his sub watching the remnant of a covert operation scrambling aboard with blood on their hands, dragging a prized prisoner, who would soon be mercilessly tortured to death before being shot out through a torpedo tube.

Gristle stirred himself from the warm stupor that was seducing him. 'I spoke to Caribbean Michael, who was collecting trolleys, later that day. He told me the head count was fourteen taken to hospital with modest crush injuries, minor burns, cuts and one lost false leg. Ten cars had smashed windscreens. A six-car crash on the entry road stopped all traffic going in or coming out. Dozens of abandoned trolleys, piled high, had to have the food in them destroyed. Forty-nine arrests were made for fighting and general disorder, with three of those for assaulting officers of the law. Vegetable displays were overturned and trampled underfoot. Six sections of shelving were knocked to the ground as customers climbed over them to gain advantage at the tills. The automatic entrance door was torn off its hinges. There was a higher than usual amount of goods unaccounted for – shoplifted – particularly electrical goods, top-end spirits and expensive cuts of meat. When Bad Breath Bailey turned up he was trampled underfoot and carted off to hospital. The manager was summoned to regional headquarters. Staff assumed the lookalike walk-around manager was the actual manager when the real manager left to meet his boss. The lookalike ran the store for the rest of the day even though he is only an out-of-work actor temping in Tango Echo.'

I could see the Commander was as pleased with the succinctness of the casualty report as he was with the content of what Gristle had said. 'Good publicity?' he asked.

I nodded. 'The local paper ran the headline, "Disturbance in Store". That was picked up by the nationals and headlined "Rampaging Shoppers Reduce Store to Rubble Over High Milk Prices and Shortage of Avocados". Another wrote, "Irate Shoppers Riot over Badger Meat in Horse Burgers." One right-wing rag headlined it as "Foreign Workers Scatter Women and Children in Ethnic Flashpoint. Deport them *NOW*". The BBC sent investigators from late-night news shows, who disrupted activities in the store for days afterwards. They concluded that the violent actions of hundreds of shoppers were a protest against EU interference in our sovereign affairs and government cuts in benefits. The situation was made worse by a false rumour that the store was offering the 10,000th shopper, expected that day, free shopping every day for six months to an amount equal to the value of whatever was in that 10,000th shopper's trolley. Some customers said they had been told by two blokes leaving the store that a second family member accompanying the 10,000th shopper would have the same benefit as the winner.'

Card Index cut in. 'The police refused to be interviewed on those BBC late-night programmes because their interviewers are biased against the forces of law and order. The chief constable of the West Midlands promised to set up an enquiry that would report in eighteen months' time with swift action to follow that would be based on any lessons learned. He guaranteed that a disturbance would never happen again.'

Cyril said, 'The Prime Minister went on TV promising draconian measures to curtail all hooliganism, especially in primary schools. He said that hooliganism was never justified and must be stamped out by the teachers. He went on to say that his Education Secretary would make anti-hooligan lessons a key part of the curriculum. He said that food riots in low-end stores frequented by the poorer classes could be stopped if shoppers frequented Waitrose, where they would find a gentler type of shopper. The PM's spokesman said that due to stringent health and food safety checks introduced by the government after the horsemeat scandal, which was caused by a bloke in Ireland, or some foreign country, he could categorically guarantee that there was no truth that culled badger meat was in the food chain. Furthermore, he said, he would be happy to be filmed live on camera feeding loads of so-called badger burgers to his two daughters, one of whom is a vegetarian and the other is a vegan.'

Gristle joined in again. 'Bill Spratt, the leader of an anti-immigration party, demanded to be invited onto all TV and radio news programmes to lay the blame at the door of the government who allowed hordes of foreign nationals to fill our schools to bursting point. Mr Spratt said, "considering where they come from, it is not surprising that these foreigners don't know nothing about proper ways to behave in our shops when they don't have no shops where they come from and they don't believe in God or wear clothes like us. Quotas on the number of benefit cheats flooding the country is the only way what will keep out all foreigners and evil ones in future. Our pure women and innocent children need our protection. NOW. I am not racist because I know two black people from Africa. I have spoken at them in the street even, one about the state of his bins. The other one drives the Number 28 bus. He claims he is a trained brain surgeon in his own country but I still have to tell him to stop the bus and let me off at my stop".'

The Commander allowed himself a slight movement of his lips that might have been a smile. 'The enemy is engaged. We have penetrated his armoured defences. However, he will be alert for our next sortie.'

I could tell he was thinking again about *The Guns of Navarone*. He loves that film. He told us it shaped his attitude to warfare at sea. Fixing Cyril with a hard stare, he asked, 'Is Task Force 2 ready to proceed as per plan?'

Cyril nodded vigorously, without a flicker of hesitation. Our war was about to escalate. We were about to enlist other Venerables in the conflict. The ability of this auxiliary force to hold their nerve under fire was unproven, a weakness that could only be tested in the heat of battle.

Trouble at the Checkout

Sunday 1st February 2015 – Ash Moon

Basher made us wait at the bar until we were all present. Gristle kept an anxious eye on the fireplace in case anyone tried to take our seats. He was always a bit tetchy about his place in life, especially his physical space. Living with his violent father all those years ago had made him like that.

Most people were leaving the pub so we were fairly safe in assuming our places would not be snatched. We had ways of dealing with interlopers. That, as it turned out, is what Basher intended to lecture us about. 'I had a formal complaint after last week,' he declared.

Not an unusual occurrence, I thought. There was that time the woman fainted. She thought she saw a dead fly in her gravy and it turned out to be a live spider. Or the time Basher was reported to health and safety for keeping three dead pheasants, a pair of partridges, a brace of rabbits and a badger (culled) in a crate behind the bar for several days. He was storing them until Older George picked them up on his way to his brother's fourth wedding as a present. Then there was the complaint from an angry dad one lunchtime. He complained about the pub being a house of ill-repute because his daughter was impregnated after drinking there. None of the complaints ever came to anything. Being an ex-police inspector carries some weight and leaves Basher connected to powerful people who see off complainants.

Basher rested his hands on the bar, leaned forward and repeated himself, as if to give more threat to his words. 'A *formal* complaint. About you lot attempting to inveigle a young couple into sexual orgies with you in the woods behind the pub.' He paused, tilted his head back a little so he could look down his nose at us, as if he was looking out from under a peaked hat. He gave us a silent stony stare.

Anyone who has had dealings with the plod knows that the stony-stare plod-look can mean anything. It might mean, 'got you', or 'save me the bother and cough to it now', or 'I know something about you and it will surprise you to know I know', or 'I haven't a clue what you have been up to but if I act mysterious you will tell me because you are now shitting yourself with guilt.' Usually it means the officer is setting up a bribe.

Cyril, who gets away with most things because he is a vicar, is quite naïve in matters to do with civil liberties. He has yet to be banged up for being naughty in the eyes of the law, guilty or not. He asked, 'What are you talking about, Basher?'

Basher nodded, trying to look sage and all-knowing. I knew then he had no evidence. When plod does the sage-and-all-knowing look, it is an act. Still, Basher's reputation for violent interrogation techniques had to be kept in mind.

Gristle, who has been around the block a few times with plod, nodded and mirrored Basher's sage-and-all-knowing look. 'Oh aye?' he said.

The Commander, being used to confrontations with the Russian fleet, attacked immediately. 'Is there any substantive evidence to support this ridiculously fallacious accusation?' he proclaimed, standing tall and moving his elbows as if preparing to launch a torpedo or fire off a broadside.

Card Index took a few seconds to work through the images running through his mind. 'A couple?' he said. 'Boys or girls? Or do you mean indeterminate or mixed gender?' He was already reaching for the app on his iPhone to look up all the possible permutations on 'couple'.

I raised my eyebrows when Basher stared at me, waiting for a response. I shrugged my shoulders. Talking in front of police or ex-police is not to be recommended.

They pick up information from the tone of your voice. Interpretations of my shrug of the shoulders are not in their interrogation manual. My raised eyebrows work as a question mark in any language without any indication of meaning or implied insult.

'I'll have none of it,' he continued. 'I run a respectable pub. I'll come down hard on anyone who drags this pub into disrepute.' I wondered how a bout of fornication in the bushes with Cyril's religious group would lower the reputation of the pub. It might boost its attractiveness. 'Don't think I will forget this. I have to prepare the lounge for tomorrow's visit by a coach party of old people—'

'We call them Venerables,' Cyril interjected.

'—or I would sort all this with you now,' he said. In other words, he couldn't be bothered to give more time to the matter, but he had demonstrated he was top dog in the place, just because he owned it.

Recognising the signs that he was finished, we picked up our pints from the bar and made our way to the calm of the fireplace.

'Silly sod,' Gristle said.

'Nothing wrong with a bit of sex in the cause of religion,' Cyril snorted.

'Man has overstepped his authority,' the Commander stated. 'He'd be keelhauled on my boat.'

'Can we get down to business?' I asked. 'There is a lot of reporting to be covered tonight.'

The Commander sat up straighter in his seat. 'Crew will come to order. Target: Tango Echo. Purpose: repeat attack. Objective: disrupt customer flow at tills. Boarding party number 2 will come to order and report.'

Gristle looked across at me. 'You ready to write this?'

I waved my notebook and pen at him. For a moment I forgot what the code name Tango Echo stood for until

Gristle started. 'Me and Cyril were outside Tesco—'

'Log keeper will strike target name from the records,' the Commander snapped. 'Code names of operatives and targets to be used at all times to preserve secrecy. Tango Echo is the title you want.' The glare he gave Gristle would have melted tar.

Gristle, never one to be intimidated, not even by Buckle Crossley's one-eyed black bull that time it escaped, glared back at the Commander. 'As I said, me and Cyril—'

'Your fellow operative,' I butted in. 'I can't put actual crewmembers' names in the record. Suppose our records fell into the wrong hands during a raid by the SAS and GCHQ, or even by the Excise men.'

'For God's sake, let him get on,' Cyril said. That was rich, calling on God's name and him a druid.

Gristle shifted on his low stool. He seemed to be losing patience with the proceedings.

'Green Goalie is correct,' the Commander said. 'Let the record show that code names and proper operational nomenclature must be used by all operatives.' I could just imagine that man standing on his conning tower laying down the law to the returning heroic assassins being lifted on board his boat as they left another Third World country in ruins.

Gristle shook his head and sighed. 'My fellow operative arranged for and accompanied the Council's *Dial A Van* minibus, driven by his cousin Billy Boobystock. They collected a pair of Venerables from eight care homes, as planned. I reconnoitred the terrain before the arrival of our troop transporter. I identified that there was an air of slack vigilance in the target zone. All boded well for our foray into the enemy's territory.'

Cyril picked up the story. 'On arrival, before decamping, the newly recruited auxiliaries were given the chance to withdraw with honour if they felt the task too daunting.' The military lingo was being given a good run by Cyril. His background as an army chaplain before he was dismissed for unbecoming behaviour inclines him to use words like that. 'One really old bloke looked like he had died, but the woman propping him up said he sleeps a lot. He was ninety-two, she said, as if that explained his narcolepsy. Grist– my fellow platoon leader and myself got the old bloke off the bus. We proceeded in an orderly fashion into the store with half a minute gap between each pair to avoid attracting attention.'

Gristle took up the story. 'At that point, I was accosted by the enemy security forces. They pinned me against the stacked wire baskets inside the door, saying I was banned from entering the store. I pretended to be outraged, which I was. By making a fuss, I drew attention away from my fellow operative, who, being a vicar and in his full clericals for the occasion, was allowed to pass unnoticed.'

I wrote as fast as I could as Cyril continued with the account, letting Gristle take a sip from his pint. 'Any anxiety that these newly recruited auxiliaries would lose their nerve at the last minute was soon dispelled. It brings tears to my eyes remembering the smooth way each pair of Venerables, having filled their trolleys, merged into our pre-arranged holding pattern, moving in an orderly line down the wine and spirits aisle, coming back through soft drinks, waiting for the next pair to arrive and merge with the flow. A traffic controller at Heathrow could not have marshalled his incoming planes with more finesse.'

The group around the fire nodded approvingly at the success of the operation, in spite of one of the leaders being taken down so early on. The glow from the fire softened our wrinkles, bushy eyebrows and drooping throat skin. The setting reminded me of a scene from a Christmas card showing the Magi gathered around the light emanating from the baby Jesus in the crib. Fires can coax out the spiritual in the most arid of souls, move the meanest of men to mystical levels and tame the heart in the fiercest of breasts. As the heroic warriors of old gathered round their tribal fires to remember their mighty deeds, so now it was the turn of Cyril and Gristle to luxuriate in the warmth of our approval, as well as basking in the heat from the fire. The images in the flickering flames held us in their thrall.

'Did they land as efficiently as the planes at Heathrow?' Card Index shattered our contemplative mood. A typical former Ofsted inspector comment, destroying our mood of awe and wonder. 'Did the plan go to plan?'

Cyril shook himself out of his reverie with a tightening of his lips that signalled his unhappiness with Card Index's curt intervention. 'Of course. These auxiliaries were like seasoned warriors, if a little overcome by the occasion. One lady cried because it had been years since she had last filled a shopping trolley. Another couple were over the moon at selecting bottles of drink that they had stopped touching years earlier because their pensions won't let them buy even one bottle. All of them, including the narcolepsy chap, said it was moving to feel some self-respect again after years of loitering around the cheap shelves, waiting for the staff to reduce prices on bruised and damaged food. I was so proud to be with them,' Cyril announced, glaring around at us as if to challenge us to say he was over-emotional.

'Go on,' the Commander encouraged him.

'As per our plan,' Cyril said, 'I had bought the luxury item each couple had asked for as a reward for their service to our cause. I waited by the door to hand over the booty to these dedicated servants of the cause.' Cyril was starting to wax lyrical at this stage, a practice not uncommon among the clergy when given the floor, coupled with the unusual experience of everyone listening to every word. 'Peeling off from their holding pattern between the wines and soft drinks aisles, each pair landed alongside a checkout as instructed. Emptying their overfull baskets onto the conveyor belt, they asked the checkout operator to wait while they picked one more item they had forgotten. Leaving everything behind, they made their way to me at the door, picked up the item they had ordered and hurried out to the minibus to be met by my fellow operative, who by this time had given the enemy security forces the slip.'

Gristle grinned at us. 'Caribbean Michael told me that consternation broke out when the checkout managers saw eight checkouts bunged up with food and drink with nobody to pay. The checkout staff refused to clear the belts. They said it was not their job to remove food, and anyway it couldn't go back on the shelves now it had been handled and discarded. Several thousand pounds' worth of food and drink were piled up, according to Michael. Checkout staff grew fractious when managers abused them in front of customers, who were railing at the hold-up with eight tills out of action. In retaliation against the managers, the checkout staff summoned union reps, peace negotiations broke down and when managers called for backup checkout staff to come forward, there were fights with the blackleg scabs. Some of the checkout staff tied themselves to their chairs and couldn't be moved.

In the melee, many customers made their way out of the store without paying, their trolleys piled high with the most expensive items they could find. Bad Breath was summoned to the boss manager's office, where a loud shouting match took place with the sounds of violence interrupting the flow of foul language. The police escorted Bad Breath off the premises with his badge of office torn from the lanyard around his neck. Shortly after that, the manager was summoned to regional headquarters. Caribbean Michael said that the stand-in part-time actor who walks around the store pretending to be the manager will be offered the full-time job when the real manager is moved to a Tesco Express in Merthyr Tydfil.'

Gristle, anxious to get back into the dialogue, added, 'The auxiliaries we recruited said it was the best day they had had in years. They want to sign up as permanent members of the VNRF. On the way back to their care homes, some of them plotted to set up a mobile shoplifting group so that they will get back to eating and drinking what they like instead of putting up with crap because they can't afford anything else. The woman with the narcoleptic bloke said it was the longest he had kept his eyes open and thinks she may have discovered a cure for his illness. Another couple agreed to join with her and her sleeping bloke on shopping disruption excursions to the other superstores around the town.'

'Like the partisans in a war,' the Commander murmured, his face lighting up with a rare smile. 'Their guerrilla activities will allow us to build up a *force majeure* of saboteurs.'

Sitting in front of a fire makes it easy to be carried away in the heat of the moment. However, fires burn as well as giving comfort and building false confidence. But what the hell! I only keep the record.

Gristle and the Dating Site
Sunday 8th February 2015 – Ash Moon

The Commander docked at his berth close to the fire without interference from Bottle Blonde. Cyril, true to his word, had thrown himself at her ample bosom to stop her colliding with the Commander. Cyril now stood between her and Skinny Slug with his back to Slug while looking into her eyes. At the same time, he was, surreptitiously, glancing down her cleavage and sighing out loud. Bottle was enjoying the encounter, judging by her frequent loud snickers and guffaws. There was great slapping of Cyril's shoulder and clutching at his arm while she leaned a breast on the bar and roared with laughter.

The Commander anchored his eyes firmly on the fire in the same way a man thrown overboard stares after his disappearing ship, willing it to return and pick him up. An unusually loud raucous roar ripped the air, sending spasms through the Commander's beer-holding hand. 'She has to die,' he muttered, repeating the words like a mantra. 'She will kill thousands. She has to die. The submarine fleet is at risk. She has to die.'

I looked at Card Index in the hope that he would distract the Commander's attention from Bottle's voice. Card Index shrugged his shoulders. I turned to Gristle for help. He has the ability to distract a murderer from his act of violence when he puts his mind to it.

'I went on a website,' Gristle said. This was not one of his better efforts at distraction.

'She has to die. She has to die,' the Commander droned, steadying his beer-holding arm against the edge of the table to prevent any further spillage.

'A dating website,' Gristle added.

Even I was distracted by that piece of information.

'What for?' Card Index asked.

'That should be fairly obvious,' Gristle said, 'with a name like "dating website".'

'I know,' Card Index protested. 'What I mean is, what does the like of you want a date for?'

Gristle squirmed on his low stool by the fire and glared at Card Index. 'What does anyone want a date for?' I picked up a slight edge in his voice as if he was upset by the question.

Card Index didn't answer straight away but was clearly working through a range of possibilities in his mind. Here we go, I thought, any moment now his iPhone will be blinking away as he scrolls through his app looking for every computation and correlation.

When he was ready, Card Index asked, 'Was this date with male or female or both?' He was right to cover all options because of Gristle's openness to every possibility life offers. There had been a time earlier in his life when his chances of fraternising with others had been forcibly denied him. People were violently intolerant of his physical presence if they were downwind of him. At that time, the only companionship he found was in walking old dogs, too far gone to smell anything, or when he joined in badger baiting and foxhunting. He was barred from those latter two activities when his body odour so damaged the dogs' senses that the hunts were called off and the hounds returned to kennels to spend two weeks in quarantine recovering their sense of smell.

Gristle discovered the use of water as a cleansing agent only after his mega-rich father died, or was killed, as some would have it, when buying a steam-driven traction engine. Gristle the only surviving member of the family, Gristle inherited his father's whole estate. In fact, Gristle was the only surviving member of his father's business contacts and acquaintances. The rest had suffered from Gristle's father arranging their unfortunate habit of disappearing down wells or stumbling into well-known and clearly signposted swamps.

The police were happy to see Gristle's father in such squashed and intimate contact with the ground after the trouble he had caused them during his criminal life. They didn't investigate too closely why he had prostrated himself in front of the rear wheels of such a monstrous beast of a machine. The police said Gristle's old man *died* when the rear wheels of the traction engine swerved over him without warning.

Less-forgiving commentators voiced an opinion that it should have been *was killed*, because they saw some slight connection between Gristle sitting in the driving seat and the sudden forward lurch of the machine that dispatched his violent, robbing and sadistic father. Gristle still displays the machine on his front lawn, the wheels washed, the paintwork gleaming, although he has never driven it again since that fateful day.

I cut in quickly to dampen a simmering volcanic eruption in response to Card's question. 'Obviously, a date with a female,' I said. 'With Gristle's good looks, his easy charm, his silver tongue and his mega-riches that even he can't count, who else would he draw into his embrace only the most voluptuous and desirable of females?' I fixed a grin on my lips to persuade Gristle I was sincere.

The Commander had stopped his mantra of 'she must die.' Totally distracted now, he stared at me, wrinkling his forehead and lifting his eyebrows at the same time, a peculiarity he acquired after many years of staring through periscopes. He was giving a good imitation of someone bewildered by what I had just said about Gristle.

I was a bit taken aback myself.

'Did you send a photo?' Card Index asked. 'Which one?' he continued when Gristle nodded 'yes' to his first question.

Gristle paused to think. 'The first time it was a photo of that young gardener that cuts my lawns. He is posing bare-chested on a horse, like Putin. Fine build of a lad he is. Looks like me when I was a bit younger. I sent that to a Cougar site.'

'The first time?' I said.

He nodded. 'I've sent a few. Just to see what happens and what kind of women are on those websites.'

'What's a Cougar site?' Card Index asked. When Gristle told him, Card Index started adding feverishly to his app and checking out websites on his iPhone.

'How many times have you been online?' I continued.

Gristle started counting on the fingers on his right hand, switched to counting fingers on his left and then went back to his right hand again. He looked at me, 'Maybe around fifteen or twenty-nine.'

'You get any photos back?' I asked.

He nodded. 'All of them a bit dodgy. Some photos show very young women with beautiful hair, lovely eyes and fresh skin while they claim they are mature and fun-loving. You can't trust the photos.'

'Like the ones you sent.'

He ignored my comment. 'I found some sites that line up younger women for older men. I sent photos of older blokes to that site. Not any old blokes, just healthy ones.'

'Why would young women want old blokes?' Card Index asked.

Gristle smiled at him and came out with what sounded like a rehearsed delivery. 'They seek the more mature man to share life with, a man they can trust, rely on and have fun with. Men of a certain age and position make better partners because they are experienced, classy, caring and financially independent. These young women want someone sensitive, respectful, generous, fun-loving in a cultured manner, oh, and rich. That's what the advice on the website says to write. I'm in with a good chance.'

There are times when all one can do is sit silently and stare into a fire and wonder about the imponderables of life, existence and the universe. This was one of those times. The old traditions tell us that we can see in flickering flames all the scenes we are likely to come across in life and some that will occur only after we cross to the other side. I searched the fire in vain for images of a classy, caring Gristle being sensitive, respectful and fun-loving in a cultured manner. All I saw was spluttering, hissing logs showering sparks when the resin in the wood met the flames. That was a more accurate image of Gristle with the young women.

The Commander stirred from his shock-induced stupor. 'You can only run deep and silent so long. Eventually you have to surface. Have you exposed yourself to any of these women yet?'

For a moment, Gristle took 'exposed yourself' in a limited meaning. 'The whole purpose is to get to that point, but not immediately, you need a bit of chat first, and then—'

'He means, have you met any of them,' I added, cutting him off before he distressed us with the details.

'I've met a few of them. Some of them are right dogs. Talk about lying photos! It's disgusting the lies some people tell.'

'How do they recognise you?' I pressed him.

'I tell them over the phone that I will carry a daffodil and a double sleeping bag. I go into the pub first without the sleeping bag and the flower in case I change my mind when I see them.'

'How do you know what the woman will look like?'

He looked at me as if he was puzzled by my innocence. 'She'll be the only woman sitting by herself, looking at the door. She doesn't need to wear anything, well, nothing special anyway. Obviously she has to wear *something*, or she wouldn't be allowed to sit there naked. Not in most pubs anyway. Mind you, there are a few pubs along the canal at Stoke Prior that would encourage that sort of thing, but it is dangerous to go into them.'

'Any women from round here?' I asked.

'No, I never shit on my own doorstep. Do it too close to home and they'd know my real name and where I live. I can't be doing with that. They would want more out of our one-off meeting and that would mess up my other arrangements.'

'If you want sex, why not pay for it?' I said.

'Don't be so disgusting,' he shot back. 'You have a dirty mind.'

'What do you get out of these women if not free sex?'

He glared at me. 'What free sex? You know nothing about seducing women, especially the younger ones. I feed them in a decent pub and, even with special two-for-one offers, those places cost a few quid. I buy them beer to get them drunk. Even the cheapest of hotels where I pay by the hour costs money. I don't use hotels much, the sleeping bag is handier. Then they need a taxi home. All that cost mounts up. It isn't free sex.'

'What is your objective in all this activity?' Card Index had finished fiddling with his iPhone app and was listening again, back to his Ofsted inspector style of interrogation.

'One site I read,' Gristle answered, 'asks that same question and gives you four answers to choose from. One answer you could tick says, "to have a wild time". That's a good reason, although it does tire me out if the wildness goes on too long. The next reason is "to have a bit of fun". That means more than going to a comedy show. Sometimes it means a change of clothes if the women are into that sort of thing.'

'Why would they want to change their clothes?' Card Index asked.

'Look it up on your app,' I told him.

Gristle continued, ignoring Card Index's snort of frustration. 'The next reason is "to find a soul mate". How could anyone expect to find one of those in a pub after they lied about their looks and age on the Internet?'

A particularly loud spark exploded from the burning logs with a high pressure hissing noise as if the fire was protesting at the hypocrisy in Gristle's comments.

'What's the fourth answer?' I asked him.

'Something else.'

'I know it's something else,' I said, 'what is it?'

'That's it,' Gristle told me. 'Just "something else." You have to write your own answer to it.'

'That "something else" is the useful question,' Card Index added. 'After the experience with my first wife, I needed to know if the second one would be any good at keeping the house clean and washing and ironing. Cooking was something I wanted to find out about as well. I forgot to check out about gardening, which is why I had to do it myself.'

'I think it means kinky stuff,' I added.

'Naw,' Gristle said quickly. 'I don't do rubber boots, bobble hats and beating women with truncheons. What's the point of knocking them out and handcuffing them to the wall?'

I ran out of further ideas. The fire gave me no clues.

With loud goodnights and protestations of friendship

all round, Bottle Blonde and Skinny Slug processed out of the bar, leaving a pool of calm behind them as the echoes of their passage faded away. The Commander visibly relaxed as the bloodlust weakened its hold on his equilibrium. He drank his pint slowly instead of gulping at it.

Cyril joined us after a visit to the toilet. 'Have you noticed I can't pee as easily as I used to do?' he said, as he took his usual place on the bench by the fire. We admitted we had not noticed any change in his peeing since we had never looked at him peeing previous to this. Without a performance benchmark, it is difficult to gauge any change.

'What's different?' Gristle asked, while Card Index scrabbled away on his app searching for options.

'I dunno. It feels different,' Cyril said.

'According to this website,' Card Index said, stabbing at his iPhone, 'the changes in peeing could be in your ease of starting, dribbling at the end so it goes on even when you think you have done, strong smell, different colour, slight discomfort in passing it, interrupted flow so there is no continuity. You need to have a medical test.'

'Five-bar gate test,' I said. 'That's the best standard for peeing. Shoot it over a five-bar gate. Then you know it is different if you can't clear the gate the next time.'

'Does wind-assisted count?' Gristle asked.

I shrugged my shoulders. I don't go into details like that.

'Did you complete your task in Tango Echo store on Wednesday?' the Commander cut in to ask Cyril, frowning at what he thought was idle chat.

'No,' Cyril told him. 'I called into the surgery to see about an appointment about the peeing thing so didn't get to Tes– Tango Echo and missed meeting my friend Geraldo. I'm seeing him on Tuesday of this week and we'll

41

do it then.'

'What did they say in the surgery?' Gristle asked.

Cyril shook his head, 'Nothing really. I have an appointment with that nice young woman doctor tomorrow to have a prostrate check.'

'Pros*tate*,' I corrected him, 'though you would probably want her pros*trate*.'

'Ever had that check before?' Card Index asked.

'I don't think so. It can't be much. I imagine it will be a blood test. They don't bother me.'

I looked at Card Index, who looked at Gristle, who looked at me. We grinned at the image running through our minds.

'What?' Cyril asked. 'What are you lot grinning at?'

'Justice being done,' I said. 'The young *woman* doctor, you said.'

Cyril nodded.

'Let's hope the sisterhood hasn't given her too many details of what you get up to with your women in the woods, or she might choose to turn a simple check into a ritual righting of the balance of who is being poked by whom.'

'You lot are weird,' Cyril said, smiling weakly as he failed to grasp my meaning. 'I'm not afraid of a simple test. I am well used to revealing my body to young women.'

We laughed so loudly that Basher glared across at us, warning us to quieten down.

The Commander sniffed loudly before pinning Cyril with a fierce gaze. 'Military discipline demands that all tasks are completed in spite of personal injury or distraction. I hope such violations will not occur again, or disciplinary action will be taken.' With that, he drained his pint and marched smartly out of the pub, leaving us in the warm embrace of the fire. I imagined pictures in the flames of the look of horror on Cyril's face when the doctor explained the prostate test.

I wandered down the road with Gristle when we left the pub. Gristle was silent, an unusual state for him. I broke into his thoughts. 'Which of the four answers on that website did you tick?'

He stopped for a minute, kicked at a weed growing up through a crack in the tarmac on the side of the road, and looked at the stars before answering. 'The "something else" box.'

'What did *you* mean by it?'

He shrugged. 'You know how it is. This age business is like…' He paused and then continued. 'Some days I see nobody. I miss talking and hearing movement in the house. My "something else" is hearing some noise. Maybe seeing someone around from time to time. No strings. No demands. A bit of movement and noise.'

'How do the women feel when you tell them?'

'All they want is sex and more sex. It gets depressing.'

I nodded my head and we continued along the road. 'It's sad really when women think only of sex. My grandmother used to say it was like that when she was young. It was like that also when she was old, so I suppose it isn't anything new. Maybe it's an age thing that affects only men.'

Gristle shook his head, 'It affects horses too. I've seen it. Old dogs as well,' he added, as we wandered in the starlight toward his house.

Cyril Laid Low

Sunday 15th February 2015 – Ash Moon

The bad news had spread. Even the fire was low and lacklustre.

Basher pushed our pints across the bar without a word as we entered. Perfunctory greetings sputtered around the fire as we took our places, each of us conscious of the empty seat. Staring at the fire gave us a good excuse not to look at each other.

The Commander was the last one to enter. He took in the atmosphere as he sat down. He hadn't run the closed community of a nuclear sub, capable of staying submerged for three months, without picking up on attitude and atmosphere. He drank half of his pint in one go and placed his glass deliberately on the table. He does things like that to be authoritative. It was a signal that a new phase was about to start.

Gristle used the sole of his boot to push a log deeper into the fire. A loud threatening cough from Basher reminded him he was not allowed to touch the fire. Gristle turned to me and raised his eyebrows. I scowled at him, shaking my head, warning him not to kick off, or Basher would heave him out the door.

Card Index flicked through the pages on his iPhone like he was flicking away flies from a piece of raw meat. His snuffling and snorting told me he was agitated and at odds with the world. He never minded being at odds with most things in the world, having been an Ofsted inspector for almost fifteen years. However, personal loss and any form of bereavement are outside his comfort zone. The way he hunched over his iPhone, peering like he was short-sighted, made me think of a badger rooting around a grassy bank in the early evening not realising a badger culler is hiding up a tree with cocked rifle.

My notebook lay on the table. Opening it and taking out my pen would break the mood. Some might regard that as being insensitive in such a melancholy atmosphere. My ability to control my sensitivity was strengthened through doing a part-time job hosing down the floor in an abattoir on the edge of Redditch.

The silence around the table was getting to me. 'Well,' I said. Nobody looked at me. 'I cut myself,' I said, waving my finger still showing the line of the paper cut.

'Did you cut it off?' Gristle asked, sounding disinterested.

I waved the digit at him. 'It was really painful. I nearly had to go to A&E.' I knew I had said the wrong thing as soon as the words came out of my mouth.

'Poor Cyril went to A&E when he was struck down,' Card Index murmured. 'Of all the things that could have happened to him, that was the worst.'

'He is like a lame racehorse. Fit only for burgers after that,' Gristle agreed.

'All those women! What will they do?' Card Index asked.

'He will be fine,' I said, trying to ease the gloom I had just deepened.

'In the old days, men who died at sea in the service of their country were wrapped in a sail and buried at sea with respect,' the Commander said. 'We had no sails on a sub. We stuck them in the freezer with the food until we passed the bodies in a dignified manner to the supply ship. That hospital where Cyril went sticks them on a trolley to die in a corridor, without any respect.'

'No more jumping over fires in the forest for him,' Gristle said, staring into the fire.

'Sobbing women. No shouts of delight and pleasure.

45

Only pity and memories,' Card Index added.

'He isn't dead,' I said, in a failing effort to lift them out of their despondency.

Gristle glared at me. 'Sometimes you are so insensitive that I wonder why we let you sit with us.'

'Now, hold on a minute,' I protested.

'Injured in the course of duty,' the Commander interrupted. 'One would expect that from a true warrior. Let us remember him with a moment's silence.'

I breathed out a sigh and sat back.

Basher came over to find out why we were sitting so quietly. 'Are you lot up to something?'

'A minute's silence for Cyril,' I said, earning a glare from the Commander because the minute was not up.

'Did he die? Good job I didn't pour his pint.'

I looked at Basher, hoping for more talk from him to break the silence. 'He's still in hospital, but with a very personal wound,' I said.

'A wound? It wasn't a wound. I heard he couldn't piss. His prostate was blocking his bladder. He couldn't pass water. Three litres of it I heard. They catheterised him. Came out like a hose pipe.'

Great, I thought, this will send the others over the edge. I should have known better than to expect a sensitive intervention from Basher.

Gristle looked like he was about to explode. Card Index clutched his iPhone to his chest. The Commander sat up even straighter than usual.

Card Index spluttered, 'He has a fifteen-inch piece of plastic tube stuck—'

Gristle cut in, 'up his—'

'—penis,' the Commander concluded.

'With a bag hanging from it and a tap to turn it on and off.' Card Index closed his eyes as if he was trying to control a pain or a spasm shuddering through him.

'What will he do for sex with that lot in the way?' Gristle said, getting to the heart of the problem.

'It has advantages,' Basher said, silencing us all.

'How can you talk about advantages of such a personal affliction?' the Commander asked.

'Had one myself once. Not for the reason Cyril has it. Mine was more a personal injury in the line of duty. My what's-its came in violent and unplanned contact with a couple of criminals' boots.'

Mentioning a wound earned in the course of duty impressed the Commander.

Gristle couldn't restrain himself. 'What advantages?'

Basher leaned over the table in a conspiratorial way. 'With the tube and the bag strapped to your leg, you can pee anytime, anywhere and nobody knows you are doing it. You could be talking to the bishop and be peeing into the bag strapped to your leg and he wouldn't have a clue what you are at. You could be talking to some stuck-up bird, smiling at her and filling your bag – no sign, no sound. Absolutely brilliant way of showing people what you think of them.'

'But you didn't actually *show* them,' Card Index said.

'Not as such. But in my own mind I knew; that's what counts. People are just a load of shites when it comes down to it, and any way I can put them in their place is fine with me.' He turned and walked back to the bar, insulting drinkers as he passed.

We looked at each other until Card Index broke the silence. 'I never thought he felt like that about people. Does that include us?'

'Is our moment's silence for Cyril up yet?' I asked.

The Commander nodded his head. I breathed a sigh of relief. 'Do you want my report?' I was given the signal to

47

proceed.

'I was not an eyewitness so this report is based on third-hand information. It is still true in spite of that. Cyril had picked up Geraldo and they were upstairs in Tango Echo. Geraldo started his Alzheimer's act. He was walking naked through the TV and computer section, carrying his toothbrush, asking customers to switch off the TVs and turn out the lights so he could go to bed. The staff wouldn't go near him. Cyril, who was keeping an eye on Geraldo, suddenly keeled over from the pain of his blocked bladder. Geraldo forgot he was supposed to be acting and ran to help Cyril, shouting for someone to call an ambulance, or to fetch the store's first aid staff, or, better still, the cleaners because they have more about them than the others. Staff realised Geraldo was a fake and jumped on him and held him till the police arrived. He was arrested for indecent exposure in a public place. Cyril was carted to hospital where they stuck a plastic tube up his... he was catheterised.'

The Commander sat still, gripping his lower lip between his teeth. He must have looked like that the time he lurked in deep water off Singapore playing cat and mouse with a spying Chinese sub, waiting for the moment to blow it out of the water. Orders from London told him to spare the Chinese sub, that time, so instead he sailed into Singapore on a goodwill visit.

He reached a decision. 'A set-back,' he said, looking directly at each of us in turn. 'Morale will be maintained. A minor skirmish, not even a battle and certainly not the war.' He was pleased with his summary. Who am I to challenge a military man of his renown? How do you correct a man who has looked through his periscope, his thumb hovering over the missile button, tempted to fly one into the middle of Beijing? I went with the flow.

Something in the back of my mind told me it wasn't as simple or as clear as the Commander said. For some reason I couldn't pin down, I knew we were at a turning point in our campaign. I should have challenged the Commander, except I didn't know what was bugging me. That would come later, almost too late, as it turned out.

Basher returned to our table. He was more active among the customers than usual. I suspected it was his police instinct getting at him. I was right.

'I just heard there's been a lot of trouble at Tesco's, with a lot of talk about who is behind it,' he said, standing so close to Card Index in front of the fire that Card had to move to one side.

No one answered. The less said to Basher, the better.

'What was Cyril doing there with that Geraldo the actor?' He looked knowingly at us, the plod technique designed to intimidate lesser mortals. 'I hope you lot aren't mixed up with what has been going on. I can't afford to have my pub associated with anything like that.'

'No, indeed,' Card Index muttered. A look from the Commander stopped Card from adding any more.

'If I thought for a minute…' And again Basher stopped as if waiting for us to finish his sentence and incriminate ourselves. Looking disappointed at his failure to prompt a clue out of us, he continued, '… out the door you will go, lock, stock and barrel. No leeway given on that sentence. Am I clear?'

We nodded. He wandered off to risk his health by breathing in the fumes of the industrial air-fresheners as he checked the toilets, leaving us staring at the fire.

The Commander resumed control again. 'All active sorties will be suspended until the enemy is confident we have withdrawn from the field. Instead, Green Goalie will reconnoitre the next store, code name MO, and report back.' He drained his pint. The meeting was over. No questions were asked. No opinions were sought. The Commander looked like he was back on the conning tower of his sub sailing the oceans of the world scanning the horizons for someone to annihilate. The world was once again in safe hands.

Card Index tagged along with me as we left the pub. Unusually for him, his iPhone was in his pocket. As we walked, he picked up a branch broken off by the storm earlier in the week, snapped a long twig off it and used that to swipe at anything growing along the side of the road. 'I can't get him out of my mind,' he said.

'Basher?' I asked. 'He's all wind and blow.'

'Cyril.'

He didn't expand. I didn't ask. Sometimes, men need time to drain away emotions before they speak, in case other men think them emotional.

After a while, he struggled to put his ideas into words. 'His thingy... with that plastic gadget stuck up it... A tap on it, for God's sake... humiliating and...'

A few more weeds and bushes lost their growing tips as he lashed out with the thin branch he was carrying.

'You ever see one?' he asked.

I nodded. 'I helped my Uncle Jack empty his a few times when he was out of it with the drink. Reduces your mobility, especially with the bag strapped to your leg,' I said.

'Oh God,' he answered.

'He'll get used to it. Tell you what, let's visit him in the hospital and ask him to show it to you. He won't mind you looking at it in a hospital. By now he will have been humiliated so many times by what the staff do because he is old, he won't care.'

'I couldn't look at anything like that.'

We walked in silence. I smiled to myself at the thought that ran through my mind. 'It might be a bit awkward to visit him,' I said. 'Knowing Cyril, he will be at it with the nurses by now. We would be a distraction.'

'I thought he couldn't do stuff like that with a fifteen-inch tube in his thingy.'

I grinned at Card Index. 'I wouldn't be surprised if they used a longer one than that for Cyril. Anyway, he will find a way around that obstacle. Do you remember that time one of the more active members of his coven fell over the edge of the quarry? She was stuck in the bushes halfway down and they had to wait for the fire brigade to come and lift her out. He climbed down, "clung to her" in space, held up only by a bush, yet she had the biggest smile you ever saw when they hoisted her up. Would you doubt that a man like him will allow a small thing, or even a very long plastic one, to get in his way?'

Card Index's iPhone rang before he could answer. 'It's a business call,' he said, shielding the screen from me. 'I have to hurry.'

'At this time of a Sunday night?' I asked.

'Arrangements for tomorrow.'

He scuttled off, leaving me to walk the rest of the way by myself. I tried to work out how Cyril might do it with the nurses and the young female doctors. Whatever I thought up, he would think of it first and discard it for something more imaginative. It would take more than a slap on his personal parts to make him lie down.

I walked on down the road in the dark on my own again.

Barred from the Pub

Sunday 22nd February 2015 – Alder Moon

A sliver of moon dodged among the scudding clouds giving sufficient light to let me follow the bridle path. I can move easily through the countryside with only a little light from the moon or the stars. The Excise men who hunt me are brought in from towns and know only roads and the country lanes. They are no match for me on the bridle paths.

Tonight I approached the edge of the car park furthest away from the pub. I stood in the shadow of the hedge searching the open space, waiting before stepping through the gap. Old habits die hard.

The light from the pub would highlight anyone walking in front of it. I picked out the normal sounds of the night, the rustling in the bushes, the sound of small animals scurrying across stones, the occasional flapping of wings, the cry of a captured animal, the solitary breathy cough of a cow hidden behind hedgerows, the whisper of the dead retracing their former paths through the grass. I listened carefully for other sounds. Such care had saved me on some of my more dangerous smuggling jobs.

Absolute silence is a danger signal, just as some sounds warn you to beware, like the sounds coming from a car immediately to my left.

Cars are usually parked as close as possible to a pub door. Only gypsies park far from the entrance, as well as those up to something shady.

I could tell by the noise from the car that there was only one reason to park this far away from the door and in the darkest corner of the car park. Someone was 'at it' in the car. Or, more accurately, some two were at it, or maybe more than two, but for that you needed a very big car and preferably a van or a lorry.

It wasn't a van but Bottle Blonde's car. Surely she could wait to take Skinny Slug home before devouring him, I thought. There seemed to be a lot of devouring going on judging by the groans, cries, grunts, exclamations of surprise and delight, not to mention the violent shaking and the way the car lurched as if people were jumping around inside it. Someone was mightily engaged in the personal pursuit of happiness, or maybe just seeking pleasure. Anyone so actively engaged in lusting after the delights of the flesh would pay little attention to me stepping through the hedge and crossing the car park.

I was about to move when there was a great shuddering and shaking of the car with two voices joining in harmony with roars of "ooh... ooh... ooh... oooooooh" and "aaaaaaaaah". I paused, not out of respect for the sensitivity of the occasion, nor for fear that I might disturb the delicacy of the moment, but so that I might not alarm the participants with the thought that they were being observed, or, as the popular press would have it, 'were being spied on by a pervert'.

I had mastered the knack of waiting when pitted against the Excise men out to catch me. I stood still.

Inside the car, the talking had started. The murmur of voices rose and fell with both parties speaking, sometimes at the same time. I thought this unusual. Skinny Slug was never heard to address Bottle Blonde in public. Maybe he was granted speaking rights in the sanctuary of the car, or as a reward for what had sounded like a world-shattering performance. No cigarettes were lit so there was no flaring match to show me the occupants. I sometimes wonder what people do after sex these days if they don't smoke. Maybe they chew a hard toffee sweet.

The voices fell silent, a sure sign that a conclusion had

been reached. I eased myself deeper into the shadow of the hedge to hide from the players in the sex-mobile. A car door opened and slammed. Bottle Blonde called out, 'See you. We must do that *again*,' and drove off across the car park and out onto the road in her usual rough fashion. As a driver she had as much respect for the gears and her engine as a jockey flogging a flagging horse in the Gold Cup in the final dash to the line.

Why was she leaving Skinny Slug behind? Surely not as a punishment? He had been congratulated on performing his matrimonials so well. Was it his reward to be left alone for not disappointing her in the car? Perhaps he was being sent into the pub to spy on us. The figure left behind started walking towards the pub. Once he moved between me and the light, I saw who it was. I could hardly catch my breath to shout at him.

'Gristle! What are you doing here?'

He spun around. 'Who's there? Who's that?'

I stepped out from behind the hedge.

'It's you. What the hell are you doing? I thought I was about to be mugged,' he protested. 'Why are you hiding there? What are you up to?'

'Never mind what I am up to,' I answered, striding towards him. 'What are you up to?'

'I asked you first,' he said.

'No, you didn't. I was first. You were shagging that woman. Where was Skinny?'

'He wasn't in the car.'

'I guessed that,' I countered, although I would not have been surprised to hear that Skinny was in the back taking photographs.

'Trouble at his new massage place in Wolverhampton. She is off to pick him up and help him get rid of the injured.'

'Why her? You said you never shit on your own doorstep,' I snapped at him. Sometimes he is so daft and does such silly things I could punch him. 'You know she is trouble.'

He stopped in the middle of the car park. 'If I tell you something, will you keep it absolutely secret and confidential?'

'Of course,' I said, although I might let some slip if it was worth my while. I am no priest or lawyer so I have no problem with stuff like that.

He looked around the darkened car park as if we were being closely monitored by GCHQ. 'She wants me to act as an intermediary between her and the Commander. That bout in the car was a sort of a sweetener, a first payment. Much more to come if it all goes well, you know, more space, more time, things hanging off the walls and sex gear to try out.'

'Are you mad?' I asked him. 'She will devour you.'

'I wish,' he sighed. He paused and stood there with his head tilted a little to one side as if he was remembering something. 'You know how she looks, sort of all pumped up and people say it is all show. Well, between you and me, I can tell you it is *all real*. God, how *real* it is. You should see it, and hold it and…'

I swallowed hard. It felt like my mouth was filling with a bad taste. 'What deal are you working on for her?' I said. 'What's all this to do with the Commander?'

'That's the secret bit for now. But you will be surprised when I tell you.'

'Go on then,' I said, 'tell me before we go inside.'

Gristle had stopped at the door to the pub, his hand on the door handle, when the Commander himself came around the corner.

'Ah, Commander,' Gristle muttered, in what sounded

to me like a guilty voice. 'Good evening to you, sir.' He only called him 'sir' when he was anxious or had been caught out.

The Commander grunted at him without taking his eyes off me. 'Well?' he said, 'What happened to you?'

'A slight issue, Commander,' I answered.

'You were arrested,' he said.

'Technically, yes,' I said, 'in the strictest interpretation of the word, but…'

'You blew your cover.'

'I was set up.'

'You lied,' he said. Glaring at me, his face coming closer to mine all the time. 'You stole and then lied about it. No one, no one, for any reason, should lie about service to his country.'

'It wasn't a lie,' I protested. 'They planted the tins of beans on me.'

'You blew your cover,' he went on, ignoring my explanation. 'A blown operative is a wasted operative, fit for nothing but to be disowned. On my boat I would put you ashore at the next opportunity and never let you set foot aboard again.' He turned and, elbowing Gristle out of the way, steamed into the pub.

'You certainly fouled *his* propeller or whatever they do at sea,' Gristle muttered, as we trooped in after the Commander, who had picked up his pint and was moving to join Card Index on our seats by the fire. A solitary poured pint stood facing us when we reached the bar. It wasn't my Guinness. I looked enquiringly at Basher, who was wearing one of his stern looks. He had folded his arms in that police no-messing-here-my-lad sort of way.

'You are barred,' he announced.

The silence around the pub was as sudden as if someone had shut a door on a noisy room. I shook my head in surprise. This was my pub, my drinking place, my friends, my fire, my Sunday night, my place of rest and sanctuary. 'You can't,' I said, which I realised afterwards was not the most telling argument to persuade him to change his mind.

'I can. I have. Leave. Now.' He had that look I have seen on policemen when they have you bang to rights and they only want you to protest so they can do you over and cause you great personal injury. The best defence is to shut up, walk away and live to fight another day.

Before I could argue or shout at him, my arms were grasped from behind. Two soothing voices spoke in my ears, which only confused me because I could not understand what they were saying since they were both talking at the same time, but I was being eased towards the door.

'It's ok, Basher,' Gristle said, from my right-hand side. 'He's on his way.'

'Just a little misunderstanding,' Card Index said, from the other side of me. 'Soon be resolved.'

'Hold on…!' I shouted.

'You hold on,' Gristle hissed in my ear. 'Don't give him the opening to have a go at you. Remember what he did to those three tinkers last year when they crossed him.'

'We will sort it when he has cooled down,' Card whispered.

'I warned you not to bring your thieving ways to this pub,' Basher shouted, as my two friends walked me to the door. 'I'll not have criminals and robbers in here. We are God-fearing and law-abiding folk.'

'Liar,' I shouted.

'The likes of you are a disgrace. I'll have none of it in this house. You are barred *for life*!'

As I was hustled out the door, I noticed the

Commander was sitting with his back to me, in front of our fire, his head bent over his pint, pretending he had nothing to do with me. I thought, you are like Peter standing by the fire with Pontius Pilate when Jesus looked at him and said, Et tu, Brutus, except there was no cock crowing outside the pub.

Card and Gristle backed me against the wall outside the pub. 'I'm ok,' I said, shaking out of their grip. 'I can manage by myself.' They stood back from me but were ready to jump on me if I made a run at the door. 'I won't go back in. Relax,' I said, straightening my coat and stepping away from the wall.

'Give it time and he'll forget,' Card Index said.

'Or we will take our business elsewhere,' Gristle added.

'I doubt if he would miss the money off our few pints,' Card said. Not the most consoling of comments, but honest.

'All that fuss over nothing,' I protested.

'You were arrested,' Card Index pointed out.

'And taken through the store in handcuffs and driven off to the police station in a police car for all to see,' Gristle said.

'I was framed.'

Gristle said, 'That excuse never worked for me. Nobody believes you, even when it is true.'

'Anyway, it will all be sorted when the evidence is heard,' Card Index said, in his Ofsted inspector obsession with evidence, real of false.

'I can tell you what really happened.'

'Best leave it till another day when everyone is calmer,' Gristle said, heading back towards the door of the pub. Card Index moved after him.

'Hold on. Where are you going?' I asked.

They paused, looked at each other, then at me. 'Inside,' Gristle said.

'But you can't go in and leave me out here.'

'We're not barred,' Card Index said. 'Our pints are waiting for us.'

'And what am I supposed to do while you lot are in there drinking?'

'You can't stand there,' Gristle said. 'Basher will maim you if he comes out and finds you loitering in the car park.'

'I'd go home if I was you,' Card offered. 'An early night will do you the world of good.'

With that, the pair of them left me.

The sharp edge on the wind told me not to stand there too long. The possibility of Basher coming out and finding me made moving a matter of some urgency.

The cloud had covered the moon and stars. I would have to head home the long way by following the road and the lane. I turned up the collar of my coat and headed off through the darkness, on my own again. This time I was not going to take things lying down. Someone would pay for the indignities I had suffered and for the damage to my reputation. At the time, I didn't know that the Commander had been more accurate than I could have imagined, my cover had been blown.

Ghosts From the Past

Tuesday 3rd March 2015 – Alder Moon

The face answering the front door was wrong. It was too bony, with piggy eyes and topped with greasy hair. It should have been a round, pink face, crowned with wild hair and lit by eyes bubbling with life. 'Can I help?' wrong-face asked.

I looked at him before leaning to the side to peer down the old-fashioned hallway behind him. 'Cyril in?'

'Cyril?'

I nodded. 'Is he in?'

'Do you mean the Reverend Smallpiece?'

Smallpiece? I paused a minute and processed the name until it clicked. I nodded. 'Aye, him, Cyril Smallpiece'

'Do you have an appointment?'

No one ever made an appointment to visit Cyril. He was either here in the house leading one of his women's group sessions, or 'groping' sessions as we called them, or doing his druid stuff in the woods, or visiting the home of one of his pliant parishioners. As long as you waited until he was finished what he was at, he always had time for you, no matter what time of the day or day of the week you called, except for a Saturday afternoon and evening when he wrote his sermon for Sunday. He never neglected his sermon preparation. He was not given to off-the-cuff extravagances like some of his ilk are prone to drone.

'Appointment?' wrong-face repeated, interrupting my thoughts.

'No,' I said, shaking my head. He had given up talking and was inching backwards, about to close the door.

'How is he?' No answer. 'You know, after the operation on his thingy.' I nodded down in the general direction of his lower body where the operation would have been carried out had it been done on the dour doorkeeper. That was when I noticed he was wearing a cassock and a clerical collar. This was new. Cyril takes the gear off. This one puts it on. The public yin and yang of the priesthood and clerical gear.

'We cannot give out personal information to strangers at the door,' the cassock-clad one said.

'I'm not a stranger,' I answered. 'He knows me.'

'We have to abide by a new diocesan rule,' wrong-face added, which wasn't helpful. I didn't know the old rule.

'I'll make an appointment,' I said, if that was the only way I would get past wrong-face guarding the door.

'Not possible.'

'Why not?'

'He's not here.'

'So why did you ask if I had an appointment?'

'Procedure.'

'Do you know where he is?'

'No.'

'Would you tell me if you did know?'

He shook his head. 'Diocesan rule.'

While I was working out my next question, he closed the door. I took it the conversation was over.

The priest's house was built in the middle of the graveyard. Only a Church with a morbid interest in death would build a house in such a place. Visitors ran the gauntlet of the watching dead as they approached Cyril's house. When I had complained about the dead people glaring at me as I passed, he reassured me they would do me no harm. 'Dying,' he said, 'has deprived the dead of any menace. They feel no malice. They regard us with pity because we have to struggle on before we join them in their place of blessed release.'

Cyril tended the graveyard like it was a show garden. 'Why would they want to be buried in a place less attractive than when they walked around?' Cyril told anyone interested. Graves were manicured, grass was cut, edges trimmed, headstones washed, bushes and trees pruned, and the sweet smells of blossoms at different times of the year testified to the loving care he put into maintaining the showpiece. Leaving food offerings for the dead, however, was a bit unusual for an Anglican burial ground. Cyril's waiter service left food on the graves for a year following the burial. After that length of time, he said, the dead had adjusted to their new way of existence and didn't need offerings of chickens, or curry, or fruit and vegetables for the vegetarians. There was one bloke who took longer than a year to get over his longing for potatoes roasted in goose fat. Cyril told me he was the exception.

Cynics in the village said Cyril had the best-fed foxes in the area. Cyril smiled at their remarks. His list of villagers with their food likes and dislikes grew longer each year as more of them registered with him to make sure their preferences would be taken care of when they took up residence in his plot. In case it isn't down to the foxes, they would say.

I didn't hang around in the graveyard. I wasn't afraid of the dead in this place, but they reminded me of other dead I thought best forgotten.

I was almost at the gate that opened onto the top end of the village high street, when two men coming in blocked my way. I recognised the type after years of meeting their kind. Cocky but quiet, wearing suits like they were uniforms, watchful as hawks riding the wind and always in pairs. These were top plod of the dangerous type. Casting my eyes down, I tried to manoeuvre around them.

'Excuse me, sir,' the one shaped like a small hillside

said, moving to stand in my way. 'My friend and I are looking for the grave of a soldier killed in the line of duty. Would you know that grave, sir?'

'Paying our respects, sir,' the bigger hillside said, fingering the pin badge on his coat lapel. 'Former comrade he was.'

'Sorry,' I mumbled, without looking either in the eye. 'Go to the house. The priest will help you.' I hurried past them, feeling their eyes boring into my back.

Both of them were wearing the pin badge of One Paras, the army's ruthless squad. These were more than top plod. These boyos were killers. I had seen them in action, close up. I wanted out of there as quickly as I could.

Why, after all the years, should they appear now?

Unwelcome Visitors

Friday 6th March 2015 – Alder Moon

Gristle was his usual unhelpful self. 'Probably they came to kill you for something you did long ago. Like Jimmy Savile and those DJ pervs. Did you play with little kids back then?'

'Don't be stupid,' I said. 'There were no little kids around when I was growing up. Do I look like a paedophile?'

'Paedophiles don't wear a badge. You can't recognise them until they are caught.' He paused, trying to dredge up something from long ago. 'I remember old man Modger Sowerbumble, his family used to have that little farm out the Hunt End road, you know the one where the tree fell down and crushed the house and there wasn't even a storm at the time. If he saw me coming from school and by myself, he would tempt me with an apple to go inside the shed behind his house. I was only a kid, about eight or nine. He was harmless.'

'Did you go in?'

'Not for an apple. I made him give me a cigarette as well.'

'And did he do things?'

'Such as?'

'You know,' I said, trying to be delicate in resurrecting a matter of such sensitivity from Gristle's past. 'Like, did he play with you?'

'Play with me? Are you daft?' Gristle asked. 'He didn't want to play with me. He wanted me to drop my trousers so he could see my todger and touch it with a stick.'

'A stick?' I said.

'What's wrong with a stick? He only poked my thing

with it. He wasn't like the ones who liked to hit it.'

'Did you feel bad?'

'The cigarettes could have been better. He bought cheap ones. They made me cough like a horse with hay stuck in its throat. Were you like Modger? Is that why these fellas are after you? Have you stopped doing it? People don't understand that sort of thing these days. You are in enough trouble with the shoplifting and the ban from the pub.'

'Of course I've stopped. No, what I mean is, I never started it to stop,' I said.

He stared at me for a moment. 'If you say so.' He thought for a moment. 'How do you know for sure they are after you?'

'I can tell.'

Gristle leaned forward with his arms resting on the top of the steering wheel. He stared out the windscreen like he was reading signals from the hedges alongside the road that ran up the wooded hill towards Stratford-upon-Avon. We had parked in a lay-by for privacy to consider my plight.

He reached a conclusion. 'If you don't want to tell me what it is about, fine. That's up to you. But if them fellas are out to kill you, then you should kill them first. Simple really. Do you want me to help? You probably haven't done much in the way of killing.'

If only he knew. 'No more killing,' I said.

'Are they hit men for the superstore you were robbing when you were arrested?'

'I wasn't robbing. I was framed. Anyway, why would they bring in two blokes built like tanks from One Paras? These are the lads the government sends out to kill anyone who gets on their nerves.'

'There's your answer,' he said. 'You upset the government.'

I sighed out loud. 'I don't know why I bother. I'd get more sense out of Card Index.'

'Please yourself,' he said, starting the engine. 'I have to get back. I've a young thing booked in for the afternoon to sort out my feet, plus a few other bits she can attend to, with some luck. Anyway,' he said with a grin, looking at me out of the corner of his eye, 'I shouldn't be sitting here with you in *this* lay-by. People will talk. I have a reputation to think about.'

Gristle dropped me at the end of the narrow lane that led to my house. The high hedges along the lane and the bend just before the house shielded my place from passing traffic on the road. Out the back of the house a long narrow strip of garden ran between tall fences that protected me from prying eyes, with space enough to grow all the vegetables I needed for the year.

The back garden ended in a hedgerow with a padlocked narrow gate opening onto a small pasture, the final home of a retired horse, the first home of young lambs each March before they were trucked off to the abattoir. Bridle paths crossed the pasture, one leading down the hill to the old oak by the pond, the other heading up towards the ancient woods that were unaffected by human interference. Both bridle paths were largely unused except by me on those excursions that required a privacy of movement the roads could not give.

My front gate was pulled to but was not latched. No country dweller would be that neglectful. I stood in the gateway and examined the front and as far down the sides of the house as I could see. Nothing was out of place. The soldiers wouldn't be that careless.

The deep layer of stone chips spread along the path showed no unusual disturbance. The depth of the layer of stones made it difficult to move quickly and made such a noise underfoot that no one approached the house without being heard. Natural security protection is simple and effective. I had a pair of geese once but the noise they made and the mound of shit they left in the garden helped me give into temptation the first Christmas that came around.

The front door might be booby-trapped if they had been inside the house. I had to assume they had been in. Any 'present' to welcome me home would be connected to the key cylinder, or primed to detonate when the door was opened. I followed the path around the house, my head bent forward as if watching the ground, but glancing in every window I passed. The back door looked secure. If there were danger at the front door, then this one would be safe. They had to come out through one of the doors.

I stood with my head tilted slightly to one side, listening to the house, before I stepped into the kitchen. The movement of the air told me someone had been there recently. Cyril had taught me the druid way to sense the silent wake of people who had passed along a path before me, a useful skill on night excursions evading the Excise men. The sense of a second presence was strong in the hallway. The air in the front room confirmed there had been two of them. They were good at what they did. Not a thing was out of place. But they didn't know about the patterns and waves in the air that marked the passing of bodies.

The front door showed no sign of interference; no wires protruding, no packages linked to the handle, nothing waiting to be ignited when the door was opened. I took my time looking around. Not a kill, this time, I thought. It was intelligence gathering; searching for documents, planting microphones and cameras. I looked at the phone on the hall table without touching it. Surely they wouldn't try that old trick.

I spent the next hour checking plugs and sockets, all electrical equipment, cupboards and under my bed for any sign they were booby-trapped. There were no bombs but I found a listening device in the hall and one on the upstairs landing. I switched on Radio 4 to cover the sound of my movements and to let the eavesdroppers think that I suspected nothing.

When I walked to the end of the back garden and stood looking across the pasture, Blazing Bolt, the ageing white horse, ambled across to nuzzle my shoulder. I twisted his ear and rubbed his neck to say welcome. 'We have a situation,' I told him. He snorted and shook his head. 'Don't argue,' I told him. 'You don't know these fellas. If you see them in your field, run to the other end and stay there. Their fight isn't with you. That won't stop them hurting you, if it suits them.' Cyril said horses could read the minds of people they liked. I hoped Blazing couldn't read mine just then. I didn't want him to catch my confusion.

It had taken me a long time to find a secluded spot offering such anonymity. The peace and calmness of this place had taken root in me. Now it was as much a part of my life as was eating and sleeping. Living here on my own, in the silence, enriched me in ways I would not put into words for fear of draining away the gift of peace I had found. Standing in the garden at night watching the changes in the sky, feeling the movement of air around me, gave me a sense of my aloneness that was humbling. At the same time, I sensed the energy moving this immeasurable dark dome and the lights scattered across it. Cyril had taught me that the same energy held me softly, sheltered me tenderly, forgave my foibles and healed the wounds of a life lived carelessly. I teased Cyril about his druid faith, but I knew the truth of his beliefs.

To leave here at this stage of my life was impossible to consider. But would I kill to stay here?

Those two killers had not come to my door by accident. It would not be chance that would send them away.

If I didn't kill them, would they kill me?

Blazing shook his head and snorted. It seems like he reads minds, after all.

Desecration of the War Memorial

Thursday 12th March – Alder Moon

Ofsted inspectors don't cry. They make others cry. Card Index, a school inspector of many years' standing, was about to change the Ofsted image. He was on his knees on the small patch of grass in the middle of the village. The forty-nine tiny wooden crosses planted in neat rows in the grass at the foot of the memorial every November were scattered, mud-stained, some broken. The plot, so sacred to the British Legion and to the people of the village lay desecrated.

Card focused on picking up the crosses. 'Every one represents a man from the village who gave his life in the Great Wars. One cross for every name carved on the memorial. Two crosses are for my father's brothers and there is one for my mother's brother,' Card Index said, almost to himself. 'Each of them was killed before they reached the age of twenty-two.'

I sat on the bench to the side of the memorial, nodding my head as the only way I could show sympathy. I was afraid to disturb his mood by talking.

He laid his handkerchief on the ground and placed the pieces of the broken crosses on it one by one. When he had wrapped them, he handed the few unbroken crosses to me and sat beside me on the bench, holding his package on his upturned palms like a worshipper holding an offering before a shrine.

Stillness hung over us, silencing any urge to speak, blocking any movement other than that of staring silently at what rested in our hands.

I didn't see Gristle until he stood in front of us blocking the sun. For once, he picked up the atmosphere and waited for us to speak. Card had his head bent over, with eyes only for the bundle of broken relics. 'Someone desecrated the crosses,' I said.

'Bastards,' Gristle said.

I nodded. 'Card has collected the broken ones. These whole ones need washing.'

'I can mend the broken ones,' Gristle said.

'No,' Card said. 'I will do it.'

No one spoke for a few minutes. Gristle sat down on the bench on the other side of Card Index. 'You can use the woodworking equipment in my workshop,' Gristle offered.

Card shook his head. 'I've to buy special wood to make the new crosses.'

'I could do that, save you the bother,' I said.

'Why are you putting yourself out?' he said, looking at me, as if seeing me for the first time. 'You're not from around here. Why should you get involved?'

'Helping a friend,' I said. 'I can show respect too.'

'But you Irish didn't fight in the war.'

'Yes, we did,' I protested. 'Not officially, but thousands of Irish men and women joined up. A great-uncle of mine was killed in the First World War. And, we have a massive memorial in the main graveyard in Dublin commemorating the dead of the two world wars.'

'I never knew that,' Gristle said.

'Well, it's true, everyone knows it,' I said. 'Hundreds and thousands of Irish chaps were killed all over the world during those wars. They even got VCs and Military Crosses to prove it.'

'The glorious dead,' Card muttered. 'Carried in triumph to their last resting places of honour.'

'Hardly a resting place of honour when some of them were blown to pieces,' Gristle commented. He often lets his mouth run away with him like that.

Card Index swung around to stare at Gristle. 'The air

for ever carries the glory of their victory and is alive with the honour of their presence.'

'Tell that to them poor lads dragging themselves around the QE hospital in Birmingham who had legs and arms blown off. Not much honour for them to imagine their missing body bits floating through the air of Afghanistan while they learn to walk on plastic legs and eat without hands.'

Card leaped to his feet clutching his bundle of broken crosses to his heart, glaring at Gristle. 'They loved and served their country. True and brave men every one of them. No cost too great, no sacrifice too far, no thought of selfish gain in the service of others. They made this country great. You are not worthy to breathe the same air as them.' He stormed off, leaving Gristle looking puzzled.

'What?' he said. 'What did I say?'

I raised my eyebrows and shrugged my shoulders. 'I couldn't even begin to imagine,' I said. 'Sometimes, you need to…' I paused and sighed, '… sometimes you need to be aware that not everyone thinks and feels the same way as you. People can be sensitive.'

'I can be sensitive too,' he protested.

I looked at him. 'Good job you told me,' I said. 'Could you raise a middle finger, or wiggle your big toes the next time you're being sensitive, just so I know what is going on. I might mistakenly think you are suffering from constipation by looking only at your face.'

Gristle thought for a moment. 'Are you taking the piss?'

'Why would I do that?' I asked.

He sat silently for a moment. 'You couldn't see me wiggling my big toes if I was wearing boots. That's a stupid signal.'

'You're right,' I said, trying not to smile, 'that is a silly suggestion.'

Arthur Stockleman, the self-appointed village supervisor and busybody, came out of the butcher's shop and crossed the road to us. 'I've been watching you two. What are you up to? Did you pull up them crosses?' he said, nodding towards the few whole crosses Card had left in my care.

'Taking them to the cleaners to be dry cleaned,' I muttered, hoping he would go away. 'They are muddy. We want them shiny clean for the summer.'

'Why?'

'Soldiers are a bit fussy about appearances.'

'Soft in the head, you are,' he said. 'There's no soldiers here, not even dead ones. It's just a bit of grass with little wooden crosses. The dead soldiers are buried miles away. They can't see the crosses. You had better tidy up this place. We can't have mud and debris on the footpath. Do you know anything about it?' he asked, looking at Gristle.

'Sod off, Stockleman,' he answered.

'If it wasn't you, I bet it was those bloody kids again. I'd kill all the little buggers if it was down to me,' Stockleman said.

'That's a peace-loving thought for a leading light on the County Children Safeguarding Board,' I said.

'Sod the little buggers. Flogging is what they need. Public flogging would be better. Knock all that insolence out of them. In my day we—'

'went off killing innocent blokes in other countries,' Gristle interrupted.

'Duty,' Stockleman protested.

'Bollocks. You enjoyed it.'

He stared at Gristle. 'They were foreigners. They don't count.'

'You were the foreigner. You were in their country,'

73

Gristle said. 'How many did you kill, personally?'

'I can't answer that question. Official Secrets Act. Security issues. I was in Intelligence.'

'You were misplaced then,' I said.

Stockleman glared at me and then at Gristle. 'Waste of time talking to the likes of you two. Bet you never did anything for your country.'

'My taxes pay for the likes of you to go and shoot the poor bastards who didn't have a chance,' Gristle said. I could tell Stockleman was irritating him. Once he went down that path I never knew where he would stop.

'Stockleman, why don't you go and flog a kid. It'll make you feel better,' I said.

He paused for a moment, trying to think up some smart reply. As he turned away, he muttered loudly, 'At least I'm not a criminal shoplifter.'

We watched him march across the road shouting at a boy to stop cycling on the footpath.

We sat still. I tried to convince myself the sun was warm. Gristle picked at the flaking paint on the bench. I stared at the collection of wooden crosses in my hands. I could feel him looking at me out the corner of his eye.

'What?' I said.

'I didn't say anything,' he said.

'You want to ask me something,' I told him.

'You a mind reader now?'

I shrugged and waited.

He was struggling to find the right question. 'Did your uncle really win the VC medal?'

'He was my *great*-uncle,' I said, 'and no, I didn't say *he* won a medal. He was killed four days after the war ended.'

'Did no one tell him the war was over?'

'I don't know. We never asked him.'

He thought for a while. 'Bit silly that. You know, waiting till it's over and then letting himself be killed.'

'Happens.'

Silence saved me from more questions, for a while anyway. Gristle was never one for the speedy repartee. Questions worked their way slowly up from his subconscious, or hatched out in response to the physical stimulus that had to assault him to be noticed.

'The Scots are real bastards.'

I didn't know what prompted this comment. 'No more than most,' I said.

'In war, I mean. Everyone is afraid of them. No mercy with their bloody big swords. They frighten the shit out of everyone. Those bagpipes with all that noise would make anyone run away and hide. What must it be like when you know the bloke you are fighting is wearing a skirt, is stark naked under it and has a sword big enough to cut you in half with one blow? Doesn't bear thinking about.'

'Scots women are the same,' I said.

'I know, but I don't mind women not wearing knickers.'

I groaned. 'They carry weapons in their handbags, to beat off blokes like you.'

'They're good fun, though.' He sat smiling, probably playing with the memories running through his mind.

I sat wondering why no one ever put crosses on patches of grass for all the innocent people killed by soldiers.

I stood up. 'I'll go and ask the butcher for a bag to carry these crosses,' I said.

'Do you think the soldiers know who did this?' Gristle asked.

'They're dead.' I told him.

'I know, but Cyril says that the dead are not completely

dead. So, do the dead soldiers know what went on here?'

I nodded. 'I expect they do. Except, being insulted won't bother them.'

'Will they come back to haunt the kids?'

'Why would they?'

'People are always killing, or flogging, or punishing someone, or taking over the next country. The Gandhi bloke preached about it a lot.'

'You're thinking of Genghis Khan,' I said. 'Gandhi believed in peace. He preached *against* violence.'

He stood up and stretched. 'Come on, I'll go over to the butcher's with you to ask for a bag.'

We stood on the edge of the pavement watching for a gap in the traffic. A large Merc was the last in the line going by. As it was about to pass, the driver caught my eye. He was one of the soldiers from the church graveyard. He grinned at me. The other soldier sitting in the passenger seat made a gun out of his fist, pointed it at me, his finger pulling a trigger.

'C'mon, hurry up,' Gristle said, hurrying across the road without me. 'Can't have you killed before you clean them crosses. The soldiers would be rightly pissed off with you.'

They might be that already, I thought.

Village Vigilantes

Wednesday 18th March 2015 – Alder Moon

I stopped inside the door, looking around The Old Saddlery. Boyd Bromley, the owner, referred to it as, 'the rustic café', or 'the village tea shop, where simple country folk gathered to discuss crops and the weather'. That was as far from the truth as the expectation of townies that the countryside is a tranquil place where you live in harmony with your neighbours. The name of the café attracted the pompous and the opinionated from miles around. They paid more for a cup of coffee here than the tourists paid in the middle of Stratford-upon-Avon.

Card Index was sitting at a table by the back wall, opposite the door. I walked over to sit beside him, facing across the room with a clear view of the door and to stop anyone going behind me.

Boyd knew my preference and sent his wife across with a black coffee and a currant bun. Boyd called the buns a posh name so he could charge more for them. She set down the drink and the plate. 'How you doing, GG?' she asked, smiling at me.

'I'm fine, Madeleine. You fancy leaving that miserable old git and running off with me?' I asked.

'Not today, my lovely. I've the chimney sweep coming to the house later, my mother-in-law is bringing around one of her mighty monster pies that her podgy son loves, and today is my bath day, so not today, sweet thing,' she said, rubbing her hand across my shoulder. 'Come round on the right day and I will be out that door behind you faster than you can say "Cock your Robin".'

'You've been telling me that for the last forty years, Madeleine Bromley. You'll be walking behind my coffin the day you follow me out that door.'

She gave me a gentle shove and headed back to the counter and the podgy dour Boyd.

'Sexy devil, aren't you?' Card said, before poking at the crumbs of the apple pie on the empty plate in front of him and licking them off his fingers.

'She likes me teasing her. Always has. Harmless fun. The only fun she has when she is locked up with that old misery guts all day and night.' I ate my bun in silence. I waited. Card doesn't respond well to being rushed.

When I had finished eating and pushed away my plate, Card leaned forward, his forearms resting on the table. 'Last week,' he said, 'at the war memorial. I was upset. I was rude to you and Gristle. I didn't mean anything about the Irish and the wars.'

'That's ok,' I said.

'No, it wasn't ok. I was out of order.'

'You were upset.'

'Doesn't justify how I spoke to you. It's just that… those little crosses are all we have to remind us of those brave men.'

I nodded in agreement. 'It's easy to forget. It's a good job the likes of you remind us what those lads went through for their country.'

'I wanted to apologise for being rude when you offered to help and for casting aspersions on your countrymen.'

I pursed my lips and nodded, as if I was giving his apology due consideration. 'Thank you for being so generous,' I said. 'I accept your apology.'

He sat back in his chair looking relieved. 'Thank you.'

'You're welcome,' I answered.

The door was snapped open and three women pushed in, looking like they were about to take over the place, their high heels snicking on the flagstone floor. Without pausing their cackling and cawing, they surveyed the room, staring for a moment at Card Index and me sitting across from the door. The one with the largest handbag pointed to a table. 'That one by the window.' The screeching of chair legs on the floor along with the noise of heels clicking and clacking and the non-stop talking filled the room.

Madeleine crossed to stand slightly behind them, her order pad at the ready as they settled themselves. They ignored her as they nattered on. Largest-handbag looked around, 'I don't like this table. It isn't clean. We'll have that one behind the door? More privacy.' The three of them decamped to the table behind the door, Madeleine following silently behind them. The women looked like they were waiting for Madeleine to pull out the chairs to assist them in sitting down. Madeleine stared down at her order pad until the three women sat. 'The menu is on the table. There is a Specials Board by the serving bar with the specials of the day. I'll take your orders when you ladies have had a moment to catch your breath.'

'Just coffee. You don't expect us to eat here. What types of coffee do you serve?'

Madeleine listed the different types and combinations of coffees and sizes of cups and calmly wrote their orders and their changes of mind.

I looked at Card, who was staring at the scene. 'I wouldn't fancy trying to manage that lot at a meeting,' I said.

'Spoiled, rich, nothing to do but to try out new places around the county,' he answered. 'People like them should be put down.'

'That's a bit harsh.'

He turned up his mouth in a sneer but didn't answer.

'What type of car do you think they came in?' I asked.

'If they came in one car then it has to be one of those big Beemer jobs. Ladder attached for climbing up into the cockpit. Bet it was driven by her with the mouth and the big handbag.'

'Nah,' I said, 'if Big Handbag is driving then it is a Ferrari four-by-four. They are as big as a shed. A woman with a handbag that size wouldn't drive anything with a lesser badge on the front.'

Madeleine came across to us. 'More coffee, boys?'

We nodded. 'Any chance you could get that lot to quieten down?' Card asked.

'I'd have more hope of persuading Russia to give back Crimea,' she muttered, as she turned away to make our coffees.

Card Index watched the three women for a few moments. 'Ever think what makes people like them tick?' he asked.

'Gave up on that a long time ago,' I said.

'Some people get away with so much that they think they are above everyone and can do what they like. I can't stand them, but you have to deal with them carefully or they will destroy you without a thought. They thrive because they know people don't like to interfere and will put up with bad things.'

'That is a bit cynical,' I said.

'Ok, then. Go over and tell those ladies to stop talking so loudly because they are being inconsiderate, and tell them Madeleine is not something nasty stuck to the sole of their shoe.'

'I can't walk over and tell them to shut up.'

'Why not? Not right to get involved, is that it? A lot of bother over nothing, or shall we pretend we don't hear them?'

'It is only a bit of noise. It isn't important enough to cause trouble.'

'What is important enough to make you cause

trouble?'

Card rarely comes out with such strong personal views and he isn't given to idle chat. When he asks questions, he is leading somewhere, but he wants you to think you figured out how to get there by yourself. This technique comes from his Ofsted inspector days when he would harry the quarry he was quizzing until the victim was backed into a corner. I thought back over our conversation since his arrival, looking for a clue as to where he was headed with his questions. 'Desecrating the war memorial,' I suggested, 'that would be serious enough to cause trouble.'

He nodded. 'Indeed. And you were ready to help set things right when you saw the damage.'

'Any decent person would do it.'

'I didn't notice many decent people rushing to help.'

There was no point in challenging a statement of fact. I sat in silence.

The cackling trio were hard at it with lots of murmured talk punctuated with cries of 'I told her, I said…' and 'No!! She didn't, did she? Such cheek…' and 'He turned up and found them and, well, what could he do only…', and 'His father was the same…'

'Someone getting it in the neck over there,' I said.

'That's fine if they deserve it.'

'You're very judgemental today,' I said. 'You still think like an Ofsted inspector.'

He smiled at me and took his time to drink more of his coffee.

'There is something that is worth making a fuss over,' I said. 'The way old people are treated. We started to make a difference on that.'

'We were blocked. You were arrested, banned from the pub and now the Commander is in league with Bottle Blonde.'

'The Commander is sailing alongside Bottle?'

'Yes. Cosy as two fleas on a dog.'

'I'd never have believed it. What are they at? Does Skinny Slug know?'

He nodded. 'He knows. I don't know what they are at. Some business deal they are putting together.'

'The fight for the Venerables is not over,' I protested. 'It will start again.'

'After you get out of jail,'

'I won't go to jail.'

He shrugged his shoulders. 'Whatever.'

'It was only a few tins of beans.'

'And criminal damage in the other store and the assault on the security staff and—'

'Ok, ok, no need to go on,' I said. All that was small-fry stuff compared to the two brutes following me around. I was needled now and unwilling to play by the polite rules of his game. 'What is it you really asked me here to talk about?'

He looked at me with one of his looks that said he was deciding whether to trust me or to walk off. 'It's hard to talk with all that noise over there.'

'Go and tell them to shut up,' I suggested.

'Ha, very funny.'

'I can listen in spite of the noise.'

He licked his lips, a sign he had decided to take the plunge and trust me. 'How do you feel about paedophiles?'

'I never fancied them much. You starting an app for a dating website?'

'Don't be stupid. Do you approve of them?'

'No.'

'Would you stop one if you found him at it?'

'Yes.'

'Would you punish him?'

'I'd tell the police.'

'If it happened a long time ago?'

'Makes no difference,' I said, puzzled by where he was heading with this.

'Would you take the law into your own hands?'

'No need. The police will sort it.'

'Why not deal with it yourself?'

'The police know how best to deal with it. It's their job.'

'Suppose the paedophile was a policeman.'

'For goodness sake,' I spluttered. 'What are you getting at?'

'I am part of a group, they call themselves the Co-operative for the Pursuit and Prosecution of Paedophiles, CPPP for short. They block any of that sort moving into the area and drive out any who are here.'

'Like a vigilante group?'

'A bit like that. Except there's no lynching.'

'That's very civilised of them. What do you do instead of the odd hanging?'

'Warn then off, mainly.'

'Do they go?'

He nodded.

'If they don't?'

'They have always gone, eventually.'

'How long have you been at this?'

He shrugged. 'Me? Not long. The group has been going a good while,' he said, looking away from me like he didn't want me pushing him on the details.

'Why you telling me all this?'

'They are inviting you to join the group.'

I leaned back against the wall behind me, glad to feel something solid pushing into me, proving I was not dreaming or imagining the conversation I was having. I had heard Card spouting about child protection and safeguarding before now, but assumed his enthusiasm for the topic came from his work as an Ofsted inspector rooting out child abuse in schools. I took in his M&S shirt, woollen tie, sports jacket, corduroy trousers and brown brogues and almost laughed out loud at the image of him leading a lynch mob. How can a man dressed like the retired pensioner he is, with his innocent-looking face, bright eyes and quiet air, turn to violence? A flash of memory killed my humour as I remembered a mob chasing a boy along a narrow street and into a litter-strewn alley, the only sound that of the slap of their boots against the cobblestones, the sibilant sound of running people intent on killing and the splintering of glass as the thrown bottles hit the ground around me.

'Well?' he said, 'you in or out?'

'Why me?'

'You live hereabouts so you have an investment in the community. You know your way around the countryside in a way that few others do, even if your comings and goings are somewhat secretive. You don't really break the law, you just thwart the Excise, a countryside tradition as old as the hills.'

'I can't stand vigilantes or mobs who take the law into their own hands.'

'They aren't a mob. They don't run around the countryside after criminals. The members of the group are at the heart of the community. They see themselves as a community service group, part of David Cameron's Big Society. They help our community, they protect our children, they assist our police and they encourage evil sex monsters to see the error of their ways.'

'I think you should invite Gristle, not me, he has more personal knowledge of what goes on around here than I do.'

Card stared at me, his eyes narrowing as he focused on some idea buzzing around his brain. 'The group thinks he is part of the problem.'

'Not Gristle,' I burst out, loud enough for the three women to stop nattering and look over at us. I grinned and gave a little wave of my hand. It's a trick old men use to turn away attention. Senile old men, dribbling or talking loudly to themselves, are considered a blight on society and best avoided.

'Not Gristle,' I hissed, turning my attention back to Card Index. 'He is a friend.'

'Harold Shipman had lots of friends. How many suspected him of killing his patients?'

'That's ridiculous and you know it,' I said. 'Gristle is a bit unorthodox, but he would never do anything like that, especially after the upbringing he had from his father.'

Images of pillars of the community swarming over the countryside armed with billhooks and cudgels searching out paedophiles to bludgeon them to death as a punishment was so ridiculous an image as to be laughable. Only, I knew first-hand what people would do for ethnic and religious cleansing, so why not be extreme to protect children?

Card Index wasn't laughing. He was waiting for my answer. I needed a starting point that made sense if I was to put my feelings into some semblance of order and give him a clear answer. Then he gave me such a starting point.

'Those two chaps following you around,' he said, leaning towards me in a conspiratorial manner.

'Who told you about them?' I asked

He ignored my question. 'As a member of our group you could depend on the group to resolve whatever problem you have with those two following you. We look after our own, first and foremost. Let me know your answer in the next few days.'

He stood up and headed out of the rustic café, pausing in the doorway, holding the door open as he turned to face the three women. He smiled at the woman with the biggest handbag. 'You remind me of a film star,' he said. 'I was trying to remember who she was. You know how us old 'uns dither a bit.'

She beamed at him, delighted, waiting for him to name the film star.

'Then I remembered,' he said. 'It was that irritating dog Lassie. Never stopped barking, that bloody dog, ruined every film he was in.' He went out, shutting the door quietly behind him.

Someone had been poking Card Index's fire. I would never see him in the same light again.

From the Frying Pan into the Fire
Tuesday 24th March 2015 – Willow Moon

The guard dogs knew I was there. That was their business. They would tear me apart if ordered. That wouldn't happen tonight. I was safe from them as long as I stayed outside the line they were patrolling until the exact time arranged for me to cross the field towards the farm they were guarding.

I was sitting on a large rock on one side of the old Roman road, now just a broken pathway through the woods. From where I sat I had a good view of the field bordering the trees. My night-vision goggles would show up any animal, or man, that might cross the field. Blazing Bolt stood beside me, occasionally jerking or swinging his head as he sensed movements in the air. I rubbed his neck and blew softly through my pursed lips to reassure him and to stay his impatience.

In exactly five minutes the dogs would be called to heel. I would lead Bolt down to the barn to collect my assigned share of the smuggled load brought in that afternoon. In the surrounding countryside, people like me were waiting for their pre-arranged time to close in on the barn and collect their allocation. There would be no greetings, no talking, no exchange of money. That would take place in a few days in a friendly village hall.

The sky was cloudless but with only half a moon showing some light, but not enough for those unsure of their path. These tracks were as familiar to me as the hallway between my kitchen and my front room. The night-vision goggles were a luxury, not a necessity. Safe movement along these bridle paths was as much to do with sound, smell, touch and feeling movements in the air as it was to do with seeing. And I knew I was never on my own.

Bolt stretched his right foreleg and scraped it on the ground. He was saying hello to my grandfather. He was here. I could sense his presence. I caught the movement of a shadow out of the corner of my eye. I never see his spirit straight on. Cyril had told me that a clear sighting would mean he had come to take me with him to the next place. Cyril said my grandfather watched over me and put me on my guard if there was danger. Everyone had a personal guardian, he told me.

Somewhere in the darkness, a cow coughed with a juddering burst of breath. Foxes barked in the distance, their calls bouncing through the night. Closer by, badgers and animals of the night hunted in the bushes, a rustling of leaves and twigs marking their passage. I sat soundless on my rock beside an ancient road travelled by many for hundreds of years before me. Wrapped in my ankle-length, heavy dark coat, my black woollen hat pulled down to my ears, I sat out the remaining minutes until my time to move down to the barn.

Cyril said nature teaches us humility when we sit in the dark looking up at the stretch of stars across the sky. It is like sitting on the outside of the world, without a cover to stop us flying off. Maybe it is how an astronaut feels, floating in the black silence, tethered outside his spacecraft as he looks out into the corners of space, so unimaginably far away. On this path, in these woods, in this darkness, I feel I can see into the corners of the universe. Is there a corner out there where I will find peace? My life has been shaped always by having to find somewhere to go to, or to escape from.

The soundless shifting in the air around me could be the wake left by those who had tramped this way going home, or the efforts of those looking for a new home. Or maybe the sounds of the night are the whisperings of those

I have left behind as I was forced to search for another home. Not all the whispers are benedictions. The two soldiers who have tracked me down would speak no word of blessing or forgiveness, nor would those they represent.

I stood up from my seat on the rock. Just one minute to go. Bolt jerked his head. He pulled back when I tried to lead him forward. He was anxious. The movement of a shadow across the corner of my eye told me my grandfather was back. The smell of his pipe tobacco was in the air so I knew I was in real danger. I searched the field. There were no figures, no noise, no movement to alert me. A false alarm, surely. Calming the horse, I turned to lead him through the gap in the hedge.

The explosion of men shouting and the baying of big dogs in attack mode blew apart the calmness of the night. The sound of a gunshot stunned me into stillness, but only for a brief moment.

I learned very early in life that there are three sounds that command immediate reaction rather than waste time looking for an explanation. A gunshot is one of those sounds.

I turned and ran, leading Bolt beside me, back through the woods. At a safe distance, I took the panniers that should have been loaded with illegal cigarettes and whiskey off his back and hid them in the bushes away from the path. Meeting the Excise at this time of night would be pure bad luck, but with empty panniers on the horse, I would have difficulty persuading them I was out for a ride because I could not sleep.

Reaching the boundary of the paddock where Bolt spent his days, I waited while I checked out the field ahead. The noise of the raid on the rendezvous farm was far behind me. The threat from it would not go away easily. The Excise had to have been tipped off, which meant there was an informer in our midst. Each of us scheduled to pick up smuggled goods would be suspects until we proved ourselves innocent. In another place and in another time I had seen the treatment meted out to informers. I didn't want to see that sight ever again, still less to be on the receiving end.

I took off Bolt's halter and rubbed his forehead. 'We were lucky back there,' I whispered to him. He snorted in agreement before moving away to his favourite spot down by the pond and the big oak tree.

The glow of the nightlight in the hallway and the soft sound of the radio I always left on when going out at night welcomed me as I walked up the path to my back door.

I sensed that the movement of the air inside the kitchen was different. I reached down for the baseball bat I kept standing behind the back door. The bat was gone. The kitchen was empty. I took the carving knife from the block on the worktop and moved back into the hall.

'For fuck's sake, stop tap-dancing out there and come into the front room.'

It was one of the soldiers from the graveyard.

The two of them were sitting in the darkened room, at ease in my armchairs while I stood in the doorway with the light from the hallway behind me.

'I don't want any trouble. If you leave now, I'll say no more about it.' Neither of them moved. 'I've got a large knife,' I added, waving the carving knife in front of me.

'Scareey!' Big Hillside said. 'I've a gun. He has too. Gun blunts knife, so stop pissing about, come in and put on the bloody light. This darkness is getting on my nerves.'

'You won't get away with killing me,' I protested.

'You're no use to us dead,' Big Hillside said.

'*We* won't kill you,' Small Hillside added.

'But we know some old friends of yours who would be

delighted to do it, if we told them where to find you,' Big Hillside said. 'You are about to help us. Put down the knife before Kevin there breaks your arm while he takes it off you. He is partial to a bit of arm-breaking and damaging other appendages when he is in the mood. So don't be a silly bugger by provoking him. We have some serious talking to do, my little Irish bomber, you murdering bastard.'

I switched on the light to see Kevin staring at me. He was not smiling.

Seeking Help

Thursday 2nd April 2015 – Willow Moon

Gristle stared straight ahead. He does that when he is thinking through complex issues. Cutting to the chase, he calls it. Being able to deal with only one idea at a time, is what I call it. Whatever you call it, he eventually gets to the heart of the problem. Once there, he says the solution is obvious, if often unpalatable.

He took a deep breath and sighed loudly, a sure sign he was nearing the end of his hunt for understanding. Then came a shallow breath, and a light sigh; he was about to speak. 'I never knew you were involved with that IRA lot when you were a lad.'

'It was a long time ago,' I said.

'Were you known as Mad Mick the Irish Killing Machine, or were you Machine Gun Kelly or Stabber Murphy, or were you the top IRA assassin, or were you…?' He paused and stared out the windscreen, his mouth hanging open as he replayed in his mind the words he had just said. He closed his mouth and straightened up his head and shoulders before turning to me. 'You bastard. You're an assassin. You never told me. I thought we were friends.'

'I'm not an assassin. I was too young.'

'You were in the IRA, they kill people.'

'I didn't kill anyone. Not really.'

'What do you mean, "Not really"? What did you do? Shout "boo" and tell them to lie down and pretend to be dead?'

'I was a messenger. I carried parcels and took messages. They wouldn't let me do any killing or shooting. They said I was too young. But if they used stuff I carried then, yes, I am guilty.'

'How many did you blow up?'

'None. I was a messenger boy.'

'How come they found your fingerprint on a bomb, or what was left of a bomb?'

I paused at the painful memories I had painted for him from all those years ago. 'It could have been on a package I delivered and the bomber must have used the packaging as part of the bomb.'

'So you can identify the bomber.'

'That's what the soldiers want me to do.'

'Is that all they want from you?'

'They also want me to spy on someone. They work for MI5.'

'Who are you to spy on?'

'They didn't say. They also want information on Martin McGuinness.'

'The one in charge of the Irish government?'

'The Deputy First Minister, yes. He isn't in charge of the Irish government. He's in Northern Ireland.'

'How do you know him?' Gristle asked me.

'I was in Derry when he was in charge of Northern Command.'

'Did you fight for him?'

'I was in his division. He was there for only two years.'

'You could put him away, if you gave evidence, just like you could put away the bomber. Is that what they want?'

'No one can touch McGuinness now. The British government would make sure of that. He is too high up. You'd be dead before you could testify. None of that information about him is new, you can find it on Google.'

'Seems to me like it's deep shit time for you.'

I nodded in agreement. 'That's why I told you everything in case you can think of a way out.'

He frowned, no sighing this time, so I knew I was probably a hopeless case.

'It seems to me that you will be killed either by the two army chaps working for MI5, or by your former friends in the IRA, or you will be arrested and sentenced to a long stretch and the other prisoners will kill you when they find out what you are inside for, especially if you pretend it is only for shoplifting. You will die sure as day unless you agree to do what the army lads want and spy for them. Even then, you can't trust them. They'll turn you in when they have finished with you, or if you step out of line, or if you tell anyone about them. It is definitely shit-creek time.'

I thought for a moment. 'That about sums it up.'

He nodded approval at my recognition of his succinct conclusion.

'Are you scared?'

'Yes,' I answered.

'You should be. The odds are stacked against you. There is no way out and you don't have a chance against a couple of lads from First Paras.'

We were sitting in his beat-up Range Rover, parked in a lay-by hidden from the main road by a line of trees and bushes, a different lay-by from the one on the hill outside Stratford. He was tapping his fingers on the steering wheel as if playing a melody.

'So, what do I do?' I asked.

'I know you don't like it, but do what they say. Spy for them and turn in anyone they want when they tell you who it is. Better that than being some brute's toy-boy in prison, or being a close neighbour to the last dead person in the graveyard.'

'The IRA will kill me if I spy for MI5.'

He nodded. 'Can't blame them for that. Nobody likes spies.'

'It's not fair. I left all that years ago. I don't want to go back to it.'

'That's not how they see it,' he said. 'Life is tough, so tough it out. If you want a quiet life, lie down and die.'

'I don't intend to die, not just yet. I could fight back.'

'And die, or you could give in, spy for them and live a little bit longer.'

'I could refuse to help them,' I said.

'And be killed now or later in prison. Even if we killed these two, there will be plenty more where they come from. All these cuts to reduce the size of the army means there are loads of redundant killer soldiers bursting to slaughter someone, but there's no one to kill. They will be lining up for their turn to kill you if it takes them to a week after next Christmas before their turn comes around. I'd give in and spy if I were you.'

I was heartened to hear him using the word 'we', but only slightly so when I thought of the thousands of killer soldiers waiting to bump me off. 'No need for you to get involved,' I said, hoping he would disagree.

'I can't let them kill you,' he said. 'I'd have nobody to talk to if you were dead.'

'What about your women?'

He shrugged his shoulders. 'They don't count. You are the only one daft enough to put up with me.'

I looked at him out of the corner of my eye. He was grinning to himself. 'What?' I asked. 'What are you grinning at?'

'You,' he said. 'You go around with me, but refuse to spy for the government as if it was a matter of principle or something. If you had principles you wouldn't be seen near me.'

'I have loads of principles.'

'Name three.'

I hesitated. 'I am against killing, that's one.'

'That's not a principle, that's expediency. We'd all kill if we could get away with it, so that doesn't count. A principle is something like, ehm, well, something you wouldn't do no matter what.'

'Such as?' I asked. 'Name three things *you* wouldn't do.'

He sucked in his top lip as if this was a mighty challenge to be thought through carefully. 'I wouldn't kick a dog,' he said 'because dogs don't do no harm even when they bite you because they know no different. Or, let me see, I wouldn't drive a train full speed into the buffers at a station that was the end of the line. Or… if I saw some bloke without his trousers and he was wearing pink pants, I wouldn't laugh at him.'

'You can't drive a train, so how could you crash it.'

'Exactly, it is a principle, that's why I don't drive the things.'

'When did you ever see a bloke with no trousers and wearing pink pants?'

'Just now, over there, going behind that lorry. The other bloke with him has green pants. Do you think they are colour blind, or is it some sort of a signal?'

I looked around, shocked at what he had said. 'Is this another one of *those* lay-bys?' I asked. 'How many gay lorry drivers are there, for goodness sake?'

'All lay-bys are *those sort* if they have lots of trees and bushes around them. I thought you knew that.'

'Can we drive out of here, now?' I asked, 'before someone sees us'.

'They already have. Did you not see Dickie Dickson scoot off when we drove in? He won't say anything as long as we don't say he was here and who he was with and what they were doing. He might work in a chemist's shop, but it wasn't pills he was giving the chap with him.'

'I never noticed him.'

He snorted. 'You're not much of a spy when you can't see what is under your nose.'

'I'm not a spy.'

'You will be as soon as you work out it is healthier than being dead.'

I bent down to tidy the floor at my feet as we drove out of the lay-by, a good excuse to hide my face in case anyone was looking. 'How come you never tidy this car? Look at this mess, spanners, screwdrivers, boxes, empty bottles, socks, bits of sandwiches, two odd shoes, apple cores, a humane mousetrap. It is like a mobile health hazard in here.'

'The seat is clean, isn't it?'

'Only because I took all the rubbish off it,' I said.

'See, it was you who made it untidy by dumping everything on the floor.'

I gave up and slumped down in the seat, overwhelmed by the injustice of being dragged back into a life I thought I had left long ago. I could see no way out.

'I don't even know who they want me to spy on,' I said.

'They could hardly tell you until you agreed. You might warn the person before the two lads killed you.'

We drove for a while until he broke the silence. 'If I call you "GG the spy", what do I call the person you spy on? Is he the "spyee" or the "spied upon" or the "spyeye"? You could report to your spy masters "Aye aye, I spied with my little eye a spyeye who didn't know I spied him".'

I didn't encourage him. Without looking, I knew he was grinning again. 'Drop me home and hurry up before you think up any more daft things to say.'

Spying Galore

Monday 13th April 2015 – Willow Moon

I had been summoned to the meeting of the village elite, convened in Card Index's front room. The woman squinting at me had the look of a hungry owl perched in a tree, waiting for its next meal to scuttle through the long grass. Her unblinking eyes staring at me through thick-rimmed glasses distracted me from her other grim features.

'Mrs Cenhelm,' I murmured in greeting.

'As postmistress, Olivia is in an excellent position to manage our communications network. We don't know how we would function without her expertise in communications. She keeps us up to date and in contact with each other at all times and at a moment's notice.'

Mrs Cenhelm flicked her eyes in Card Index's direction, possibly a sign that she approved his public acknowledgement of her key role. He turned to the next member of the group.

'Ms Philomena Luge, as you know, is a highly successful businesswoman running the village flower shop. She is our head of logistics. Our group functions efficiently because of the skills she learned flying killer drones in the RAF. On becoming a Jehovah's Witness, she resigned her commission and now devotes herself, in a different way, to cleansing and purifying our corrupt society.'

I nodded in greeting, giving her a feeble smile of recognition. For some reason, she reminded me of a bed of nettles and tangled briars growing against the side of a cow byre.

'Mr Arthur Stockleman, as you know, is a true pillar of the community,' Card said, indicating the man sitting in an armchair in the bow window. 'Arthur is our Head of Suspects Profiling. He serves on the County Children

Safeguarding Board and also engages actively with the county council to make them do their duty of keeping the village tidy and clean.'

Arthur seemed to take a bow without standing up. 'Can't allow standards to slip,' he piped. 'Zero tolerance is what we practise. Self-respect, respect for others and pride in where we live are the keys to a happy community. Intolerant and selfish people have to be driven out. Unacceptable standards will not be tolerated.' Especially if you have a liking for flogging kids who step out of line, I thought, remembering our conversation near the war memorial.

'You do keep the village in wonderful condition,' I said, imagining him like a petulant cock robin intolerant of visiting birds when a new arrival crossed his territory. 'I love the window displays in your picture-framing shop,' I added.

He beamed broadly. 'Do it all myself. I have an eye for what is right, a sense of balance and perspective and, of course, an artistic temperament and a generous endowment of good taste.'

Bill the butcher stood with his back to the fireplace, dominating the room by his bulk. 'Bill you know well,' Card said by way of introduction. 'Who doesn't know Bill, eh?' he added. 'A well-known pig farmer, proprietor of his widely acclaimed organic butcher's shop, leading member of the local Farmers Union, key player in the Countryside Alliance, community representative on the police board and leader of the Neighbourhood Watch. All his roles put him in a good place to gather information about what is going on in the area. Such a selfless man has to be admired as a leader of the community, so dedicated to the service of others.' I imagined him as a big black dog rooting in bins and crapping on people's lawns. He replied to my greeting with a cold stare.

Card continued, 'Bill's sons, Barry, Bradley and Brutus, are our direct action facilitators when we need extra support. They are associate members of the group.'

Having seen the three sons in an affray outside a pub in Alcester, I knew 'brutal enforcers' would be a more accurate description of their direct action facilitation.

I turned towards the weedy-looking man perched on a hard kitchen chair to the right of Mrs Cenhelm. Cyracuse Cactus Chadwick had been given his middle name in celebration of his father's reputation as the grower of the best cacti in the West Midlands. Gristle used to joke that Cyracuse had got off lightly with his middle name, considering what he might have been called had his father been a top consultant on testicular cancer.

'Cyracuse, in his role as an estate agent, checks out all incomers and keeps records of home owners and their habits.' And keeps copies of keys of the houses he sells, I thought, so he can visit the houses later to spy on the newcomers. I had seen him around the village, obsequious with potential buyers, but behind their backs scurrying like a grey squirrel, collecting and hoarding information.

Cyracuse crossed his legs and folded his arms. 'Enough of the introductions. We have business to sort.'

'Of course,' Card said and sat down in the armchair by the fireplace. There was no seat for me. I stood to the right of the door and gradually inched back until my back rested against the wall behind me. All eyes turned to Bill the butcher.

The butcher looked at each of them in turn. 'The purpose of this meeting is to consider offering our visitor the privilege of associate membership of our Co-operative.' The lack of warmth in his voice made me think he was reciting lines someone had written for him. He glared at me before launching into the next part of his memorised script. 'Normally, according to the rules of our constitution, you would not be eligible to join because you were not born here, nor has your family resided here for three generations and you have not lived here continuously for twenty-five years. However, force of circumstances demands we waive the normal procedures.'

'Can we just get on,' Cyracuse interrupted. 'I have a meeting with a prospective buyer for the old station cottage in an hour.'

The butcher looked up at the ceiling before continuing. 'I am sure brother Chadwick will remember the need to abide by the rules of the constitution when we are considering such an important move.'

Cyracuse grunted and twisted on his chair.

The butcher turned his attention back to me. 'We are a Co-operative. That means our work is under the direction of the full members only. We are not beholden to outsiders or outside influences and we are accountable only to those holding full membership of this Co-operative. Only full members are eligible to receive a dividend when the profits are declared at the end of the financial year.'

He shifted his weight. He was enjoying his command of the meeting. 'We pursue paedophiles, pure and simple. We root them out of our community and drive them away. We are the Co-operative for the Pursuit and Prosecution of Paedophiles. We do what the title says.' He fixed me with what he must have thought was a domineering look. I could think of more appropriate words for the title CPPP. 'As an associate member, you will help in this activity by collecting information and data on those we suspect of being part of this disgusting sexual trade in young children and vulnerable young adults.'

'Do I have to find them, or is there a list of the ones

you suspect?' I was there only because Card had told me in the café that they suspected Gristle was a paedophile. I wanted to find out what they knew and warn Gristle. Asking a question had taken the butcher by surprise.

The butcher recovered quickly. You develop that skill if you are killing pigs that are notoriously reluctant to co-operate in their own slaughter. 'There may be one or two we know about, but it would be your job to find others. You move in unsavoury circles where these filthy criminals gather.' I thought to myself that my smuggler friends would object to being called 'unsavoury' or 'filthy'.

'Do we go to the police with the evidence?' I said.

The tension in the air shifted up a notch.

Philomena Luge butted in with a more winsome tone in her voice than that used by the butcher. 'We are more benign and Christian than that. Even disgusting sinners should be offered the chance to repent and to seek forgiveness for their filthy lives.'

'What? You make them go to church?'

Shifting of eyes and shuffling around on chairs followed that question. I was going somewhere with my questions that they had not anticipated. I was enjoying unsettling these hypocrites. Arthur the picture-framing expert broke the silence. 'We fine them.'

'Actually,' Card Index broke in, 'we give them a choice. They can repent or we go to the police. If they repent and give up their illicit activities, they pay a fine and gather information on others who indulge in such filthy ways.'

'Who sets the fine?' I asked, realising that this was the dividend they shared at the end of the year.

Again there was a reluctance to answer.

'Is it a fixed fine?' I prompted.

By now they were all staring at the floor apart from

Mrs Cenhelm, who looked more and more like that hunting owl ready to pounce on me for her next meal.

Philomena Luge sat up straight. 'We are not unfeeling people. We take account of the dirty sinful perverts' circumstances. The Bible guides us when it says, "from those who have been given more, much more will be expected". Everyone according to his means, as it were.'

'Not according the severity of the crime, then?' I asked.

'We take all circumstances into account,' Cyracuse snapped at me. 'If you were given the choice of being exposed as a paedophile or allowed to repent and pay a fine as a sign of repentance, which would you choose? We give these degenerates a chance to be respectable members of society.'

'What if they won't pay?' I said.

The pig-slayer found his voice again. 'We report them to the police and they pay a higher price and suffer in jail, where they should be locked up to rot. Now, are you with us or not? We were led to believe that you were against these animals and would help us.'

'What's in it for me?' By the look on their faces I knew I was at last talking their language.

'We have influence with the supermarket manager,' the butcher said with a smirk. 'He will drop the charges against you. As well as that, we can help ease your relationships with your smuggler friends. You are their prime suspect because the raid took place just as you were due to arrive. I am sure you are aware of what they are likely to do.' I was staggered. How did he know about the raid and that I was on the point of heading to the barn when the raid started? 'We will also have you reinstated in the pub.' He grinned at me in what I thought was a nasty way. 'It might be more in your line to ask what will happen if you don't help us, or shall I spell it out for you? Especially if your friends the smugglers pick up wrong messages about you.'

'Who do you want me to investigate?' I asked. Self-preservation trumps high principles every time.

'Gristle,' the butcher answered.

'I can tell you now, Gristle is not one of those lads.'

Cyracuse spoke up. 'He has abused at least two underage girls. He visited the primary school and encouraged the children to have sex and he took photos of them on his phone. He can afford to pay a large fine for his sins.'

'He talked to the children about growing up in the village years ago. He wasn't talking about sex,' I protested

'We have evidence to say he did,' Cyracuse said. 'What about his filthy illegal activity with two underage girls? They will swear it happened.'

The butcher intervened. 'We want to know who are his criminal contacts, how widespread is his evil group and who are his other victims. He has been seen loitering in lay-bys and his reputation for seducing young women is well known. His behaviour is reprehensible for someone living in a God-fearing village such as ours. You are closer to him than most so you will find the evidence we need. Or, would you prefer time in prison for your misdeeds?'

There was no sympathy in any of the faces looking at me. I shrugged my shoulders. 'I'll see what I can do.'

'We will look forward to your findings,' the butcher added with a grin.

Cyracuse raised his hand for attention. 'There is one other issue I want to raise with the Co-operative. Two strangers have visited me. They are ex-soldiers. They claim to be looking for a big house to lodge soldiers injured in war, soldiers with missing body parts, like a Cheshire

Homes set-up. Has anyone come across them?'

I kept quiet. It sounded like my soldier boys were going public.

'Will these crippled soldiers be officers or squaddies?' Mrs Cenhelm asked.

'They didn't say. What difference will it make?' Cyracuse asked.

'Think about the quality of visitors who will descend on us if these cripples are housed in our village,' she answered. 'Imagine the families of ordinary soldiers arriving to visit them. Not the type we want wandering through the village. The amount of petty larceny, drunkenness and pilfering would be intolerable.'

'I agree,' Philomena Luge added. 'The families of officers would be so much more acceptable. Better class of persons in every sense of the word. I suggest you should be careful which houses you show them, Cyracuse.'

Mrs Cenhelm nodded in approval. 'Maybe it would be better to point them to properties outside the parish boundaries, possibly in Alcester. We don't want busloads of visitors from the slums of cities every week. In addition, imagine what it would be like seeing some of the cripples walking around the village with missing arms and legs. I visited the QE hospital in Birmingham a few weeks back and saw several of those crippled soldiers in the entrance hallway with bits of iron for arms and legs and no covers to hide their deformity from visitors. I found the sight quite distasteful.'

'How awful for you,' Philomena Luge said. 'Did you protest?'

'Naturally. The young lady behind the desk was quite sniffy about it and acted as if the fault was with me. I wrote a severe letter to the hospital authorities on my return home, but typically I have had no response yet.'

'Quite right to make a stand,' Arthur added. 'The level of depravity and lawlessness in the country is down to too many people not caring enough to stand up for decency and Christian values. We certainly don't want cripples and deformed people wandering around the village, with God knows what type of visitors arriving by the lorry load from Birmingham to see them. Stick to the aims of our Co-operative, I say. Keep the village neat, tidy and pure the way we like it.'

The point was greeted with approval by the group.

I thought, what sort of group have I been drawn into? Could I really betray Gristle? On the other hand, would I rather go to jail, or take whatever punishment the smugglers would dish out? How could I deal with the threats from the soldiers? My quiet hidden life was growing more complicated each day. This time there was nowhere to run to and hide.

Coming Out

Monday 13th April 2015 – Willow Moon

I hid in the bushes at the end of the lane until the last of the CPPP members had driven away from Card Index's house. I waited another five minutes in case anyone came back.

I rang the doorbell twice before I heard him coming down his stairs. He stood in the half-opened doorway, surprised to see me. 'It's you.'

I didn't say anything.

'Did you forget something?'

I shook my head. 'Am I allowed in, or do I stab you out here on the doorstep?'

'Ah. Best come in if it's stabbing you have in mind.' Stepping to the side, he gave me room to go past him. He peered up and down the lane before closing the door and leading me into the room I had left a little earlier.

I stood in the middle of the room and faced him. 'What did you get me into?'

'You said you wanted to help deal with paedophiles.'

'Only because I wanted to know what you lot suspected about Gristle. I didn't expect to meet extortionists and blackmailers. You never even hinted I would be asked to spy on a friend, or that I would be threatened.'

He shrugged. 'That's just their way.'

'What do you mean, "just their way"? They are crooks and sanctimonious bastards who delight in destroying people. They ignore the law, they take matters into their own hands, they think they own the village and can do anything they want. I am amazed they don't issue visas to visit the place. As to imposing fines, my arse! They are extortionists who rob people they catch out. They talk about sharing out dividends at the end of the year; more like divvying up their spoils. Their main aim is to feather their own nests.'

'You agreed to help them.'

'I didn't have a choice.'

'You're in now.'

'I don't have to stay,' I said. 'I can walk away any time I want.'

'You can't,' he said. 'They will do everything they threatened and hand you over to the police, or to the smugglers.' He paused for a moment. 'Or to the two soldiers who are asking about you.'

'They know nothing about me or the soldiers,' I said.

'They know the soldiers want something. Once they find out what is going on and you are connected they will put real pressure on you. This is only the start of your problems, believe me.'

'They know nothing about me.'

'They soon will, or they will make up information. They never let facts or truth get in their way. Rumours and innuendo are their key tools. Go against them and you might as well throw yourself into a shredder. They will spit you out in little pieces, whether or not you deserve it.'

I walked across and stood in the window looking out across his front garden.

'Do you want a coffee?' he asked.

I shook my head.

'A drop of something? I've a bottle of whiskey hidden in the kitchen. Come on, there's no point staring out that window. The smell of them is still in this room.'

I heard him go through the hall into the kitchen. Bottles were moved in a cupboard, a drawer was pushed home and the noise of glasses being shifted drew me after him.

'Sit down,' he said, pointing to the chair opposite where he was standing at the table. He poured a generous measure of whiskey. 'Water?'

I shook my head. 'I hope this is proper stuff and not mixed with body fluids.'

He poured his own drink, sat down across from me and put the bottle on the table between us. 'It's the real McCoy.'

'To your good health and all the luck you will need,' he said, raising his glass to me.

I lifted my glass to touch his in reply to his toast. We sat in silence while my mind worked through the implications of what Card had just told me. I didn't know what questions to ask or where to start to make sense of it all.

Card must have sensed my confusion. 'Start with Gristle.'

I looked at him. 'What has he done?'

'Not "what", try asking "why" questions. The so-called Co-operative will make up the "what". You need to know the "why". The paedophile accusation is the "what" and only the last in a long line of tactics they have used, and not just against Gristle.'

'I know he can be difficult and outrageous and sometimes he acts as if he—'

'They hate him. They despise him. They resent him and his wealth. They will never forgive him because his father and his father before him ran the whole countryside around here and rode roughshod over them and their families. Family grudges mean a lot in a village and are carried on from generation to generation. Old scores will always be settled eventually. On top of that, Gristle has a lot of money and they want to get their hands on it.'

'This is about greed?'

'No, settling old scores first, then greed is a close second. That there is a lot of money in it is all the better.'

'Gristle isn't a paedophile.'

'They say he is and that he had sex with underage girls and is grooming the kids in the local school. They have the statements of the two girls he assaulted and they want you to get the proof he is grooming and photographing little ones for kiddy porn.'

'Who are the underage girls?'

'Grown up now. It happened a long time ago.'

'Who are the women?'

'Bixey Halligan and Maudie Millstroom.'

'They are ancient,' I protested.

'So is Gristle. It happened a long time ago, according to the women. Under 16 they were, according to their story. They will swear to it.'

'No case to answer, it is their word against his,' I said.

'There are two of them and God knows who else will come out of the woodwork, either because it is true, or because others will think there is money for them in the publicity.'

I sighed as the full weight of what he said hit me. 'Thank God for whiskey,' I murmured and took a long swig of it.

I picked up his suggestion about asking 'why' questions. 'Why me, why not get you to find the information? You are one of them already.'

'I tried. I couldn't get what they wanted. You are the closest to a friend Gristle has. He trusts you. Plus, they think you are too stupid to figure out what they are up to.'

'Stupid?'

'You're Irish and you're not from around here.'

'All Irish are stupid, is that what they think?'

He nodded. 'Once this is all over, they will get rid of you, run you out of the village, or whatever. You have no family to fight your corner or get back at them.'

The 'why' questions were flying across my mind now. 'Why are you mixed up with them? I hadn't put you down as a money-grabbing, family-feuding arsehole.'

He shifted in his chair and poured more whiskey into the two glasses. He took a long drink, looked down at his glass, waited a moment, took a deep breath and let out a quick sigh. 'I am not a full member of the Co-operative.'

'But they meet in your house.'

'Part of the fine I pay.'

I paused while I checked to be sure I was putting together the clues he had been giving me.

He nodded his head as if he was reading my mind. 'Say it,' he said.

'You're one of their victims, paying the price for your sins.'

He grunted in agreement.

'You are a paedophile!'

'Not exactly. But I had too much to lose from bad publicity. I had to go along with them. It reached a point where it was too late to escape.'

'Either you're a paedophile or you're not. You can't be "not exactly". It isn't like catching the flu that lasts for a few weeks and then goes away.'

He fiddled with his whiskey glass, twisting it around and tilting it slightly from side to side. I was looking at a man who was making big decisions in his mind.

'After my second wife left me... I don't know if you are aware that I was fairly senior in Ofsted inspections and... The point is, I had led some very high-profile school inspections with a lot of publicity in a few cases. I was expected to be whiter than white. My second wife left me and it was as if—'

'They found out you were into kiddy porn.'

'No! Nothing like that.'

'What, then?'

'I took up with a young teacher I had met on an inspection. I sent some indiscrete emails and they found out about it.'

'You mean she grassed you up.'

He looked me straight in the eye. 'She was a he. And he didn't grass me up. They found the emails on my computer.'

'You mean you are…'

'Gay.'

'Oh.' That word is such a stupid sound. What other sound could express my astonishment that my perception of someone had been turned upside down, inside out, back to front. 'Oh,' I repeated, playing for time while my brain worked out how to make my mouth move in a sensible way. My next words did not represent cutting-edge repartee, nor the savage put-down I would have aimed for had the perpetrators been in front of me. Nor did they convey the depth of anguish and the surge of sadness I felt for my friend. 'The bastards!' I drained my whiskey and pushed the empty glass across the table towards him.

'You didn't know?' he asked.

I shook my head.

'Oh,' he said. Now he was making the simple sound that said so much.

He poured me another whiskey like it was some intricate rubric to be observed. His hand was steady, the pouring slow, the measure generous, the bottle never touching the glass. We both fixed our eyes on the operation as if it was the most important act we could witness. He pushed the glass slowly across the table until I could wrap my fingers around it without having to stretch out my arm.

I stirred myself. 'Am I the first you came out of the cupboard to?'

'Closet,' he said as he nodded. We were into limited word communication by the sound of it.

'But you married twice.'

'I thought it would cure me.'

The sharp, iodine, sea-fleck taste of the whiskey was softening as my mouth welcomed the drenching of my taste buds, while at the same time the relaxant power of the distillation began working on my brain.

'At least your fine was easy, letting them use your house for meetings.'

He shook his head. 'That is only part of the fine.'

I think I raised my eyebrows in a questioning way because he answered before I asked.

'Each of them have equal shares with me in the proceeds from the app I designed and I had to sign over my house to them. It's in my will so they get that when I die. No one to leave it to, they said, if I am gay.'

'Change your will, go to a solicitor and... and... tell them to... to shag off.'

'Can't,' he said. 'It's all tied up in a trust deed and I am not one of the trustees.

'The bastards.' I knew about trust deeds, the last resort of deceivers, legal robbers and greedy gobshites. Trust deeds put you in the deepest shit.

He nodded his head and we sat silently for a few moments staring at the whiskey glasses.

'Do you think Gristle is a paedophile?'

'No,' he said.

'But you said he was.'

'I said *they* think he is. They want him to be one.'

'So why drag me into this mess if you knew he is innocent? Why not tell Gristle?'

'You know Gristle. He would kill them.'

'Sounds like a good idea.'

'That would get him locked up? Can you see him surviving that?'

I shook my head.

'Anyway, I thought if you were involved you would find a way out for all of us. I need you to help me turn over the greedy bastards. I could get the better of them if you helped me.'

'Me? Me, help you find a way out?'

'You can find your way out of a thick wood on a dark night so you'll find a way out of this.'

'Do you realise I could end up in a box with the lid nailed down on a lorry heading to Ukraine, or in a sack on the way to First Paras headquarters in Wales, or looking down the wrong end of an IRA rifle outside Derry, or hanging out the door of an MI5 helicopter saying my last goodnight before dropping five hundred feet into the Irish sea? You think you have problems?'

He smiled at me. 'You forgot one other problem you have.'

'What's that?'

'Let me put this delicately. How do you think people will feel about you when they find out that you have one friend, Gristle, who shags every passing woman looking to get at his money, one who likes to shag blokes, me, and Cyril, who shags women and trees in the name of religion?'

'Compared to what you don't know about me, all that is nothing. Is it any wonder I am mixed-up?'

He smiled. 'I take it you are with me.'

I smiled back. That whiskey was weaving its magic and we still had half the bottle to work through.

Bert's Bestest Bacon Butty Bar

Friday 17th April 2015 – Willow Moon

'Ok,' Gristle said, 'I promise not to kill you.'

Card Index breathed a sigh of relief.

'Not just yet,' Gristle added.

'Hold on, Gristle. He told you everything. He could have kept it secret,' I said.

'Am I supposed to be grateful that he confessed he spied on me behind my back? Now you intend to spy on me as well as him. I should kill both of you.'

'I don't want to spy on you. Listen to what I'm saying. Stop going on about killing if you want to hear the full story.'

'I don't need the full story. It's enough to know that that crowd of arseholes are setting me up. I'll kill them too.'

'I told you he'd be like this,' Card said, opening the car door. 'I'll walk home. That way, I won't have to listen to the mad ravings of a loony.'

I reached back over the seat and caught Card's arm. 'Wait, wait for a minute. We can sort this out if we talk about it.'

'He doesn't want to talk. He intends to murder everyone.'

'At least he doesn't plan to kill *you*. Walk away now and you will be like the others and I'll kill you.'

Card pulled in the car door until it snicked shut. He settled himself back in the seat. Gristle leaned forward, resting his forearms on the steering wheel, a typical pose when he is thinking and similar to the way he drives on motorways. He stared at the mobile café in front of us in the lay-by as if he was expecting something remarkable to pop out of the serving hatch. The A-board at the entrance to the lay-by told us we were looking at *Berts Bestest Bacon Butty Bar*. The steady flow of customers, mostly men, climbing out of vans and lorries testified to the accuracy of the word 'Bestest'.

'So?' I said, breaking the silence. 'Now what?'

'I could do with a cup of tea and a bacon butty,' Gristle said, releasing his seat belt. Pulling the release catch, he shoved the door open with his elbow. 'Are you two coming?'

I opened my door to follow him.

'I'll have a cappuccino,' Card said.

Gristle stopped and looked back in. 'You can have tea in a *big* mug, or tea a *small* mug. That's the choice Bert gives. Just wait till you taste his bacon butties; pure magic.'

'The place doesn't look very hygienic,' Card said.

'I'll ask Bert to wear his Marigold gloves when making your sandwich,' Gristle said, 'and naturally the whole lot will be served on a beautiful tray covered with doilies, while his wonderful assistant, Aggie the Teeth, regales us with her wit and repartee. That's her with the eye-patch and the fag in her mouth.'

We waited our turn in the queue with no mention of killing or spying.

'What do *you* want?' Aggie said, when it was our turn, staring at Gristle with her uncovered eye, flicking the fag end over his shoulder.

'I want the chance to look you in your fair eye, before whisking you off to some exotic beach, where I will play my fingers on your naked flesh and smother every part of your beautiful body with kisses in the light of the setting sun, breathing in the whiskey fumes on your breath, entranced by the quiet murmur of the gentle waves lapping around our naked bodies passionately entwined on the sand.'

'Fuck off, Gristle. What d'you want?'

At the sound of Gristle's name, Bert turned round from the worktop at the back of the mobile hut where he was making sandwiches.

'Hi, Gristle. Usual? Wholemeal, no sauce, double bacon, crisply done, sea salt only and freshly ground black pepper, a side of three fat sausages and a large mug of Earl Grey?'

'Hi, Bert. Make it sandwiches for three with one large mug, two small. Don't be so crude about the tea. It's past 11 o'clock, it has to be Ceylon Orange Pekoe.'

'Eating in or taking away?' Aggie asked, without a smile cracking her face.

Gristle took in the once-white plastic garden tables and chairs scattered around the lay-by. 'I think, on reflection, we will eat in today, Aggie. The sumptuousness of your décor is too enticing to take our food elsewhere. Will you grace us with your presence when serving Bert's supreme cooked delight?'

'Fuck off, Gristle.'

Card used his handkerchief to wipe the chair before sitting on it. 'Can you ask her for some serviettes and a cloth to wipe the table?' he said to Gristle.

He frowned at Card. 'In your dreams.'

We sat without speaking, looking at the cars and vans pulling in around us, or gazing at the steady line of customers lining up for Bert's butties. When his name was called by Aggie, Gristle brought across three plates, each heaped with monstrous slabs of fresh bread with layers of bacon holding the slabs apart and the fattest sausages I had ever seen oozing grease around the base of the wall of bread and bacon.

'Any knives and forks?' Card asked.

Gristle nodded towards the serving hatch. 'Plastic ones.

Help yourself.'

Gristle pushed down hard on his sandwich with the heel of his hand, picked up the flattened mountain of food and took great bites out of it. I lifted off the top layer of bread and ate that as I picked up and munched my way through the slices of bacon. Card was not used to this alfresco style of eating and starting cutting the sausages into bite-sized pieces.

'Pick the sausages up in your hand and eat them from the end, sucking them as you bite,' Gristle advised from behind a barrier of bread and bacon held in a two-handed grip in front of his mouth. 'You get the benefit of all the fat that way.'

Seeing the success I was having attacking my sandwich in a piecemeal manner gave Card the courage to do the same. He drank from his mug. 'God, God, this is real Ceylon Orange Pekoe tea.'

'Ah, I should have asked what you wanted,' Gristle said. 'Bert has a full range of loose-leaf teas. I assumed you would go with the Orange Pekoe at this time of the day. He buys it from Ringtons of Newcastle. Do you want a different one?'

'This is fine,' Card said, looking puzzled. 'I wasn't expecting it.'

'This bacon is superb. Home reared?' I asked.

'Bert doesn't rear them any more. Takes up too much time, he said. He sources his meat from several smallholders, all with the best of home-produced meat. Bert used to be a Michelin-star chef so he knows good food.'

'What happened?' Card asked.

Gristle munched through another mouthful before answering. 'Gave it up. Long hours. Didn't get to see the customers. Owners were arseholes. Loves it here, works half days, only five days a week, knows all his regulars, is held in high regard and knows more about what is happening than MI5, MI6 and GCHQ put together. A good bloke to have on your side.'

'What about Aggie?' I said.

'She's his life-long missus.'

Card frowned at the idea, 'But she is so…'

'Ugly?' Gristle said. 'The eye-patch is false, the greasy hair is a wig, the teeth are blackened every morning and the rough manner and language are put on. I've seen her dressed up at functions. You would let them drain every last drop of your blood in transfusions just to be allowed to stand near her and look at her.'

'But why…?' I asked.

'At the start, when she looked like her real self, there were too many fights among the customers because they held up the queue wanting to talk to her and gaze at her. She invented Aggie the Teeth. Problem solved.'

'Do you know the problem with this country?' I said.

'You're about to tell us,' Gristle said.

'Nothing is ever what it looks like, no one says what they think and you all pretend to be someone you are not.'

'You're a fine one to talk,' Card said. 'Put the words, kettle, pot and black together in a sentence, little spy master and secret assassin.'

'I'm different. I have to hide.'

'Because you killed people,' Gristle said.

'So did you,' I answered.

'I did it because I had no choice; you did it because you wanted to. Big difference,' he answered.

After that, we sat drinking our tea, ignoring each other, watching new customers spilling out of cars and lorries following the smell of cooking bacon and sausages.

I leaned forward, my forearms resting on the table so

119

that I could speak quietly. 'So where are we up to with our other… er… issue?'

'He promised no slaughter,' Card said.

'I didn't, I said I wouldn't kill *you two*, not yet anyway. How do you read the "other issue", great mastermind?' Gristle asked, leaning forward to look at me directly.

'It seems to me that we are each exposed and we are being picked off one at a time. Alone, we are easy targets with little by way of defence – other than killing everyone in sight,' I added, glaring at Gristle. 'Killing doesn't solve anything.'

'It clears the ground,' Gristle said. 'You see who you are really up against.'

'Bigger killers,' Card added.

'Card is right,' I said. 'As I see it, the CPPP is our common enemy. I will have to sort out the problems with the smugglers and with the soldiers, none of that is your business. We need to be united if we are to see off the CPPP without resorting to wholesale slaughter. I don't know how to do that yet. I know we have to work together and not let them drive us apart. We should play along with them for the moment, until we are ready to move against them. Look how effective we were when we operated out of the pub and worked together to challenge the supermarkets. We could do it again if I moved back into the pub, but with a different target this time.'

'You're barred from the pub,' Gristle said.

'His lot said they will get the ban lifted,' I said.

'They aren't "my lot",' Card protested.

'Pity Cyril isn't around. We could do with his help,' I said.

'Why not visit him and see how he is and ask him to help us?' Card said.

'Because we don't know where he is, you daft so-and-so,' I answered.

'Yes we do,' Card said. 'Philomena Luge said he is locked up in some special hospital the diocese runs for wayward priests. They hide paedophile priests among the mad ones until they can smuggle them out of the country.'

'Why didn't you tell us?' I demanded.

'You never asked. I didn't realise it was important.'

'How did that lot know where Cyril was locked up?' Gristle asked him.

'They were responsible for putting him there,' Card said. 'Didn't you know that? It's the kind of thing they do. That Philomena has connections in the diocese. She pulled a few strings and Cyril was whipped off.'

'Where is this hospital?' I asked.

Card shrugged. 'Philomena wouldn't say. Said it was secret, but from the few bits I overheard it is somewhere near Ashby-de-la-Zouch, up the motorway and off to the right. A big house of some sort, lots of high walls and barbed wire.'

Gristle pushed back his chair and walked across to the mobile café, giving Aggie a nod as he passed, before knocking on a side door. Bert peered out and, after a few words, stepped down and went round the back of the café with Gristle.

I piled the debris of our meals together and dumped it in the bin at the side of the lay-by. Card was wiping down the table with his hand when I returned. 'What is he up to now?' he asked me, nodding towards the mobile café where Gristle had disappeared round the back.

'Probably buying a gun,' I said, before realising it was a tasteless comment. 'Only joking,' I added.

Three mugs of tea, one big, two small, were plonked down on the table, catching me by surprise. Aggie the

Teeth was glowering one-eyed at me.

'We didn't order more tea,' I said, being as deferential as possible.

'On the house,' she grunted. 'Are you good friends to Gristle?' she growled.

'I think so,' I said, while Card nodded vigorously.

Her eye flicked from one of us to the other. 'Any harm comes to him, I'll fucking kill the pair of you.'

We watched her stalk back to her place behind the counter. Card cleared his throat. 'You know where you stand with that lady. Nice turn of phrase she has. Do you think she meant it when she said…?'

I nodded my head.

'Does that mean she is on our side?' he asked.

'As long as we get it right.'

'Dear me,' Card sighed. That phrase goes down with my 'Oh' as one of those sounds that says it all while saying nothing out loud. I thought, 'Dear me' indeed!

He sipped at his tea. 'Still Orange Pekoe,' he said. 'I wonder at what time of the day Gristle switches to his next preferred brand?'

'Stop wittering on.'

'I'm nervous.'

'We all are, so shut up.'

The flow of customers was slackening off. More tables and chairs were available. It must be near closing time, I thought, time to cash up and head home for Bert and Aggie. 'That reminds me,' I said. 'You know you said you had to pay the CPPP a share of the proceeds from your app? How much does that come to?'

'You told me to shut up.'

'Talk again. It can't be much. You told us one time that you sell the thing for £1. Not many people would want to buy something like that. What would they want it for?'

'Do you know how it works?' he asked me.

I shrugged because I wasn't sure.

'I designed it for old people who go to do something and then forget what it was they were going to do. You know, you walk upstairs and wonder why you went up. Or you walk into the bank and can't remember why you went there. Most apps tell you answers to your questions, my app asks you questions and suggests what you were about to do. Dementia sufferers, busy business people, carers with many clients to visit, a whole array of professionals working with elderly patients buy them. Once they buy one they receive an update for 50p every six months.'

'Even so, there must be only a small number of people who will want it.'

'I have been selling it for two years now. In the first year I sold over fifty thousand programs; last year I sold in excess of one hundred and fifty thousand. The great thing is there is no postage, packaging or carrier costs. It's all done online.'

I sat stunned. Fifty thousand sold and then another one hundred and fifty thousand, at a pound each, with 50p for repeats every six months, which amounted to over… a small fortune! 'How are sales this year?' I managed to force out.

'Good, fifty per cent up on this time last year. I am about to launch the Chinese version. I have had to pay a substantial amount to persuade the best Chinese translator to work for me. Apple offered to buy the business for several million, but I said no. The members of the Co-operative will make me sell it when the price is right. I could improve it further, but they don't care about the good impact it has on the life of elderly people.'

I was still sitting stunned, trying to work out the percentages and the rate of exponential growth when

Gristle came back. 'What's wrong with you?' he asked when he saw me staring straight ahead.

I shook my head, unable to find words to describe what Card had just told me.

'Bert got on the phone to a few of his customers. He knows blokes who go all over the country and come through here. The place we want is the *Lakeside Rest in the Lord Home for the Clerical Elderly*. It's like a high-security prison, they told him. He gave me the GPS coordinates. We can trot up there in less than an hour and whip Cyril out before they know what is happening. He also said he can get me a gun if I need one.'

'Slow down, Gristle,' I said. 'We need to plan this properly if we are to pull it off.'

'He is only joking about the gun, isn't he?' I heard Card mutter.

'He doesn't joke about things like that,' Gristle said as he sat and tasted his big mug of fresh tea. 'That Aggie! A body to kill for and she makes tea like this. When you see her in a bikini you know there is a God. Only God could make a woman so perfect, and she makes tea like this.'

I struggled trying to work out the amount of money Card was giving away intermingled with the image of Aggie the Teeth in a bikini, while Card seemed to be having trouble with Bert offering us a gun.

'Cyril will be delighted to see us,' Gristle said. 'I wonder if he is up to his druid stuff with the women in that place. Do they have women in a place like that? "Rest in the Lord", my eye. Knowing Cyril, it will be more like "Wrestling in the Bed".'

Lakeside Rest in the Lord Home for the Clerical Elderly
Friday 17th April 2015 – Willow Moon

'I thought your lot kidnapped all the time.'

I groaned loudly at Card Index's remark. 'I keep telling you they are not "my lot".'

'I used to kidnap horses and sheep,' Gristle added.

'That's called rustling,' Card Index told him. 'Anyway, we are not kidnapping Cyril, we are setting him free.'

'Like a jailbreak.' I said.

'They used a vaulting horse for that in the film about the British POWs,' Gristle told us. 'Seen it fourteen times, I have. Steve McQueen rode off on a motorbike. That's how he escaped. Will Cyril manage a motorbike?'

'He's in a hospital, not a prisoner-of-war camp,' I said. 'He can walk out any time he wants.'

Card shook his head. 'Not really, not if someone has committed him. Doctors need to clear him and say he is ready to go back into the community.'

Gristle twitched in his seat, a sign he was having an idea. 'Do you remember in *The Guns of Navarone* when the Nazi gunboat made the fishing boat with the main characters pull over and boarded them and the good guys pulled their guns and—'

'No shooting!' Card Index said, cutting off Gristle in full flow. 'No blowing up either.'

Gristle sank back in his seat looking disappointed.

We were sitting in Gristle's battered Range Rover parked in a lay-by half a mile past the entrance to the *Lakeside Rest in the Lord Home* for naughty clergy. Coiled razor wire ran along the top of the high wall that enclosed the property. The front gate was open when we drove past, but the entrance was barred by a red-and-white-striped pole, guarded by a burly-looking security chap wearing an earpiece and a collar microphone. Signs proclaimed the privacy of the grounds and warned trespassers they would not be welcomed with open arms.

'What do you suggest?' I asked Card. If anyone could find a way in and get Cyril out he was the one. He had the sort of mind that worked out the best way of beating the queue for the toilet at half-time during an international rugby match.

I was sitting in the front passenger seat among the usual debris, half turned with my arm over the back of the seat, looking at Card, willing him to ignite his logistical brain and find a solution. He was rubbing his chin with his thumb, occasionally nibbling at the thumbnail.

'I could ram that barrier thing,' Gristle added. 'This old machine can tear five-bar gates off their hinges.'

'What a sneaky way to get in! Why didn't we think of that? Imagine the element of surprise,' I said, as I threw my arms in the air, miming amazement. 'They would have no time to recover by the time we burst through their barrier, drove the half mile from the gate to the house, searched through all the rooms for Cyril, got him dressed, picked up his medicine, hustled him down the stairs, bundled him into the heaps of rubbish in the back of this rust bucket and raced back out the gate and away to the motorway. All over in half an hour, before they could catch their breath or lock the front gate, which looks like it is made of solid iron bars a mere twelve feet high and twelve feet wide. Not enough time for them to position the police at the entrance to stop us getting out, or to set up roadblocks once we outwitted the guards at the gate. What a simply brilliant idea!'

'I wish you would stop going on about the state of this car. Anyway, some of the rubbish belongs to you and him,' he said, nodding back towards Card.

'Show me which pieces are mine,' I demanded.

'That's not the point. It's impolite to comment on the state of someone's car, especially when that someone is driving you everywhere.'

'Will you two shut up,' Card ordered from the back. 'Gristle, which of your Bentleys are you running at the moment?'

'The blue one.'

'Is it taxed and properly insured.'

'Of course it is. What do you take me for?' He paused. 'I'll ring Gerard and check. He does all that stuff for me.'

'Which of the blue ones is it?' Card wanted to know.

'The soft top,' Gristle said.

'You have a plan?' I asked.

He smiled at me. 'Of course. We'll be back here tomorrow.'

As Gristle started the engine, I commented, 'I see we are parked in another lay-by.'

'What's wrong with this one? It's at the side of the road and not a tree or a bush in sight, just like you asked.'

'I don't like being exposed like this. It's too open.'

'I should have known your IRA lot preferred well-hidden hiding places, in spite of what you said about gay lorry drivers meeting in lay-bys behind trees and bushes.'

'How often do I have to tell you they are not "my lot".'

'Excuse me! You are the only bomber and assassin here, so who else do the lads with guns and bombs who lurk in bushes belong to?'

I gave up hoping he would tire of tormenting me because I had agreed to spy on him. I shuffled my feet around in the debris that was ankle deep in the foot-well, hoping there was nothing liquid or sticky waiting to attack a defenceless ankle. At least I could look forward to the Bentley for tomorrow's ride. Gerard kept the Bentleys spotless for the rare occasions Gristle took them out.

Three to the Rescue

Saturday 18th April 2015 – Willow Moon

Gerard, wearing his chauffeur's peaked cap, eased the Bentley over the last half mile towards the gate of the Lakeside home for deviant and knackered clergy. 'Remember your lines,' Card told us. He turned to Gristle sitting beside him on the back seat 'No making up anything extra and do not give any details. In fact, don't talk unless you are asked a question and then let me or GG answer.'

'Did you search him for a gun?' I asked Gerard.

'Do you think I am stupid enough to bring a gun?' Gristle protested.

'I took it off him and hid it before we left the house,' Gerard added.

Gristle sat back and fumed loudly in the back of the car.

Gerard let the blue Bentley glide to a silent stop, short of the barrier and lowered the driver's window.

The security guard let his eye wander over the car, lingering on the shape and size and the way it oozed wealth. He bent down and looked through the driver's window, taking in the four of us in the car.

'Party of the Archbishop of Woomerama, visiting a patient,' Gerard announced.

The security guard looked down his list of expected visitors and shook his head. 'No bishop of Woundobama listed here. They expecting you?'

I leaned across Gerard so that I could catch the guard's attention. 'Excuse me, young man. I am the archbishop's personal assistant. I will deal with your queries.'

'I can't allow in nobody what isn't listed on my visitors' sheet,' he said, taking a quick look at the two in the back of the car. Card was reading what looked like a prayer book and Gristle was staring straight ahead.

I slipped off my seat belt and climbed out to meet the guard, who was walking around the front of the car towards me. Taking him by the elbow I gradually turned him so that he was not looking into the car. 'My name is Reverend Scrubishly. Our mission here is rather delicate,' I said to him in hushed tones. 'The archbishop in the back of the car, he is the one in the cream linen suit behind the driver, is in the country for a secret meeting with the Archbishop of Canterbury. Obviously, I cannot disclose the details but he is a negotiator between Canterbury and the African bishops over the issue of homosexuality, clerical celibacy, ordaining women and bringing witch doctors into the ranks of the clergy. You know how these African bishops are, you must have had some of them come through here at some time.'

He nodded. 'Aye, dare say we might have.'

Putting on my best conspiratorial voice and inclining head and shoulders towards him, I continued, 'There is a priest who is… er… shall we say, a resident here. He is an old family friend of the archbishop. The archbishop would like to see him before he flies out of Birmingham this evening.'

'Neither of you is wearing clerical attire, sir.'

'We have to travel incognito. Rather hush-hush business, as it were.'

'Visitors must book these visits in advance,' the guard said, sneaking a look back at the car.

'I should think so too,' I assured him. 'We were with the Archbishop of Canterbury at a meeting all day yesterday that went on late into the night. His Grace the Archbishop of Woomerama did not know about his friend being here until we were leaving this morning and then we did not know how to get here. We were texted only half an hour ago and given directions. The Canterbury office said they would phone ahead and clear our visit.'

'I don't want to be difficult, sir,' he said, 'but duty is duty. It's more than my job's worth to break the rules.'

'I know,' I assured him, 'especially with the rather delicate issues you have to protect here, if you know what I mean,' I said, giving him a knowing look.

He looked at the Bentley again, and shot a glance at Card and Gristle in the back seat. 'I could phone the main house, I suppose.'

'Good man,' I said. 'The sooner we sort this, the quicker we can get out of your way and the archbishop can go to his next meeting in Birmingham.'

He walked away from me, fiddling with the microphone switch on his collar and speaking quietly so that I could not hear him. He came back. 'Could you please confirm who you are, sir?'

'The Reverend Nicolas Scrubishly, diocese of Truro, seconded to be His Grace's personal assistant throughout his visit.'

'The name of the other gentleman in the car with the archbishop, sir?'

'I don't know if I can reveal his name,' I said. 'He is one of those Foreign Office types.'

'Actually the office here had a phone call fifteen minutes ago and they was given his name. I've to confirm it's the same gentleman whose name they was given.'

'No problem in that case,' I said with a smile, 'that averts a diplomatic incident, doesn't it?'

He didn't smile at my quip.

I cleared my throat. 'He is Lord Anklebury of Lothian and the Borders, from the Foreign Office. His role is to expedite the passage of the archbishop; something to do with enhancing trade relations with Africa and Australia, but that doesn't concern the likes of you and me. We just do our duty.'

'That's all in order, sir. Please sign my visitors' sheet next to the registration number of your car, if you would, sir, and I will be happy to allow you access.'

'Thank you, George,' I said, peering at his name badge. 'Your strict observance of the procedures has been noted. We will comment favourably to your superiors.'

'Thank you, sir. Enjoy your visit. Keep to the driveway until you reach the front door of the house. Maude the receptionist will greet you and point out where to park your car. Wonderful car, if you don't mind me saying, sir.'

'Not at all. Loaned to His Grace by the Archbishop of Canterbury, who is using public transport while his car is at the disposal of His Grace. Isn't it a wonderful gesture of solidarity with the common people that the Archbishop of Canterbury will travel by bus in accordance with the teaching of the Scriptures?'

I breathed a sigh of relief on climbing back into the car and we moved gracefully through the entrance, heading towards the large mansion house off in the distance.

'What was all the gabbing about?' Gristle asked.

'Another humble person falling victim to my charm,' I said.

'Bollocks,' he answered. 'More like you couldn't stop blathering on.'

'Just one little issue,' I said. 'He noted our number plate. He will be able to trace the car back to Gristle.'

A broad-beamed woman with more than a trace of a moustache on her top lip was leaning against the jamb of the heavy front door, with her arms folded, watching our arrival. As we walked up the steps to the door, she turned and, without a word of greeting, led us across the worn stone floor of the entrance hall. Gerard, following

131

instructions from Card, moved the car around to the south side of the building.

'I'll tell the director you're here,' hairy lip said over her shoulder, as she slouched into an office behind a glass screen from where she could observe us without having to speak.

The bare reception hall had all the warmth of an unmanned railway booking office on the Welsh borders. A dog-eared notice informed the staff of the date, place and starting time of the 2012 Christmas party. Another notice warned visitors not to upset patients by smuggling in presents, food, clothes, drugs, pets, pornographic magazines or instruments that could be used to cause self-harm or inflict actual bodily harm on other patients. The last line of the poster, just above where it had been torn off, read, "Visitors are asked to note that sexual activities...", giving us food for thought as we stood around waiting for whoever had been summoned to greet us.

The only other poster proclaimed the mission statement of the *Lakeside Rest in the Lord Home for the Clerical Elderly* to be 'creating a home from home in the pursuit of holiness, health and happiness in the loving bosom of the Church'. The smiling face on the poster on which the mission statement had been superimposed had two black holes where someone had gouged out the eyes with a pointed blade.

Firm footsteps in an echoing corridor announced the approach of a person used to being in charge. The man who strode through the door suggested his authority was more to do with his post than with his physique. He had the look of a failed jockey, one who had been let down by his weight and his height. Too tall to be a jockey, he had accentuated his failings by carrying more weight than a sensible horse would tolerate on its back as it jumped over hurdles or fences before being hauled off to the horse burger factory.

'Archbishop, Your Grace, you are most welcome,' he announced, looking at each of us in turn wondering which of us was the boss man.

Card stepped forward to shake the man's hand. 'G'day to you cobber.'

'My secretary has just informed me of your arrival,' the fat one spluttered, sending a fine shower of saliva in front of him so that Card stepped back to avoid a wetting. 'Had I been forewarned, I would have been here to welcome you myself. Australia, she tells me. Imagine, all the way from Australia. The diocese of Boomboomabanga, she says. Is that near Sydney, or is it near somewhere else?'

I stepped forward. 'Good morning, my name is the Reverend Nicolas Scrubishly, personal assistant to the archbishop during his stay. He is from the *arch*diocese of *Woomerama*, which is north of Brisbane, ministering to the aboriginal peoples.'

'Lovely, lovely, how lovely,' he murmured. Turning to Gristle, he nodded. 'You must be the gentleman from the Home Office.'

'Good Lord, no! It's the Foreign Office,' Gristle rasped at him.

'Of course, of course, how lovely,' the too-tall-to-be-a-jockey simpered. Apart from the slight turn in his left eye, the other noticeable feature in his eyes was the lack of human kindness. It was as if he had two glass eyes, with one not sitting squarely where it ought to be.

'Now, your visit,' he continued, his eyes darting around the three of us, the good eye travelling faster than the other one. 'Lovely of you to call, lovely, really lovely, but rather difficult to grant your request, what with being out of visiting hours, indeed outside our visiting *day*,' he droned. 'So difficult at such short notice, not that there would be a problem had you turned up on the second Sunday of the month between 2.00pm and 3.00pm. *That* is our regular visiting time. Would it be possible to rearrange your visit to coincide with those times? So much easier for the staff and less disruption for the patients. You know how they are. Absolutely dependent on routine, order, predictable rhythms in their daily day and weekly week, as it were. So healing, so lovely for them to have rhythms, absolutely lovely for everyone. They live for the second Sunday of the month, looking forward so much to that hour filled with the laughter of visitors, walking in the gardens, playfully gambolling on the lawns, taking tea on the terrace, all the delights of home from home on which we pride ourselves. Lovely sight, absolutely lovely sight, lovely for everyone. But so difficult and disruptive of their healing when visitors turn up out of the blue without warning'. I expected him to wring his hands.

Card glanced at me and then at Gristle, as if he was considering the proposition we had just heard. He fixed the oversized failed jockey with what we called his Ofsted-eye. 'You haven't told us your name, sir,'

'Ah, Macintosh, executive director of the *Lakeside Rest in the Lord Home for the Clerical Elderly*,' he announced with a slight bow of his head.

'Is that "Doctor", "Professor", "Mr" or are you a member of the clergy?'

'Er… *Mister* Macintosh.'

'You are not a doctor?'

'No, Your Grace.'

'*Mr* Macintosh, I flew into this country from Nigeria three days ago. Prior to that I spent five days in six African countries, two of them ravaged by war and internal strife. I was bombed, shot at, chased through two jungles and across three rivers by hostile gangs intent on disembowelling me with their bare hands. During my stay here, I have been locked in delicate and prolonged negotiations on matters to do with the well-being, if not the future, of the Church. This evening I will board a plane for a twenty-five-hour flight back to Australia. I have jet lag on my jet lag on another jet lag, except I do not know which jet lag fatigue is the first and which is the last. Your suggestion that I return at a time of the month to suit your schedule is one I would *not* like to comment on at this stage in my current state of tiredness. You might find my reply a touch tetchy. I am sure you did not know my recent history of personal suffering when you suggested I come back on the second Sunday of next month. I will point out, however, that my last meeting before I fly out this evening is with the Bishop of Birmingham. I believe he is your boss, since the diocese owns and funds this operation. Due to lack of sleep, with my nerves frayed and my patience in tatters, I would not be a good spokesperson were he to ask if my visit here was to my liking.'

I stepped forward. 'What I think His Grace the archbishop is trying to say is that he would appreciate if you sent someone to bring him a chair, while you make the necessary arrangements for a brief visit to his close friend, who is blessed to be looked after so well by you in this wonderful establishment. A hard chair would be best,' I said, 'anything soft and he will be asleep as soon as he sees it.'

Card turned to Gristle. 'Lord Anklebury, I am sure your superiors at the Foreign Office will want you to record the details of this meeting for their investigation after I leave. I have to say I encountered nothing like this, not even when I visited our troops fighting in Afghanistan.

Please make sure you have the correct spelling of the names of the individuals we have so far met. Their Christian welcome leaves a lot to be desired.'

The too-tall, overweight director stepped back from Card, who by now had swelled into what he called his Ofsted-domineering-stance. It had taken Card a whole weekend training course to acquire that stance and to develop the Ofsted-eye that he had used to such good effect over the years to beat down those who dared challenge his authority. Bigger men than the failed jockey had buckled in front of Card in that mode.

I knew we were in. Now all we had to do was to get out, taking Cyril with us.

The director scampered ahead of us like Gollum in *Lord of the Rings*, insisting he was distressed in case anyone might wrongly imagine he had meant to delay the archbishop's visit in any way, bemoaning the fact that such misunderstandings occurred and avowing that he was a devotee of all things Australian and African, having spent three days in Australia on his round-the-world trip, following his private college course in social care management.

We were ushered into a room with dowdy wallpaper, carpets curling at the edges and a complex pong of body odours and mildew that a howling gale would not dissipate. Hard-backed chairs were placed in a line along the two walls opposite the door and the windows.

'I will send down the senior doctor with your colleague in just a few minutes,' the director said, bowing and fawning all over Card, who was giving him the cold-eye treatment. 'Would you like tea or coffee after your long trip across the world?'

'Thank you,' Card answered. 'Please serve it on the terrace as you do for the formal visiting times on the second Sunday of each month.'

'Certainly, that would be lovely, just a lovely venue for you to meet your colleague. If you will excuse me I will sort out... and... take care... and...' he said, his voice fading as he backed out of the door and hurried down the corridor.

Gristle smiled. 'That was a piece of cake.'

'That was the easy bit,' Card told him. 'Stick exactly to the plan and we should be out of here in half an hour.'

The door opened and a tall, thin man with a comb-over that had lost the battle with baldness came into the room, taking in the three of us with a squinting look.

'The archbishop?' he said.

Card stepped forward. 'You are?

'Dr Murchison. Senior medical person.'

'G'day,' Card said. 'You heard why we are here? Just a quick visit to see an old friend before I fly back to Australia. How is Cyril?'

The doctor looked at Gristle and me.

'It's fine to talk in front of them,' Card assured him. 'This is Lord Anklebury of Lothian and the Borders from the Foreign Office and this is the Reverend Nicolas Scrubishly, my personal assistant during my stay. You can speak freely in front of them.'

'Please, gentlemen,' the doctor said, ushering us to take seats. 'Cyril is one of our success stories. On arrival he was very disturbed, with vociferous outbursts and demanding to be freed from the clutches of the evil one, his name for the Bishop of Birmingham. These are not unusual symptoms displayed by patients on arrival. Cyril was slightly different in that, while he threatened the staff who restrained him, he offered them no physical violence. Instead, he warned them that the spirits, the guardians of the trees and the sprites of air and water who had followed

137

him into the room, would wreak havoc on them unless he was released immediately. Obviously, we had to sedate him, but since then he has been calm, keeps very much to himself and only speaks to say "they will come and set me free". I don't suppose you are the spirits and guardians of the trees, are you?' he said, with a grin.

None of us smiled. 'He was not referring to us,' Card answered, 'Cyril lives in a world of his own when it comes to the spirits and guardians of the trees. It is best not to interfere with that world.'

'Ah, of course,' the doctor said.

'Can we see him?' I asked. 'Time is of the essence. I have to keep His Grace the archbishop to a tight schedule.'

'Of course, my apologies. I will get an orderly to bring Cyril to you. I would ask you not to over-exert him, or to agitate him in any way. Best to humour him, no matter what he says. The orderly can stay with you at all times and return Cyril to his room when your visit is over.'

'The orderly will not be necessary,' Card informed him, standing and stretching his back. 'Cyril may wish to make his confession to me.'

'High Church,' I added quickly. 'The Australian Church is big into confessions. Strong history because of their penal past.'

The doctor raised his eyebrows at the request.

'We will take good care of Cyril,' I assured him. 'We will return him untrammelled by anxiety at the end of our visit. He will be safe with us. We can call on one of the security guards if there is any need.'

'If you are sure,' the doctor said, 'it is unusual to…'

'Absolutely no problem,' Card informed him. 'You have my word as archbishop that we will return him to his proper place at the end of our visit.'

'I'll have him brought down to you immediately.'

I followed the doctor into the corridor. 'You said about the orderlies who restrained Cyril when he arrived and what Cyril said to them... about the spirits...'

'Yes?'

'Do those orderlies still work here?' I asked.

He paused for a moment. 'No, actually, they don't. One was taken ill shortly after that day and left us, hallucinations, I believe. Another suffered constant pains as if he was being pinched on the back of the neck. The other one left one night, talking loudly to someone no one could see. It was strange that the three of them came down at the same time, but there was no link between their illnesses. Is there something I should know?'

'No, I was curious if any of them saw any spirits, that Cyril alleged. Natural curiosity for a man of the cloth.'

He smiled at me in what I thought was an indulgent manner. 'Reverend, every room and corridor in this building is full of little green men with bulbous heads, riding on multi-coloured dragons and wielding awesome swords. Spaceships land on the lawns at regular intervals disgorging aliens and kidnapped humans, who catch the bus at the end of the drive. Any of my patients will fill you in on the details. A few spirits, tree guardians and free-flying sprites are run of the mill here. I leave spirits to you, Reverend. I have enough to do to bring my patients back in touch with reality without bothering with their fantasies about fairies. I'll have Cyril brought down to you.'

Some people never learn, I thought, as I watched him walk off, not even when the evidence is under their noses.

The Escape

Saturday 18th April 2015 – Willow Moon

There was a sharp intake of breath from Gristle at the sight of the stick figure in the doorway. Card started forward, his arms out, then stopped. I was conscious of the need to lift my drooping jaw.

No fat prisoners came out of concentration camps, my father used to say. Looking at Cyril standing in the doorway, I added *Lakeside Rest in the Lord Home for the Clerical Elderly* to that saying. A gaunt replica of the Cyril we had known stood beside an orderly, who was holding him by the elbow, either to stop him falling over or to prevent him doing a runner, except this pathetic figure was out of running juice.

The orderly nudged him. 'Oh look, Cy, these nice gentlemen have come to visit us. Aren't you the lucky boy today? Think of the wonderful tales we will share with your friends on the ward when our visit is over. Say hello to the nice gentlemen, Cy.'

Cyril stared at the floor because that was where his head was directing his eyes. Every part of him seemed to droop, hanging from his head, as if his head was the anchor point that kept everything else in place, barely.

The orderly spoke in a loud whisper, 'You'll have to excuse him, he is a bit sleepy. We weren't expecting you. His drugs, you know how it is. Best to keep them calm at all times. Being a bit drowsy helps them pass the time, long day otherwise.' And here he raised his voice and slowed down the words as if he was speaking to a young child, 'Isn't that right, Cy, we like to be calm and quiet, don't we.' He looked at us and mouthed, 'They prefer it that way.'

Gristle's lips were tightening and loosening and his

fists were clenching, sure signs he was about to kick off. Card had turned on his Ofsted-eye, glaring at the orderly, who did not sense he was about to be grievously harmed.

I cut in before Gristle or Card launched themselves at the man they had marked down for slaughter. 'Thank you for your kindness. We will take it from here,' I said, as I crossed over and took Cyril by the arm. 'He will be safe with us.' I smiled at the orderly.

'It's your safety I worry about, not his,' the orderly said. 'Still, there are three of you, you should be ok.'

Cyril stood motionless, his pyjama sleeves hanging off the end of his arms and the hems of the trouser legs catching under his carpet slippers. The shabby, woollen dressing gown, once white, hung open without any belt to hold it in place. 'Now, Cy,' the orderly said, releasing Cyril to my care, 'be a good boy with these nice gentlemen. They will look after you and give you a lovely time. But no being naughty, or we will be so disappointed with little Cy. And we don't want that to happen, now do we, Cy?'

'He will be fine,' I said through a forced smile, restraining myself from punching him in the face. 'We will take him now. He will be no bother. Thank you for your time and for your care.' I moved Cyril away from the door, encouraging the orderly to leave. 'Bye, bye, Cy, see you in a teensy weensy while,' the insulting man said, as he went into the corridor closing the door, leaving us in the heavy silence that filled the room.

I licked my lips and swallowed, conscious that my mouth was dry. On top of that, I didn't know what to say. Card looked as shocked as I felt. Gristle seemed to wipe his eye before striding over and grasping Cyril in a bear hug. 'You silly old bugger,' he said, 'running off like that, not telling us where you were. We even missed you for a few minutes.'

Card joined the hug and when I wrapped my arms around the three of them it felt like a wave of delight, anger, relief, joy and sadness swept through us, knotting us together in an intense emotion that could never be captured in words.

Card broke the silence. 'Enough of this carry-on. We have work to do. If that sanctimonious bastard comes back I claim first crack at killing him.'

'That's not fair,' Gristle said. 'We should at least toss for it.'

'For feck sake,' I added, 'we can kill him afterwards. Let's get Cyril out of here.'

We walked slowly across the entrance hall, mainly because Card and Gristle were holding up the silent and unsteady Cyril between them. I acted as usher and guide. Card and Gristle kept up a steady flow of conversation that made little sense but suggested they were engaging Cyril in a fascinating conversation. I smiled and nodded at hairy lip behind the glass partition, who gave us a disinterested glance as we passed. On reaching the fresh air, Cyril stiffened and resisted forward movement, as if he was aware something strange was happening. Card and Gristle urged him forward, forcing him to take faltering steps. He walked like an old man who had been lying too long in a bed. 'It's ok, Cyril,' Gristle said reassuringly. 'Just a few steps in front of you and then we will sit and have a rest.'

'It would be quicker to pick him up and carry him,' I said, in a loud whisper.

'Of course it would,' Card said, through clenched teeth, 'but we need him to look like he is stepping out voluntarily and is enjoying himself rather than being bloody kidnapped.'

'How can it look voluntary when you and Gristle are almost carrying him between you?'

'Will you shut up,' Gristle said. 'And smile, for God's sake. This is supposed to be a group of friends out for a walk. You look like a crow dancing around a road kill trying to keep out of the way of the cars.'

'Smile? We are kidnapping him,' I protested. 'We could go to jail.'

'Bit late to think of that now. Would you rather we took him back in there?' Gristle said.

'Round to the right,' Card ordered, as the three of them began to turn in unison like a large ship deciding to change course and finding it couldn't be done quickly. 'The car should be round there.'

'It's too early for the car,' I said. 'We are supposed to follow your fiendishly complex plan and substitute a ringer and then help the ringer get out and then—'

'Change of plan,' Card interrupted me. 'We don't know how to get past that room and down that long corridor and that was a key part of the plan. Our ringer would be lost and might be locked up. Invention now called for. GG, go ahead and tell Gerard to get the boot ready. We will head off as soon as we get Cyril in the car.'

Gerard had parked the car on the blind side of the house. He put down his newspaper as I approached him. 'I thought you were going back in as a substitute,' he said.

'Change of plan. They will be here in a minute and we will scarper a.s.a.p. Get the boot ready.'

'All done,' he said. 'The bottom panel is out. I'll lower the roof as soon as they are ready.'

The trio of conspirators shuffled round the bend in the path, the speed dictated by Cyril's inability to walk properly. Gerard gasped when he saw Cyril. 'Good Lord, some bastard should pay for doing that to him.'

'There's a queue on any killing,' I said.

I kept guard while Gerard helped Card and Gristle load

Cyril into the boot of the car. The tenderness with which the three of them worked showed a different side of their characters not normally on display.

'Tuck him in well,' I said. 'Will he fit? Is there enough room for him?'

'Will you shut up and get in the car,' Gristle said. 'No wonder the IRA want to kill you if you were such a worry pot.'

Gerard was already in the car and lowering the roof that folded into the boot. We climbed into the car and Gerard headed the car down the drive towards the gate, the most hazardous part of the rescue operation.

The security guard was on my side of the car as we approached.

'Hi there,' I said, smiling as widely as possible. Card was back to reading his prayer book. Gristle stared ahead in a good imitation of a government official showing no interest in his surroundings. Gerard sat like a well-trained chauffeur, ready to take orders no matter how irritating or how stupid.

'Everything go well, sir?' the guard asked.

'Indeed, wonderfully well, thank you. Could stay only a few moments. The archbishop is in a hurry, you know how it is, one appointment after the other. We need to hurry on our way, so if you could, you know…' I pointed to the security pole and mimed lifting it.

'In a moment, sir. Need to check the car first. Escaping patients and all that, you know how it is.'

'But you can see inside the car, the roof is down and there is nowhere here we could hide anyone. Why would we smuggle anyone out when they receive such wonderful treatment here?' I shut up then, worried I had gone too far in telling that lie, but he seemed not to notice.

'Need to check the boot, sir,' he said, having

scrutinised the interior of the car by leaning over and staring into the foot wells.

'But the roof of the car folds into the boot,' I said. 'Nobody could fit in there when the roof is down.'

He hesitated, unsure of his response.

I tried to look as if we were strapped for time. 'Think of all the time and trouble of putting it up and then taking it down again and imagine how late that will make the archbishop.' I was banking on him not knowing how smoothly and quickly the roof of the car could be raised or lowered.

Card butted in using his best Ofsted-I-demand-the-truth voice. 'Reverend Scrubishly, is there another problem? Pass me your mobile. I will ring the Archbishop of Canterbury or, better still, the Bishop of Birmingham, who owns this place, and sort out this delay. Your name, cobber?' he demanded, staring at the security guard.

'Only doing my duty, archbishop, sir. Wouldn't want to delay you, it's just—'

'Well, as we say in Australia – open that bloody Sheila of a gate, get this surfboard off the beach or I'll get my kangaroos in a twist and disrupt someone's didgeridoo. Like pronto, mate, or it will be fair dinkum Alice for anyone within reach of my boomerang.'

The security guard hurried to the pole and threw it quickly into the air, saluting the archbishop as we eased out into the road. We were pushed back in our seats as Gerard took the car up to speed.

We pulled into the forestry track where Gristle had parked his battered Range Rover on our way to the hospital. No one moved for a moment as we took in the success of our kidnap mission. Gristle broke the heavy stillness. 'When did you learn to speak fluent Australian?' he asked Card.

He shrugged. 'I saw a film on sheep farming on the telly. Picked up a few words.'

'It's a good job it was an eejit on guard,' I said. 'Come on, get Cyril out and let's clear off. They will soon raise the alarm.'

Gerard raised the roof out of the boot. We lifted Cyril out, none the worse for wear, and bundled him into clothes that were too big for him. We had underestimated how slimming his experience in the home would be. We pushed and pulled him into the back seat of Gristle's Land Rover, where he lay and continued to sleep. I sat in my usual place among all the rubbish in the passenger seat and we sped off as Card and Gerard climbed back into the Bentley.

'I hope they will be alright,' I said, after a few miles. 'They might not be spotted if they keep to the back roads like we planned.'

'They'll be fine. Gerard is the best driver there is.'

'What about the number plate? That guard on the gate wrote it down. The police or the road cameras will pick it up and the two of them will be done for.'

Gristle looked across at me and grinned. 'Gerard has a button on the steering wheel that makes the number plates revolve so that he can choose one of four numbers that best suits him. Got the idea from one of the James Bond films. Gerard will wind back the mileage when he reaches home so the record he keeps of mileage shows it has not been out since before Christmas. Sit back and enjoy the ride. Your big part in this kidnap is about to start.'

He called it a kidnap just to torment me for fussing earlier. He can be like that. Good job he isn't a real gnome or there would be no peace anywhere.

Safe House

Tuesday 21st April 2015 – Hawthorn Moon

I sensed someone in the room behind me. I lay still, my eyes closed, listening and trying to figure out how to reach the baseball bat behind the door. A hand touched my shoulder, making me jerk upright in the bed. Cyril was leaning over me.

'Jesus, Cyril, don't ever do that again. You nearly gave me a heart attack.'

'GG, why am I in your house? What happened?' He sat on the edge of my bed. 'My head is full of... I was some place else but... I'm here. How?'

I looked at the clock. 'Cyril, it's only four in the morning. Go back to bed. I'll answer all your questions over breakfast.'

'Would you like a cup of tea?'

'Tea?' I said.

He nodded. 'I made a pot.'

'How long have you been up?'

He shrugged his shoulders. 'Not sure. A bit. Where did I get these pyjamas? They make me look like a prisoner.'

'They're my hospital pyjamas. Yours were so filthy we threw them out.'

'Were we drinking last night?'

'Why do you ask?'

'I can't remember anything. I should be at home in the vicarage.'

'You went away for a little while,' I told him.

'Did I die?'

'Do you think you did?'

He looked puzzled. 'It felt like it. I was buried somewhere. I saw my friends, you know, the ones from the graves. They were smiling and...' He stared at the wall.

'Did anyone die?'

'Not yet,' I said, thinking of the director of the home and the smug orderly who had brought Cyril to us. 'How do you feel?'

'I'm not sure. A bit fuzzy in the head. Legs feel wobbly. I can't remember things. Where did I leave my clothes? Was I with a female? Does she have them?'

'You're getting better if you remember women.'

'How long have I been here?'

'Three days. Sleeping all the time.'

'I'm hungry,' he said.

I looked at the clock and sighed. 'Come on, let's get something to eat. There's no way I can sleep now.' In a normal week I would be going to bed at this time, not getting up. Smuggling makes harsh demands.

Card and Gristle arrived together shortly after I phoned them. 'Did you have to phone us so early?' Gristle asked.

'This isn't early,' I said. 'It's only six o'clock. I've been up since four.'

'I'm retired,' Card said. 'I don't recognise this time of the day any more.'

'Stop moaning. Cyril has come round and is ready to talk. You can help him come to terms with what happened.'

'Where is he?' Gristle asked.

'In the kitchen,' I said.

'You making any tea?' Card asked.

'Been doing little else since four this morning.'

'Do you have any bread?' Gristle asked.

I nodded.

'How about a sausage or three?'

'Could manage that.'

'And some bacon and a couple of eggs while you are at

it. You could throw in a thick slice of fried bread. I bet you have tins of beans. Some black pudding, maybe? Go down a treat that would.'

'This isn't Bert's trundling café,' I said.

'I know,' Gristle said. 'No Aggie.'

'I suppose you want a feed too,' I said to Card.

'Too early for me. I'll wait for a while. Just tea for now,' he said over his shoulder as he headed to the kitchen and the waiting Cyril. 'You got any Earl Grey or Darjeeling? This time of day they are the only teas I drink.'

'Would one even consider anything other than those at this time of the morning?' I asked, my sarcasm echoing in the hall as I followed them towards the kitchen.

'Basically, you kidnapped me,' Cyril said.

'Technically, no,' Card said. 'It wasn't against your will.'

'You didn't have a will because you were sozzled out of your mind on drugs,' I added.

'More like a jailbreak,' Gristle said. 'Then he did his Anne Frank bit,' nodding towards me.

'How?' Cyril asked.

'Hid you from the Gestapo.'

'People from the diocese you mean?' Cyril asked.

'No, the plod,' I said. 'A big search was on for you.'

'Technically, you are on the run. You can't walk out of a secure mental institution where you have been committed. You still have to hide,' Card told him

'No, he doesn't have to hide any more,' I said.

'Why?'

'We spoke to the bishop. Cyril told him he would go to the press with some very personal details of the bishop's life. He called off the police, telling them Cyril was safe and his incarceration had been a misunderstanding.'

149

'When did you sort this out?'

'About an hour ago,' I said. 'We rang the bishop and Cyril had a chat with him.'

'He was very understanding,' Cyril added.

'You rang the bishop at five in the morning, to blackmail him!' Card said.

'Blackmail is a bit harsh,' I said. 'It was more like a friendly chat. Cyril outlined the damage he could do. The bishop thought it sounded draconian. They agreed to forgive – like a truth and reconciliation tribunal.'

'Thank God that is sorted,' Card said.

'There is one other little thing,' I said. 'Your impersonation of an Australian bishop might be a touch more difficult to smooth out. The Australian ambassador is somewhat huffy at the indelicate headlines in the newspapers. She also protested about the heavy-handed retaliation by the police against Australian citizens working illegally in brothels and strip joints. In return, the police are calling for a public enquiry into the ambassador calling them 'Thick Pommy bastards'. The police are a bit sensitive about being called names after that MP chap had a go at them.'

'The Aussies should be used to being called names,' Gristle said. 'You got any more tea?'

'I'll make *another* pot,' I said. 'And before you ask, I haven't any more grub to fry for you.'

'That's ok. I'll make a decent breakfast when I get home,' Gristle said. 'I can hold out till then.'

'Never mind all that,' Card interrupted. 'What are we going to do about the village gang? Before you say it, Gristle, killing is not an option.'

'I didn't say a word,' Gristle protested.

We all glared him into silence. We knew he was thinking that.

'So? Any ideas?' Card asked.

'Cyril and I have a few suggestions.'

'Is killing one of the ideas?' Gristle asked.

'Not to start with,' I said. 'That might be a long-term option.'

'I like the sound of the long-term option,' Gristle murmured. 'Maybe a garrotting, or hanging, drawing and quartering, or a touch of hacking, or slow dipping in acid. Nothing spectacular, nothing ostentatious. None of that lot deserve a fanfare when they go.'

'The whole point is to make their going spectacular, not to death, but to disgrace.'

'Could I add just a little bit of slaughter?' Gristle said.

'No,' we all replied with one voice.

Gristle Hears All

Tuesday 21st April 2015 – Hawthorn Moon

'Before we go any further, there is something we need to clear up.' Card usually comes out with pompous statements like that. Because I said it, the others stopped talking and looked at me.

I wasn't sure I should go on. Even though Gristle was a close friend, I couldn't be sure he would control his temper when he heard what I was about to say.

Cyril raised his eyebrows. 'Well?' he said, breaking the silence I had started.

I cleared my throat, scratched my nose and asked if anyone wanted more tea. No one moved. I had stepped into the spotlight and had no choice but to press on. I took the bull by the horns, which would have been safer compared to what I was about to do. 'Gristle,' I said, 'we need to clear up, sort out… or if you like, establish an accurate picture of… just between ourselves, as it were… What happened when you visited the primary school.'

'Why?' Gristle asked.

A good question, I thought. Indeed, a very good question. Card shifted in his chair and checked out the layout of the kitchen, probably looking for where I kept the sharp knives and other instruments for penetrating or battering bodies, or maybe he was working out the quickest way to leave the danger zone if Gristle kicked off.

Cyril joined in, in what I thought was an unhelpful way for a man I had rescued from the diocesan stalag, given shelter in my house and poured gallons of tea down his throat since four o'clock that morning. 'Why? What happened in the school?'

'Gristle went to talk to the children,' I muttered.

Gristle nodded. 'So?'

'How did it go?' I asked.

'Fine,' he said. 'Kids were fine. Bastard teachers have not changed since my time. Toilets are not much better these days either. They smelled something awful when I was a kid.'

'You didn't use the kids' toilets, did you?' Card asked. I could imagine his Ofsted plumage rising on the back of his head.

'I didn't use them. Some of the kids took me there to show me. We took some photos. Turned out really well.'

Oh God, I thought, this was going to be as bad as the crowd in the village claimed.

'Whose idea was it to take photos?' Card asked, now getting into his Ofsted hunt-the-paedophile mode.

'Kids,' Gristle said. 'They wanted me to see the terrible state of the toilets.'

'Did you do anything else while in there?' This from Card, who was now skating on thin ice, I thought.

'Don't be stupid. What else could we do in there? It's only a loo. It's not exactly the entertainment hub of the world.'

We shook our heads, agreeing with his judgement.

'What did you talk about?' I asked.

'In the loo?'

'In the classroom.'

'I was asked to tell the kids what it was like to be old and what it was like growing up near the village. One kid said they knew all that shit, seen it on television till they were sick of it. Another one said that parents are always going on about how lucky kids are these days and don't know it and teachers do non-stop moaning that kids should be grateful for all that is done for them by the school. I said it was the same with me when I was a kid. We had a laugh after that. Those kids are great when you let them have their say.'

'What did the teacher say when the kid said "all that shit?"' Card asked him.

'She wasn't there. She cleared off to the staffroom for coffee when I started.'

Card looked indignant. 'That's illegal, wrong, she isn't allowed to leave her class with a stranger.'

'I wasn't a stranger. She knew me, the kids knew me.'

'I don't mean it that way. Suppose something had happened. Everyone would turn on you and blame you.'

'What could happen? It was just me and the kids in the classroom – apart from when they gave me a tour of the bogs, and even then, I went into the boys' bog not the girls'. I thought that would have been out of order. The kids knew that and the girls said they were fine with it. Knowledgeable little sods they are. They know all about those paedophiles and that porno stuff on the Internet. Know more than me, I reckon.'

Cyril sat through the exchange looking puzzled. Having been on the receiving end of interrogation by the diocesan Gestapo on a number of occasions, he knew innocent questions were anything but innocent. 'Where are you going with these questions? What are you not telling us?'

I turned to Card for an answer. Playing pass the parcel by staring is not a useful way of getting out of deep shit. Unless I gave the next piece of information delicately, that was exactly where I was going to be. I reached around the table, collecting the empty breakfast plates and, more critically, the knives and forks, until they were all under my control. I took a deep breath, hoping it would not be my last. 'While you were away, Cyril—'

'Illegally locked up.'

'Indeed. Illegally locked up. I was asked…

erm… forced, blackmailed, threatened with loss of life and being murdered—'

'You never told me they threatened murder,' Gristle intervened.

'Can I finish this? It is hard enough without you all butting in.'

'He was forced to spy on Gristle,' Card added, impatient with my shilly-shallying. He can't stand wasting time, a hangover from his Ofsted days when everything had to be done in less time than was needed. 'He was forced to spy on Gristle by the crowd of shites who run the village. Gristle knows. We told him.'

Gristle nodded. 'That's right. I promised not to kill GG, for the time being. The village crowd will be dealt with in time. I would top them all today but those two said I should wait. Maybe I'll do it tomorrow or the day after that.'

'You never told me that earlier on,' Cyril said to me.

'I needed the two of them here so we could get the whole lot out in one go,' I answered, hoping he wouldn't notice my embarrassment at lying to him.

'I bet he didn't tell you he was in the IRA until he ran away from them,' Card said. 'The village mob will send him back to them unless he spies on Gristle.'

'Were you?' Cyril said, looking at me with concern. 'The IRA will kill you for deserting them.'

'If I don't do it first,' Gristle said, with what I hoped was a slight tinge of humour in his voice.

Cyril folded his arms and sat back in his chair, thinking through everything he had heard since gaining consciousness that morning.

Gristle offered to take the plates, knives and forks off me and put them in the sink. I circled my arms around them and protested I couldn't let a guest do jobs like that in my house. I was not handing over weapons that could inflict bodily harm.

Cyril reached the nub of the matter. 'So why are you interested in the school?'

'What I am… er… actually, what Card and I are doing, is making sure Gristle is, as it were, you know how you have to cover all bases, especially if there is the issue of guilt by association, or implication, or indeed even no guilt at all because the person has done nothing except attract rumours and innuendo.'

'Would you talk sense,' Gristle demanded.

'What I am trying to say is that there are other people, evil people, you know, people with no scruples, who, if they would threaten someone as innocent as me, well!' I paused, trying to find a way of saying what I had to say without provoking violence towards myself. 'Just imagine how far they would go with someone they were convinced was, well not actually convinced, more like making it up. So you have to, I decided, or rather Card and I decided.' If I was to be stabbed or beaten to death by Gristle it seemed appropriate to have it done in company.

'What are you babbling on about?' Gristle asked. 'Decided what?'

'To protect you,' I blurted.

He grinned and looked at the other two. 'Him protect me! As if I needed protecting and as if I would depend on him to do it.'

I could tell from the way Cyril was now looking at me that he had figured it out, including the possible danger to my well-being if Gristle got the wrong end of the stick. 'You said they forced you to spy on Gristle. Did they tell you what to look for?'

I nodded. 'Money laundering, tax fiddles, scams with cars, deals he made, where he goes, who he meets, the women, sex and stuff like that.'

'You tell them anything?' Cyril asked.

I shook my head. 'Only a few bits I made up, or things that everyone knows.'

'So there is nothing they can use against him?' Cyril asked.

'That's right.'

'And you made things up and told them lies?'

I nodded in agreement

'Even though you know that if they find you are lying they will hand you over to the IRA, who will kill you.'

'You never told me that,' Gristle said.

'He didn't want to alarm you, or set you off,' Cyril said before I could answer. 'That's what a *real friend* would do. He risked being killed because of you.'

Gristle went quiet in a way we don't normally see. His eyes glazed over as if he was going deep inside his mind. He twitched, prodded by an unruly thought. His eyes focused on me again, 'Would that IRA crowd actually kill you?'

'Stone dead,' Cyril said. 'Bullet through the back of the head, in a cow shed, blindfolded, hands tied and then fed to pigs, or buried at sea, or on top of a mountain, or in a deep bog, with not a prayer being said and him a deeply religious man.'

'Holy shit,' Gristle said and lapsed into silence and stillness once more, a unique combination for him.

We sat in the unusual silence of my kitchen. Murder, mine, had been averted by Cyril's quick talking. Even more remarkable was the long silence that wrapped us all as we sat and watched Gristle think.

Cyril interrupted the silence once more. 'Now you're doing it again, aren't you?'

I nodded agreement.

'You are building a strong defence, like a good barrister, or a true and loyal friend so you can prove your friend is innocent of all charges and that the accusations are down to malice and personal antagonism. Isn't that the truth? They are building a case against him because of his visit to the school. That's what you are fighting. That's why you are asking all these questions.'

I nodded again, deciding the less I said the better. Cyril was building the case so much better than I could.

'What defence? What accusations?' Gristle asked. 'What has this to do with the school?'

Cyril took a deep breath. 'The village mob intend to accuse you of being a kiddy-fiddler, but GG is proving you are not. But they will have him killed before he finishes the job.'

I could hear the faint sound of a tractor across the fields. Some crows in the trees along the lane were squabbling. The sheep in the next field waiting to be transported to an abattoir were bleating to each other. The tap over the sink was dripping. I was holding my breath.

Gristle sat, his hands on his lap, looking at Cyril with the look of a man lost in a complex maze without any idea of the way out. His head turned and his eyes found mine. Cyril says you can sometimes see into a person's soul if you look through their eyes. I could see Gristle's soul. I was looking at images of him being hurt, tumbled up with emotions of loneliness and rejection and a few scenes of laughter and slivers of friendship. It was like looking down a tunnel that was so full of movement and memories that it was pulsating with the noise, the vibrations of strange places and the agitation of surging people thronging along it until... everyone disappeared and there was only one image left, that of a boy sitting alone by a camp fire on a cold night, crying while he looked at the house where his father lived. Gristle's eyes closed over and blocked the path into his soul. His eyes blinked open and he focused on me. 'Would they really kill you?'

I nodded, yes.

He bit his lower lip, waited for a moment, stood up and walked out the back door. Card stood up.

'Leave him,' Cyril said. 'He needs some time by himself.' He looked at the knives lying on the plates piled in front of me. 'You can put those in the sink now. I'll go out and talk to Gristle in a few minutes. We could probably do with another cup of tea.'

Numero Uno Old Git

Tuesday 21ˢᵗ April 2015 – Hawthorn Moon

'That was touch and go with Gristle,' I said. 'You did well to get me out of it.'

'My escape from that horrible place was down to you lot. It was the least I could do to repay you. Gristle gets heated sometimes. He doesn't think before he acts.'

'That's what I was afraid of,' I answered, 'but I had to find out what happened in the school. The village gang are sure they have him on paedophile charges.'

'Asking him straight out would have been like pulling the pin on a hand grenade and passing it around a group of drunks. The dead and dismembered would be everywhere.'

'Did you ask him about the allegations he had sex with underage kids years ago?'

Cyril nodded. 'He laughed when I asked him. Seems the two young innocents from those years ago were older than Gristle. It was them that led him on and took advantage of his innocent body. Mind you, he didn't describe it like that. I think from what he said, it was the two of them who showed him some of the wilder delights of intimate personal relationships.'

We sat with our thoughts, watching a robin pecking through dead leaves alongside the path.

'Did you have any doubts?' Cyril asked, looking down the garden towards the pasture behind the hedge. He lifted his right hand in a little wave as if there was someone passing. The only movement beyond the gate was Blazing Bolt munching his way around the field taking his morning feed.

I thought before answering. 'When that crowd in the village told me to spy on him and said they had him on paedophile charges, their evidence seemed rock solid. Then

I thought about the Gristle I have known for so many years. There is no side to him, nothing badly immoral, just a bit of normal criminality here and there. I have never felt uneasy in his presence. I have never seen him in any unusual situations with kids. If anything, he loves being with lively kids, without ever trying to control them. When he is around them he always looks like he is having fun and making up for all he missed when he was growing up, being beaten by his bastard of a father. He is disgusted by people who take advantage of kids or abuse them in any way. His sexual appetites are entirely normal, but even there he plays by the rules of the game and is good to those he goes with.'

'In other words, no doubts in your mind,' Cyril said, turning his head to look at me. He smiled at me. 'I agree completely. Still, it could have gone very wrong if he imagined we were accusing him of fiddling with those kiddies.'

'Tell me,' I said. 'That's why I was terrified to raise it. What did he say to you when you sat out here with him?'

'He didn't say anything for a while. He sat and stared down the garden. I think at one point he was crying.'

'Crying? Gristle?'

'I think so. I waited a good while until he was ready to talk. He was very moved that you would risk your life to defend him. No one has ever done much for him, unless they wanted something back. He has always depended on himself. I know the three of us knock him around and tease him, but that is fun. What you did was serious. He has never known anyone do that. He needs time to get his head around it.'

'Did he tell you what he said to the kids in the school?'

'Do you remember he said one of the kids told him that talking about the old days was a "load of shit"? What they actually wanted him to talk about was what would he do different if he was young again, if he was like them now.'

'Go wild and start younger than he did,' I suggested.

'No, no, he was taking it seriously. The kids lapped it up. They said it was the best advice they had been given by anyone.'

'Bit strange that, Gristle giving advice to kids and them thinking it was fine.'

'Well, it worked. They thought he was magic. They voted him their NUOG – Numero Uno Old Git. He loved it. At that point, the kids started on about technology. They knew a lot more than he did so the kids showed him how to use his phone and what they do on the Internet. They were taking pictures of him and each other. They showed him websites and some of the photos they send flying around. He told them they were too young to be looking at some of the photos they had. Then the teacher came back and called a halt to the whole thing. That's probably where the accusation about being a paedophile came from, plus he toured the boys' toilets with them and took photos. The kids texted the photos to him. They told him to ignore the teacher because she is an arse. That was the most common word they used to describe her. Maybe it is physically accurate, or her attempts to broaden their vocabulary have been useless. Schools get more shit-like every day.'

'Because of all that, he is now banned from every school in the county?'

'Seems so. His name is on the banned list along with speakers from all the world religions, but not Muslims so as not to cause offence. He is now lined up alongside the BNP, UKIP, English Defence League, payday loan operators, William Hill and anyone supporting Free Schools or academies and any idiot who thinks Education Secretaries are sensible and do a good job.'

'Did he say anything about retaliating against the gang in the village out to get him?'

'I talked him out of murder, torture and full-frontal attacks on property with firebombs. He will delay running them over, poisoning or garrotting, which would be his preferred mode of execution. I made him promise to wait for my signal before he does anything. I said we wanted to know what else they have dug up, or what else they will make up about him. Is there more?'

'Just that accusation of sex with underage girls when he was younger,' I said. 'But we know that will go nowhere.'

Cyril sat back on the garden bench and stretched out his legs. He raised his right hand as if he was giving another wave to someone at the gate, but only the horse was in the field. 'When I was in that diocesan prison, each day, just before my next round of medication was due and my mind came back to me a little bit, I used to imagine sitting here.' He paused and looked around him. 'I love this garden, it's my second favourite after my cemetery. I pictured the ordered rows of vegetables, the line of fruit trees, the smells, the sounds, the birds and insects doing their business as if their lives depended on what they are doing, the peace, the warmth of the sun.' He smiled at me. 'And the good company, of course, and the busy ancient road through the bottom of your garden and all the people who love to stop here and rest. I can sit on this bench and see the whole of life, past, present and to come, stretching like a great highway on either side of this place. It is a gateway to the cosmos through which all time moves, a passing place for all those who have been here in the past, or who will come through in the future. It makes you the gatekeeper between the past and the future. If you lived in parts of Africa you would be a key man in the clan, the gatekeeper easing souls into the company of their ancestors.'

I thought the after-effects of the drugs were still bothering him. That, or the sun was getting to him. 'I can get you a hat,' I said, 'to keep the sun off your head, or you can lie down for a while. The others won't be back until this evening.'

He laughed. 'I'm embarrassing you, aren't I? All this talk of your heroic deeds and generosity of spirit. It doesn't fit with your self-image of being a loser on the run, does it?' He raised his right hand in another little wave.

I looked down the garden, searching for anyone hiding there. 'Who do you keep waving to?'

'Travellers on the other side,' he said. 'The time road runs across the end of your garden. Very popular stopping-off place this was in the old days. They stop here to pass over or to rest awhile.'

'I can't see anyone.'

'You haven't learned to look properly. It will come to you.'

'Are you seeing ghosts?' I asked him.

'I prefer to call them old friends, still wandering until they are freed and move through the tear in reality, their gateway back into the energy of the galaxy. Your garden is one of their gateways. Always keep it beautiful and full of colour, for their sake. It reminds them they will take shape again.'

I never know if Cyril is winding me up when he goes on like this. How can anyone see ghosts in the middle of the day?

'I'd like to go home to my own house,' he said out of the blue. 'I miss my neighbours. I worry they might not be looked after.'

I remembered the cleric who had taken his place.

'There's a new priest down there since you went... since they locked you up. Maybe he will look after your neighbours.' Or maybe not, I thought. He hadn't stuck me as being a cemetery man. 'He wears a clerical collar and people need an appointment to see him.'

'Does he cut the grass and trim the edges? Are the gravestones clean? What about the food for the recently dead? Does he visit them and talk to them?'

'He might not do every little bit of those things.'

'You don't understand. How would you feel if someone came in here and smashed your vegetables and flattened your fruit bushes.'

'I'd have to get over it. It's only a garden. I tell you what,' I said, seeing how anxious he was about the cemetery, 'stay here for just one more night. Your dead neighbours will wait another day. They are hardly going anywhere, are they? Or maybe they have gone there already.'

He glared at me in utter seriousness, or was it in disappointment?

Maybe I had overstepped the mark.

'Another cup of tea?' I said, standing and turning towards the house.

The Kitchen Cabinet

Tuesday 21st April 2015 – Hawthorn Moon

'Someone should call the meeting to order,' Card insisted. 'How else can it be a proper meeting?'

'Oh, for goodness sake, we don't have to do that shit,' Gristle grumbled.

'Cyril, what do you think?' Card asked.

'I think we should have an air of formality about what we do. A lot is at stake here. Afterwards, it would be a strong defence when questioned by the police to demonstrate we had not acted mindlessly.'

'What's wrong with acting mindlessly?' Gristle asked.

'Most of the time it doesn't matter, Gristle, but we are heading to some serious stuff now. I propose that GG chair the meeting,' Cyril said.

'I can't do it,' I protested. 'I'm the secretary, I take notes and keep a log of our work; minutes and all that stuff. I propose Cyril chair the meeting,' I said, 'and I second it so you all know it is a serious proposal. Gristle will provoke disorder instead of keeping order. Card will talk through his arse all the time and keep us here all night.' I paused for dramatic effect. 'Cyril was the one who was locked up. That to me is the clincher.' I wasn't sure how it was the clincher but it made it look as if I had thought the proposal through.

I gave Cyril the nod. 'I call this meeting to order,' he said.

Card gave a sigh of relief. Gristle harrumphed. I started taking notes.

'Are there any apologies?'

'No, reverend chairman,' I said. 'All members are present and correct.'

'What about the Commander?' Card asked. I said Card

could be an arse.

'The emergency nature of this meeting and the short notice did not allow the secretary's office to contact the Commander,' I said. 'I propose we send him full minutes and notes of the meeting and make contact in time to invite him to the next meeting.'

'Proposal accepted and agreed. Let the minutes show the reason for the Commander's absence,' Cyril announced.

'Minutes of last meeting?' he asked.

I shook my head.

'Good,' he said, 'that means there are no matters arising, so we can get down to the main topic of the meeting. How do we deal with those bastards in the CPPP?'

We went at it for three hours after that, stopping only for a quick wee, allowing extra time for Cyril, who was still recovering from the effects of his prostate operation.

What stood out most clearly was the amazing creativity, deviousness, cunning, bloody-mindedness, thirst for revenge and the denunciation of all those who were evil, greedy, spiteful and exercised foul and vindictive deeds in their thirst to control others and steal all they could get away with. We were on a roll.

By the end of the meeting it was determined to prepare Gristle's defence against the charges being brought by the CPPP, Card to take the lead on that, and having succeeded in that, to then proceed to punish the CPPP members. To that end, we drew up a list of proposed actions.

Firstly, that Basher should raise the ban on me immediately, or we would inform the brewery that he bought spirits from the supermarkets and beer from cheaper rivals.

Secondly, that Gristle would lead a publicity campaign

against Arthur Stockleman and, with the support of the kids from the school, expose his rottenness.

Thirdly, that Cyril would subject Philomena Luge to a religious inquisition of some sort and destroy her standing with the Jehovah Church crowd.

Fourthly, that we would use Basher to resurrect a dead crime case against Mrs Cenhelm, the post office owner, brought to our attention by Gristle.

Fifthly, that I would deal with Bill the butcher and land him in deep trouble with the smugglers.

Sixthly, that the Commander be persuaded to be active in the operation and deal with the machinations of Cyracuse Cactus Chadwick.

Seventhly, that Card would proceed with his plan to set up a scam that would lead to litigation with Apple that would destroy the finances of the CPPP members.

Lastly, that each member of the group be responsible for the strategy, the execution and rendering an account of the outcome of their area of responsibility. It was agreed that should anyone be arrested he would plead insanity and feign Alzheimer's and all sorts of dementia and mental instability until we could mount a prison break and set him free. Cyril's rescue had given us a confidence boost that would brook no failure.

We were wreaking havoc on a second bottle of Lithuanian genuine scotch whiskey from my illicit store when Cyril announced he was going home the next morning. Gristle said he would send Gerard in the hardtop blue Bentley to collect him from the end of my lane and drive him to the rectory in style. It was agreed not to provoke plod by touring around in the soft-top version for a while yet.

As we neared the end of my second bottle of whiskey, I remarked to myself through a whiskey glow on how we had all changed in such a short space of time. Sometimes you can sense a feeling of power in a group. You can tell when individuals have changed, grown in some way, overcome some hurdle that was blocking them before. Your body feels different, more content, or more energetic, or just more capable of doing stuff. When I noticed them staring at me I realised I had been talking aloud. I cleared my throat. 'We had a good result is what I am saying. Cyril is back safe and as sound as he ever was, which isn't saying much, but he is here again. Card is more human and admits to having a strange tendency, or a personal orientation, I think they call it, and we hope he will find happiness. Gristle is… well, still Gristle, but more Gristle than he ever was. We know now for definite that we prefer him like that; that is a big change. And me, I suppose my change is that I know where I want to end my days. No more running for me.'

We sat staring into our whiskey glasses. I felt awkward at making such a long speech and for speaking so personally about each of them. Cyril swigged off the remains of his whiskey, lifted the bottle and said, 'Enough here for a drop each for a toast.' The bottle was passed around and drained by the last man in the circle. Cyril stood up. Like all priests, he prefers to stand when he is preaching. My grandmother used to say if we made priests sit when they preached on Sunday mornings we would all be home in half the time. 'I give you the Fearsome Four,' he announced, 'may we never waver, may we never give in and may none of us die roaring in pain and may the power of the cosmos bring us safely home when our time is up. I give you the Fearsome Four.'

'Hold on a moment before you drink to that, I want to add a bit.' This from Gristle, who never speaks at formal occasions. 'To good friends and especially to any one of them who would risk his life for someone.' He never would get the hang of the personal emotions thing.

'And I want to add, in thanksgiving for the company and friendship of understanding people,' Card said, looking more relaxed than I had ever seen him.

They all looked at me, waiting for me to add my bit. For once, I was overcome and could only say, 'Amen to what you all said. Good luck.'

In the Garden

Tuesday 21ˢᵗ April 2015 – Hawthorn Moon

I saw Card and Gristle out the front door. 'Close that gate behind you,' I called as they reached the end of the path. 'I don't want Carey's cattle wandering into my garden.'

Gristle made a big display of closing the gate and pretending to load it with many padlocks. 'Certainly, Your Lordship. Is that secure enough for you now, sir? Anything else you would have us to do, Your Lordship, before we head to our lowly hovels?'

'Feck off, the lot of you,' I called. 'We don't want you riff-raff round here. I'll have the estate manager set the dogs on you if you darken this lane again. Be off with you, you band of scoundrels.'

Their catcalls and laughter faded away as they made their way down the lane to the main road. I stood on the doorstep looking up at the thin crescent of the moon moving between the clouds, as if it was looking for a hiding place. There was unseasonal warmth in the air and gentleness about the night that said the day had been warm. The smell of the countryside hung in the air mixed with traces of animals and the deep background touch of woodland, muddy ditches and streams. Night noises started up again after our rude interruption. Shuffling, scurrying, snuffling, and the occasional animal cough or bark and the sharp cry of a startled bird or small thing cut the air. The place was as much alive as it had been during the light of the day.

I found Cyril sitting on the bench in the middle of the garden where we had talked earlier in the day. 'You ok?' I asked, easing myself down beside him.

He nodded. 'I'm fine.'

'Would you like anything?'

'I've got what I want,' he said.

We sat in silence looking at the hedge at the end of the garden. Bigger gaps were appearing in the clouds, letting the moon spread its light across us.

'Many travellers going past tonight?' I asked, teasing him.

'Just a few. One came in through your gate. He was happy to have reached the end of his journey. The others still have issues to sort out. They'll be back when they are ready.'

'Oh,' I said, not knowing what to say, or what to ask. 'Good job the garden was tidy,' I said.

'Yes, they liked that. A woman who went through the gate earlier remarked on it. Quite impressed she was.'

I gave up teasing him. He had an answer for everything.

'What do you think are our chances against the village gang?' I asked after a while.

He took a deep breath and let it out slowly. 'Justice and goodness will always prevail. That's what we believe. Sometimes the process needs a good kick to make it work. Sometimes it takes longer than we hope, because evil people are not stupid and they are good at fighting dirty. Sometimes those who start the process aren't always the ones to see the success.'

It was my turn to pause and be reflective. 'So in the end we will be successful, only it might not be us enjoying it. Is that what you mean?'

He nodded his head. 'Aye.'

'We had better make a good start then,' I said. 'I hate to think of the ones taking over from us complaining that it took so long because we made a feck of the start.'

He laughed. 'You could put it that way. The timing has to be right. We must start before the other side know what is going on. We need to be well into making them pay for being so evil before they know what is happening.'

In the pasture behind the hedge Blazing Bolt snorted and shuffled around. 'That'll be a fox,' I said, 'he doesn't like them.'

'Foxes are hunters,' he said. 'We don't like hunters much ourselves, especially if we are the hunted.'

I didn't know if I was supposed to answer that.

'Tell me about the trouble you are in with the two soldiers.'

'You're not very subtle tonight, are you?'

'You're too clever to fall for subtle,' he said. 'You would talk your way around it like a cat climbing through the branches of a tree.'

I paused, reluctant to dig too deep.

'I joined the IRA. I was a young lad. It seemed the only thing to do at the time. It was either do that or be picked off by the other side because I was on my own without protection.'

'In Londonderry.'

'Derry, yes.'

'But you left them.'

'Yep.'

'Dangerous to do, that,' he said.

'Can be.'

'Without permission it is very dangerous.'

'So they say.'

'Why did you leave?' he asked

'Something went wrong.'

'What happened?'

'Do you mind if we don't discuss this, Cyril? It's my problem. I will sort it.'

'By yourself?'

'Yes, by myself.'

'But you joined the IRA because being by yourself was dangerous. You're in danger now. You have been for years. It's why you hide.'

'Cyril, let's drop it, ok?'

'How can we help you if we don't know what happened?'

'Nobody can help me, ok?'

'Ok.'

We went back to staring down the garden.

'How come you claim to see the ghosts during the day?' I asked him, trying to steer the conversation away from my past. 'Surely they are only visible at night?'

'Do you think they sleep during daylight?'

'No one sees them in daylight,' I said. 'If, and I mean *if*, anyone does see them, it is always at night. You never hear of people bumping into them in the middle of the day.'

'Doesn't mean they aren't there,' he said. 'Could be that people are more open to the possibilities at night. Darkness takes away some of the filters we use to control what we experience in daylight.'

I thought that one through before answering him. 'What you mean is, we are more gullible at night because it is dark. Our imagination takes over, is that it?'

'You would see the same in the day if you knew how to look, smell, feel or touch the experience.'

'No one sees anything during the day.'

'No? You left the IRA because you saw something. Loads of other people saw the same thing but they didn't see what you saw. You saw your ghosts, didn't you?'

'I was there on Bloody Sunday. I was young. I saw the dead and injured.'

'That should have made you hate the British and stay in the IRA. What else did you see that others didn't?'

'Jesus Christ, Cyril, will you let it go? I can't tell you any more, or you will be damned as well.'

'Damned is such a loose word.'

Night noises filtered into the gap left by our silence.

Picking at memories is like picking at sores, you start the bleeding again. My feeling of guilt never goes away. My secret is part of the guilt. It leans heavily on me, invading dreams, pushing cries and screams into my head when I least expect them, and always tricking me into wondering where the guilty ones would be now if I hadn't kept quiet. I know where I would be if I had told the truth. I'd be buried in a bog, or in sand hills within sound of the sea, my words buried with me. Words can't bring back the dead. But my unspoken words come back to haunt me every day. Damned might be a loose word but it summed me up.

'It's like having a stone in your shoe, isn't it?' Cyril said

'What is?'

'Holding on to one little truth makes you limp. It would be so easy to empty your shoe.'

Maybe it was the garden, the time of night, the passing spirits or the fact that he was a priest and a man who knew suffering. Whatever it was, it felt like a rush of wind gushing up through my body rattling my brain, loosening my tongue and knocking down all the barriers I had carried all those years. By the time I finished telling him my story, there were no more stones in my shoe. He knew about the gun I had carried and handed over to the man I later discovered was not who he said he was, about the people who had died needlessly, as well as the lies, the cover-up and hypocrisy that maintained the lies all those years. We sat in silence for a long time, allowing the power of confession to do its healing work.

175

'You're definite about the gun?' he asked me.

'I gave it to him.'

'And he fired it?'

I nodded.

'The soldiers said they came under fire and that is why they shot at the crowd.'

I paused at the enormity of what I was about to tell Cyril. 'He didn't shoot *at* the soldiers. He shot over their heads.'

Now it was Cyril's turn to sit still and work through what I had told him. His eyes opened in surprise when he caught on. 'Holy shit! He did that on purpose. He provoked the military on purpose and put them in the wrong when they were unable to produce a gun, or even bullets, to justify the shooting.'

We sat in silence.

'All them people, his own people, killed, just for a propaganda victory,' Cyril said.

I shrugged my shoulders. 'He said it was war.'

'You said he wasn't IRA. Did he work for the Protestant paramilitaries?'

I shook my head. 'He was with a secret group we didn't know about. They belonged to no one but used both sides against each other to create trouble. That way they got rich and powerful.'

'What happened to the gun?'

'He gave it back to me. I took it away, buried it and never went back when I realised what he had done and what he was up to.'

'Does anyone know where it is buried?'

'Nobody knows, only me.'

'Is it still where you buried it?'

'I would imagine so.'

'That might just save your life.'

There was nothing more to say. We sat still, letting the drawing in of the night find its way onto us, shrouding us in the comfort of its calmness. The long dark shadows of my memories were now shared, but that didn't make them any easier to bear.

Cyril nudged me. 'Look there, by the gate into the field. See them?'

I stared at the gate. 'What am I looking for?'

'A small group of spirits, about four of them. Three of them are coming in, the other is going on his way.'

I looked at him to check if he was winding me up. 'Are you telling me they are lost and can't agree on which way to go? Don't they use SatNav?'

'Stop talking silly,' he said.

'*Me*. How come *I'm* the one talking silly? I'm not seeing a gang of ghosts standing inside my back gate looking at an A–Z to find another world.'

'You wanted to see them, this is your chance.'

I stared at the gate. I could see nothing. Maybe there was a slight shadow, or a movement in the hedge, probably the fox working his way along, or a badger rooting for worms. 'I can't see anything.'

'Focus your eyes, like you were looking at something five inches in front of your nose so that the images further away look a bit fuzzy. Go on, try it, humour me.'

I grunted and did as he told me. 'I'm going cross-eyed,' I said.

'Point your eyes towards that corner, just by the gate, in front of the old yew tree, but keep looking at the point close to your nose.'

I did as he told me, anything to shut him up. 'My eyes are starting to hurt,' I said. 'How long do I...?' Four people were by my gate! They huddled together talking about something. I couldn't see them clearly, their bodies moved between appearance and disappearance, as if I was watching smoke meandering into and out of shapes. 'Good God,' I said. 'Can you see them? They are looking this way.'

'They sense you can see them. Three of them are at the last step before going through the rent into the energy of the cosmos.' He waved at them. 'Lift your hand to them, like you were waving thanks to a driver who has given you right of way.'

I did as he told me. The four nodded towards me. One of them turned and seemed to walk out through my gate into the field. The other three smiled at us and then walked into the old yew tree and were gone.

'Where did they go?'

'Back to the start,' Cyril said, 'where we all go and where you need to be again.'

Meeting with the Village Gang of Five
Thursday 30th April – Hawthorn Moon

I sat in Card Index's kitchen drinking strong tea. 'There they were, four of them, bright as buttons. Maybe not that bright, but they were there, four spirits.'

'So you and Cyril went back to the whiskey big time after we left?'

'No, we didn't take any more drink. We sat in the garden talking and these four ghosts just, you know, appeared inside my back gate.'

'You're going as soft as Cyril.'

'No, honestly, I saw them with my own eyes.'

He sighed and raised his eyebrows. 'It would be more in your line to keep your eyes on this meeting, or you will be joining your mob of ghosts at the end of your garden.'

'It wasn't a mob. There were only four of them. They were spirits not ghosts.'

'For goodness sake, GG. You'll be telling me next they talked to you and asked you where was the nearest pub, or they explained that they were looking for a concert to go to, or maybe they were hoping to find someone dying a spectacular death so they could watch. It must take a lot to hold their attention once they have shuffled off their mortal coil.'

'They didn't talk. They nodded to me. The woman who went through earlier told Cyril that she thought my garden was a credit to me.'

'More likely it was some woman complimenting Cyril on what he had done *with* her in your garden.'

'No, she was for real.'

He frowned at me. 'A ghost, and she was for real? Would you listen to yourself? If I were you I'd hide the whiskey and lay off the drink for a while.'

179

'Bollocks,' I muttered, realising I was wasting my breath.

'This meeting we have in a few minutes, you know what to do and what you have to say?'

'Yes, yes, yes. We've been over it several times. Don't worry about me. I know what I am doing. It's you who needs to get your story straight.'

He stood up. 'I'll get the room ready for the meeting. Stay here in the kitchen until they all arrive and then I'll bring you in.'

'Why won't you believe me about the spirits?'

'Because I'm not a fruitcake. I have too much on my mind. I am a realist and a pragmatist. I advise you to be the same when you meet this lot coming for the meeting. Bloody ghosts! You'll be preaching about heaven and hell next.'

'No, I won't, because there isn't a heaven and hell as such. What you have is…' I was talking to myself in an empty kitchen. Nothing new, then, as my grandmother would have said. She believed in ghosts, even though she would not believe men had landed on the moon. All made up, she used to say, trickery with cameras to make it look like the moon. She was right about the ghosts. Now I'm wondering if she was right about the men landing on the moon being a con. In spite of Card, I know what I saw. His browbeating Ofsted inspector ways wouldn't force me to change my mind. What is more, Cyril isn't completely soft in the head now that he has me as a witness.

The front door opened and closed a few times, letting in the cooler evening air. Voices ebbed and flowed around the hallway and in the front room as the CPPP gathered like magpies hopping towards an unprotected nest.

'Help me with the drinks,' Card said, as he bustled into the kitchen. 'I've got a sherry and a soft drink for the ladies. Take in the whiskey for the blokes. Cactus has water with his, the other two take it neat. Be generous with it, they like good glasses of it.'

'What are you doing? You're giving them fifteen-year-old Talisker,' I said, reading the label on the bottle he handed me.

'Don't be stupid. It's a Talisker bottle filled with cheap stuff. That lot would drink piss and think it was pure Islay malt if it was in the right bottle.'

I looked at him bustling around and wondered. 'You ever do that?' I asked.

He turned his head and grinned at me. 'Just fill their glasses. Let's start them on the road to ruin. Follow me, my good man, into the presence of your betters.' As we headed out into the hallway towards his front room he stopped. 'Best not touch a drop of the stuff you are pouring.'

I raised my eyebrows at him.

'In case you get tipsy,' he said with a straight face. 'You need a clear head.'

I didn't know why he was so chirpy. I was shaking at the thought of what we were about to do. Maybe I had more to lose than Card Index. He would still be alive if we got it wrong. Me, on the other hand?

Best not think too far down that road.

I followed him into the room where I was greeted with the spiteful indifference young children use on each other when they have fallen out. I was a hair's breadth from turning that indifference to murderous intent if I played my cards badly. Pouring the whiskey helped ease my way around the room.

The meeting opened with each of them whinging about some aspect of village life that didn't suit them. Bill the butcher stood in front of the fireplace, pontificating over the moaning meeting, grinning at any mention of discomfort or aggravation any of the group had visited on their neighbours. I was allowed to stand inside the door as I had done on my first appearance.

Then it was my turn. 'Right, you,' the butcher man said. 'What did you find about the pig you go round with?'

I was ready with a smart answer when Card caught my eye. I took a deep breath. 'Nothing of substance to report on the paedophile angle you asked me to look at.'

'You're a waste of space.' Cactus said. 'Don't forget the stake you have in this.'

I interrupted them. 'I didn't say I had nothing, just not enough to make the paedophile charge stick.'

'What more do you need?' Arthur asked.

'I know something happened when he visited the school. He said a few things that made me realise he was grooming those kids. What I needed was to get among the kids and ask them what happened when Gristle visited them. That's where it got impossible. I can't go into a school and start interrogating kids about sex. I haven't one of those CRB things and—'

'DBS is what they are called now, you ignoramus,' Arthur butted in, drawing on his training as a member of the County Safeguarding Board.

'One of those,' I continued. 'Anyway, I couldn't see the school allowing me in among their kids to ask if they had been sexually assaulted. Before you ask, it is a waste visiting the kids at home because parents wouldn't allow it and *he* has groomed the kids to say nothing to strangers like me. You know how his lot work.'

Arthur nodded vigorously. This was his home territory. Now that I had his interest, I hurried on. 'What we need are the photos he took of the boys in the toilets and—'

'Did he definitely take them?' the postmistress asked, squinting at me as if I was soiling the room.

'Yes, ma'am,' I answered politely, as I imagined picking her off through the sights of a rifle and shooting her through her right eye. 'When I asked him how the visit went and did they take any photos for the school magazine, he grinned at me and said the magazine won't show the photos he took in the boys' toilet. Then he laughed like it was a joke.'

'Good gracious,' Philomena Luge snorted. 'The hand of the Almighty will strike his heinous hide and cast him into hell.'

Not before he stuffs hell with shit-steeped hypocrites like you, I thought, you sanctimonious old cow. 'Indeed, ma'am, but we need hard evidence to prosecute or destroy him and then the Lord will smite him mightily in his unforeseen and mysterious ways.'

Her eyebrows narrowed to focus on me as she worked out if I was taking the piss. I kept my best poker face as I turned my well-tried naïve look on her. 'It seems we are stymied on proving he is a paedophile,' I said, 'without the expert help only an expert could give. Maybe one day, if we wait long enough, he will slip up. By then he will have had his lustful and sinful ways with hundreds of young children and older women. I find it so frustrating to know we have him almost in our grasp. We will eventually catch the evil, bottom-feeling, boy-groping pederast as he works his evil ways on young boys. We mustn't forget the way he cajoles and misuses young girls, preparing them for domination and abuse when they are older, bending them to his naked and sinful ways. There is no need for me to go into detail on his activities with grown women, which are well known to all of you. He didn't learn about them tricks off the back of a Corn Flakes package. You are so close, yet he slips away. It is so maddening to think how badly I have failed and not measured up to your trust in me.'

'*You* might have failed, but we have an expert on these issues and one who has right of entry into the school as a governor.' Arthur the paedo expert beamed as he looked around the room. '*Me*.' I couldn't imagine him ever beaming again if our plan worked and he finished up in a prison with some boyos who would wipe the smile off his face, having wiped a few other parts of him first.

'Gosh,' I cried, 'Nobody told me you are such an expert. Why was I asked to check it out when there was a brilliant person already well versed in it all?' I thought I might be going too far with the praise but Arthur was too vain to notice.

The pig butcher stirred himself. 'We needed an outsider to make the initial running. Arthur is like an expert advisor.'

'But if he can get into the school I can tell him the information we need to tie up the loose ends. There will be no escape for the paedophile scumbag. I could do all the legwork if Mr Stockleman allowed me to pursue the matter, all under his direct direction, of course. He would put the icing on the cake. What a triumph it would be for whoever put the final touches to throwing such an evil person behind bars,' I paused, 'or putting him and his ill-gotten wealth in your hands.'

I could see Arthur revelling in the idea of taking the credit while the others were thinking of the money. 'I think it would be appropriate if I took over the overall management of this part of the investigation,' Arthur said. 'I know the ropes around this issue and I am a persona very grata in the school. Nobody is allowed to stand in my way if I go in as a governor and as a highly respected member of the County Safeguarding Board. Him there can do all the legwork and then I will bring the necessary finesse and add the final touches. Yes, I can see it all working out just as we want.'

The little Hitler wouldn't even call me by my name. He would find out that "him there" deserved respect as well as the use of his name. I gritted my teeth and smiled before pressing on. 'I can give Mr Stockleman the names of the key kids to target. That will save Mr Stockleman using his expert knowledge needlessly and spending time that he could use so profitably elsewhere,' I said, looking around the rest of the group for support. A few nods signalled I was heading down the path Card and I had agreed.

The pig killer looked at Arthur and then took in the rest of the group. 'Everyone ok with going ahead on those terms?'

Nods of agreement all round.

'What about his moneymaking games and other things he gets up to?' the postmistress asked, squinting at me. That woman does need shooting through that right eye, I thought.

'You were right,' I said. 'He robs, cheats, fiddles accounts, doesn't pay all the VAT he should, he uses some tax avoidance scam through some up-market accountancy so there must be a lot of money involved. I suggest we tip off the Revenue.'

'No Revenue,' the pig killer snapped at me. 'Er... we will deal with this one, in confidence, by ourselves to start with. Later, we will consider the implications of involving the taxman.'

The others nodded agreement with him. Like most crooks, they stayed as far from the Revenue as they could even when they were not breaking the law. More importantly, they wanted Gristle's money rather than giving it to the taxman.

'You can clear off now,' the pig killer ordered. 'We don't need you here for the rest of the meeting.'

'Thank you for giving me your time,' I said, turning to head out the door. 'I presume you will deal with his plan to take over some trust or other in the village. He remarked how much money he will make out of that little piece of piracy and pillaging.' I left a stunned silence behind me as I stepped out into the hall.

As Card and I had expected, the butcher man shouted, 'You, get back in here.'

I sighed and thought, they really should get into the habit of calling people by their given name. I returned and stood inside the door with an open and trusting look on my face. That face never works when being interrogated by the Excise because they are hard, heartless bastards who have heard every lie going and seen every variation on lying faces. This lot were not half as smart as they thought.

'What did he say about the trust?' the pig butcher asked.

Card cut in. 'Actually, I wanted to raise that point with the group. GG doesn't know the entire plan. I do. The immoral thief approached me with an offer, more of a demand, actually. I have given considerable thought as to how we will foil his plans and thwart him. Plus, I have an angle on that story that GG does not know about. I know how the thief intends to take over the trust and steal all your money.'

Card was definitely into his Ofsted mode with words like 'thwart' and 'foil' and he had their full attention. He has a way about him when he does his Ofsted stance. When he turns it on he frightens the hell out of teachers and commands respect from the public who do not know any better. With this lot it was difficult to know if the silence he created was because of Card's Ofsted bearing, or if it was down to the threat to their money. Card paused, glanced around the group with a slight raising of his eyebrows, and waited. He has the use of raised eyebrows and deliberate pauses down to a fine art.

'Well?' demanded Cactus. 'What does he want? What is he after? How does it affect us? What have you thought through?'

The flower shop woman got to the heart of the problem. 'How does it affect our financial position?'

The postmistress, being more practical, asked, 'How do we stop him?'

Arthur was still wearing his Safeguarding hat. 'This is a disgrace and should not be allowed. It must be stamped out.'

The butcher glowered and growled. 'Get on with it. Give us the details.'

Card took his time, making it look like he was thinking through how best to answer the barrage of questions. 'GG had tipped me off that the evil robber had hinted about some trust or other and that there would be a lot of money for the taking. I was not surprised when he approached me, after GG's warning. He had the nerve to come round here to the house and put his demands to me. He sat in that chair where you are sitting now,' he said, pointing to Cactus, who squirmed in the chair as if some nasty creepy-crawly was nibbling at him.

'He came straight to the point. He intends to buy my app, whether or not I want to sell it.'

The group gasped at the thought of their enemy getting hold of so valuable a source of income.

'You told him to bugger off, didn't you?' the butcher said.

Card nodded.

'He can't force you to sell it to him,' the squinting postmistress said.

'He said he would blackmail me,' Card said, but

omitted adding, just like you lot. 'He has found out I am gay, and since I don't live with my friend, he said it must be because I had a good reason to keep it secret. He threatened to broadcast my sexual orientation and add all sorts of details to make it sound much worse than anything I could imagine.'

The group was now locked onto his every word.

'I told him the app was not worth a lot. In that case, he said, he would not pay much for it. Then he told me how much he calculates it earns a year. He was within £30,000 of what came in last year.'

'He had asked me one time how much Card earns from his app,' I said. 'I told him I didn't know but thought he sold over a hundred and fifty thousand in his first year.'

Card picked up the next line in our choreographed tale. 'And he knew how much I sold each one for and the price of the updates. He did some fairly accurate calculations. You have to give it to him, when it comes to money his head is screwed on the right way.'

The flower woman glared at me. 'You and your big mouth,' she snapped.

'It was nothing to do with him,' Card told her. 'Gristle didn't need GG to work out the figures.'

'I didn't know why he was asking me the questions,' I protested. 'At least I had told Card and he was ready when he was approached.'

'Without GG's warning, I would have been caught flatfooted,' Card added, keeping to our carefully worked-out script.

'Then what?' This from the postmistress with the narrow outlook on life seen through her squinty eyes.

'I told him I did not own the app, I only owned a share in it and therefore I couldn't sell it to him,' Card said.

'That stopped him,' the butcher said, grinning at the

group.

'Not really. He said he would buy my share. He asked how much was my share and who owned the other share. I told him to mind his own business.'

The group were satisfied and began to relax until Card added, 'He threatened to go to the taxman if I didn't tell him the size of my share and who else was involved. I told him I owned fifty per cent but I was not prepared to say who the silent partners were.'

Talk of the Revenue poking around set all of them worrying as they worked out the implications of the taxman being involved in any way. I could sympathise with anyone at the thought of the Revenue coming in. All those cold-hearted government inquisitors needed was one loose thread and they would unravel far more than they were entitled to without any comeback by the victim. Not that I felt any sympathy for the robbing bullies in front of me, even if the Revenue trampled all over them and their brothers, sisters, aunts, uncles, cousins to the third remove, along with dead grandparents, a place the Revenue would go if they felt the need, or were having a quiet day with all their victims dispatched ahead of schedule.

Then Card turned up the heat. 'The problem is this. If I sell him my fifty per cent share he will turn on each of you. He needs only one of you to sell him your share and he will control the lot. He will dig and dig until he finds some little thing one of you does not want brought into the open. If he finds nothing on any of you, he will dig into your family and your family background until he finds a stone you do not want turning over.' He paused again with one of his loaded silences.

The postmistress blinked several times.

Philomena the flower woman bit her lower lip and frowned.

Cactus twisted and turned in his chair again, which can't have been doing the upholstery any good considering his size and weight.

Arthur the safeguarding expert stared up at the ceiling.

The pig killer coughed loudly.

Card's point had struck home.

As planned, I butted in at this point. 'If I prove he is a paedophile, will that stop him?'

Card shook his head. 'No, he could still make me sell my share even if he was in prison.'

'Looks like he has you all by the short and curlies,' I said, playing down to my loser image for the meeting.

'Not necessarily,' Card said, our superhero to the rescue. 'What if I didn't sell my share because I don't have one?' He was back as the centre of all eyes and had their full attention. I had to hand it to Card, when it came to the test, he stepped up to the mark.

'How will you do that?' the pig killer asked.

'I give over my share to the trust, to all of you, without cost, completely, legally, without any clauses or restrictions so I cease to have any ownership or control of it. You will own all of it. He will have to negotiate with you as a group if he wants to buy in.'

I could almost see their minds working – full control; no buying, so free and without cost; total ownership of the money; lots of money; rich to mega-rich all in one step; loads of cash coming in each month; rich enough to put Gristle in his place and possibly run him out of the village – everything they wanted and all without fuss, opposition or any cost to them.

The squint-eyed postmistress nearly pricked the balloon. Gristle had warned us she would be the one we would have to watch, 'Why would you give it all away? What's in it for you?' She would never understand why anyone would give away so much money, or any money, if it came to it.

'I have developed the app as far as I can go with it. It will generate shed loads of money from now on by itself. I am pushing on now and I want to spend the last years of my life relaxing and trying to be happy. Most of all, I want to live openly with my friend, in my own house and know that if I die before him he will be able to live in my house until he dies. Give me your promise that I will be able to do that and I will turn over the ownership of the app to you. I will update it every six months but you pay me only an hourly rate for doing that.' I could see them working out what that might amount to as Card carried on.

'That way, you get to own the lot. Gristle can't force you to sell because he would need to buy out all of you. You will have a great income flow to look forward to. Gristle will be enraged to think you got the better of him. He will no longer blackmail me because I will live openly with my friend.'

Knowing the selfish and greedy minds in the room, I was sure they were thinking about the money that would be theirs, how to protect it and how to make sure there were no flaws in what they had heard. I was confident that not one of them would wonder how Card felt about giving away such a valuable asset, letting go of something that was so close to his heart and that he had spent years developing. Greedy bastards are like that. We had counted on it so that they would not notice the attack being mounted on their flank that would bring about their destruction.

'We need time to consider this proposal,' the stamp and envelope seller said, giving the nod to Bill the butcher.

'Right,' the pig killer said. 'You two leave the room while we consider this proposal. We'll call you when we need you.'

We made our way to the kitchen and sat at the table. 'What do you think?' I asked. 'Did they fall for it?'

Card put his finger to his lips. 'Let's wait and see, but I think we will have a result.'

We sat in silence like two patients waiting in a dentist's waiting room, unwilling to talk to each other in case we showed how fearful we were. I could have done with a good slug of Card's whiskey, although in the light of what he had said earlier, I would always check the authenticity of any whiskey he served up from now on.

A bellow from the front room summoned us back in.

'Right, you two,' the butcher man started. 'Card, we agree to you signing over your share of the app to us on two conditions. One, that it is done legally and by a proper solicitor selected by us and you will pay the legal costs. Secondly, that if you move your nancy boy into your house you will not flaunt him around the village, or in any pub within a five-mile radius. Above all, you will not do one of those men-only marriage things. These conditions will be written into our agreement so you will be legally bound to keep to them.'

'Do I get to leave my house to him when I die?'

'Probably not a problem because most of you lot get Aids and he could die before you.'

'Is that a yes to him having the house when I die?' Card asked.

Butcher Bill looked around the group and saw no opposition. 'Yeah.'

'Is that part of the written legal agreement too?' Card asked him.

'No need for legal doings and carry-on,' butcher man answered, 'a gentleman's agreement is all you need. You can trust us.'

You say that to the pigs when you stand over them with your knife, I thought.

'I need a legal document to back up my part in this,' Card said. 'What if Gristle found out about it and used it against me in some way? You know how devious he is. He will spike me and you if he can.'

Nice one, Card, I thought. That will appeal to their overriding sense of self-protection and selfishness.

The pig stabber paused for a moment. 'Ok, we can live with your lack of trust. We will do as you ask as a sign of our goodwill. Now, how about lots more drink to celebrate our new ownership.'

'I'll drink to that,' I said.

'I wasn't including you in the invitation,' the pig killer snapped. 'In fact, you can clear off now. You have work to do, so get on with it.'

'Sorry,' I said, 'presumptuous of me. I'll be leaving you, then. Cheers, everyone.'

A wave of indifference followed me out of the room. Card followed me out, squeezing my arm in what I took to be a form of congratulations. 'Nice one. Brilliant,' he whispered.

As I walked down the road, I wondered if the CPPP would go around together when they became spirits in the next life. I would never allow them into my garden if they wanted a gateway back to the energy of the cosmos. They could bugger off and find another gate.

Readmitted to the Pub

Sunday 3rd May 2015 – Hawthorn Moon

Basher was showing his hard eyes to greet me on my return to the pub. Greet was hardly the word. He was readmitting me because of pressure from the CPPP. We didn't mention our threat of telling the brewery of his shady dealings. The CPPP had a hold over him but that made him hate anyone who was on their side. Card and Gristle accompanied me like two acolytes walking on either side of a virgin sacrifice to a pagan patron god of torment, tears and wild drinking.

Basher glared at me as I approached. Two pints stood on the counter. He pushed them towards Card and Gristle. I looked around for mine.

'What would you like to drink, *sir*?' he asked me.

'The usual please, Mr Brannigan,' I said.

'And what would your usual be, *sir*?'

'Pint of Guinness, please.'

He poured the pint too quickly and slapped it on the counter. '£3.45, *sir.*'

My reinstatement was not getting off to a good start.

'Look,' I said, 'I apologise for the disgrace and any damage to your reputation and to that of the good name of the pub. I am really sorry that all this has happened. It was all a misunderstanding. I promise I will never do anything that is offensive, disruptive or contrary to your rules, ever again. I promise, honestly. Solemn promise.'

Basher glared at me. I could see the urge to brutality in his eyes. I was on a narrow line between health and serious bodily harm. I knew his hostile attitude now was as much to do with the CPPP making him toe their line as it was with my original shoplifting charge.

Card and Gristle moved me away from the bar counter

to our place by the fire. The fireplace was empty and black. 'He won't light the fire in the summer,' Card said before I could make any comment. 'Imagine it is there.'

That was like imagining a chap was alive when his heart had stopped.

'Where's Cyril?' I asked.

'Delayed by some problem with his assistant vicar, who is still living in the rectory,' Gristle said. 'The other chap started the evening service a few minutes early. Cyril marched into the church telling him to stop because he was not allowed to hold services because it was Cyril's church. The bloke kept going, so Cyril called down loads of his druid curses on him to force him to stop. When that didn't work, Cyril physically attacked him. The church was packed with Cyril's women and they were delighted to see him in action. Cyril chased the interloper off the altar. Some of the more excitable women joined in and trapped the chap in the vestibule and literally defrocked him before chasing him out of the church. Cyril intervened and saved him. He told the women he was the only one they should defrock, but not in the middle of a service. The Anglican practice is different from the druids in that regard. The druids build it into the ceremony. Much more streamlined system, Cyril is always saying. I can't see the Anglicans taking it up.'

'Catholic vicars do it with their altar boys,' Card said.

'But not during the service,' Gristle answered. He stood up and, picking up his pint, nodded to Card. 'I'll talk to the mad fella now.' He sauntered over to the end of the bar and waited for Basher to move down to him.

'What's he up to?' I asked Card.

'Winning over Basher to give you a warmer welcome and to join our crusade.'

'How come none of this was discussed with me?'

'You were too busy with attacks and watching out for the army, the IRA and spying on everyone for the CPPP. We decided to leave you out of it for the moment.'

At the end of the bar, Gristle and Basher leaned over the counter, their heads close together looking like they were concocting some outrageous crime. From time to time they would look over at Card and me. Gristle would nod his head in my direction and say something that made Basher stare or look at me with raised eyebrows, as if he was hearing something surprising. 'What are they on about?' I asked Card.

'Best leave it till they finish and we know if Gristle has pulled it off.'

'Pulled what off?'

Card looked at me with one of his irritated looks. 'Stop going on and wait. Gristle is trying to persuade Basher to work with us, that's all.'

'What are you asking Basher to do?'

'Don't you ever stop?'

I glared at him, 'I only want to know how Basher will fit in. Maybe *I* don't want to work with *him*.'

Card snorted in a half-laugh. 'You are not in a good place to have many options about who you work with. Take whatever help you can. Anyway, there is no point in telling you unless Basher agrees to work with us.'

'And you sent Gristle to persuade him? He is hardly Gristle of the golden mouth and the honeyed words.'

Card sighed again, letting me know he was near the end of his patience. 'They know the same criminals, they deal with the same murky side of life, both of them have contacts with dodgy and useful people on either side of the law so they have a lot in common. As well as that, the two of them know Bert and Aggie, and Basher has a thing about Aggie. Gristle will bribe him with an introduction to the real Aggie not the one who dresses up for the mobile café in the lay-by.'

A tempting bribe, I thought. Basher will go for that.

The door was opened by a wild-looking figure almost running in. 'Sorry I'm late,' an out-of-breath Cyril announced. 'Few things to sort out at the church.' He collected his pint from the bar where it had been standing awaiting his arrival. Plonking himself on the bench next to me, he took a deep drink, sat back with a satisfied sigh, stretched out his legs and said, 'I miss the fire in the summer. Personally I think we should keeping it going all year even if it is only in a little blaze. Perpetual flame, as it were, never allowed to go out, always there to remind us of the power of light and of the fire that gives life.'

'It was nice and peaceful until you blew in,' Card said. After a pause during which Cyril drank more of his pint, Card asked him, 'Did you sort out the fracas at the church?'

'It wasn't much really. The poor chap was thrown by the action of the women. Mind you, some of them wanted to do more than throw him. I don't think he has ever been surrounded by a gang of women while he was nude. They were either passing comments about his personal bits or telling him what they wanted him to do with them. He thought they were rude and aggressive. Goodness knows how they train priests these days when he could misinterpret their intentions and attitudes the way he did.'

'Where is he now?' I asked.

'He was hiding under the stairs when I left. He was waiting for a taxi to take him into Birmingham. No sense of fun or feeling for life about him. Mind you, he had no feeling for the dead either. Did you see the state he let my graveyard get into? How could he bury people in such an unkempt and untidy place? I've sorted all that so the ones buried there are much happier now.'

Gristle came back from the bar and took his place on his stool by the empty fireplace. 'All done.'

'He agreed?' Card asked him.

Gristle nodded. 'I told him everything, well, a good bit of it. He doesn't need to know everything.' He nodded to me, 'I told him you work for MI5 and are working undercover for army intelligence infiltrating the IRA. He was surprised because he always thought you were a wimp.'

'Bloody cheek! What gave him that impression?' I asked.

'Maybe because he saw you doing a lot of writing in that book of yours. You know he doesn't hold much with writing or reading books; he was in the police too long. He knows a chap still in the police and he will get him to work on Olivia Cenhelm. They will dig out the file on the murder of a Hells Angel in Stratford all them years ago. She was in a motorbike gang in her young days and the story in the village was that she was the cause of the fella being murdered. Plus, they will see if she was in that computer scam in post offices where the returns were all out of kilter.'

'That murder was years ago,' Card said.

'Basher said they never closed the case,' Gristle said. 'There was always something dodgy about it. If they can pin something on her after all these years it will make Basher look good again. Even if they can't make it stick there will be a load of hassle for the bitch and her licence to run the post office could be withdrawn. She only won it in the first place because the others in the CPPP fiddled it for her when it should have gone to the Patel family who had always held it.'

'Did you tell him about Cactus keeping the spare keys

of the houses he sells?' Cyril asked.

'He gave me the name of a CID sergeant in Redditch who would be interested if we contact him. They will do Cactus for burglary if they find any trophies from the houses he visits after he sells them. He said not to go to the beat copper in the village cos he is bent.'

'Basher knows all about being bent,' Card said.

'Hold on, that is a bit unfair,' Gristle said, ever the one to defend the downtrodden and those he has done a deal with. 'Nothing was ever proved. Basher walked away with a clean sheet.'

'Only because he did a deal and took sudden early retirement,' Card answered.

'Keep your voice down,' I said. 'I don't want to be barred again if he hears you.'

Cyril went to the bar to buy our second pint, our last for the night.

'Looks like we are all set,' Card said.

'It'll be a piece of cake,' Gristle answered.

'If it was only that simple,' I said.

'What can go wrong?' Gristle asked.

I shrugged.

The Garden Attack

Wednesday 6th May 2015 – Hawthorn Moon

My grandmother fell out with God, often. She said he was spiteful because he waited until you weren't expecting it and then smote you with a great smite around the ear. She had endured a lot of hardship in her life. She was an expert on God smiting her.

Most of the time I avoided being unexpectedly smitten because my grandfather, Big Ter, protected me from the hand of God. Following his death many years ago, he would tip me the wink when it was about to happen. I never went public about Big Ter's interventions. Cyril was the only one I told. He understands things like that. I told him one night when we sat guarding a newly inhabited grave in the graveyard outside his rectory. The care home had forgotten to take out the buried woman's teeth, many of which had gold fillings, before they sealed the coffin. The family, none of whom had attended her funeral, were planning to dig her up and recover the gold teeth.

I told Cyril I sensed my grandfather was around if something was about to go wrong. I couldn't *see* him, I said. I *felt* he was there and sometimes there was the smell of his pipe tobacco which had been his trademark when he was alive. Cyril told me I probably did see him but didn't know what I was looking at, so while I didn't look at him I was indeed seeing him.

The twisting of language and the meaning he put into his explanation confused me. It was either that, or the empty whiskey bottle told us we had been going at the drink with gusto during our vigil over the new grave. The point is, as I told Cyril, it made no difference whether I saw him or just felt he was there. His message was the same; get your arse out of there before it gets scorched. Maybe

Big Ter had an inside track on what our smiting God was about to do and saved me from being smote by warning me of danger. I always was Big Ter's favourite.

I walked up the lane towards my house. I sensed my grandfather was looking over my shoulder. I tried the trick Cyril had taught me of looking out of the corner of my eye or focusing on a point inches in front of my nose while looking into the distance. I thought I saw a figure in a rough-cloth brown jacket and heavy trousers. When I tried to look properly he wasn't there. The smell of pipe tobacco lingered in the air.

What possible danger could there be? It was a bright summer's evening. I wasn't on a dangerous smuggling trip. Gristle had told us of the successful start to trap Arthur the paedo hunter. The news of that would be broadcast on the Internet when we were ready. Cyril was safely back in his house, even if he was at serious odds with the diocese over his temporary replacement complaining about being hounded out of the house by him and his marauding women. The bishop ignored the complaint, being more worried about the information Cyril could dish up. Card had snared the CPPP into accepting his app without them suspecting what was happening and it was only a matter of time until that shit hit the fan. My ban from the pub was lifted. We were on a roll.

I didn't need Big Ter's warnings when I reached my house. My front gate was pulled off its hinges and thrown on the lawn. The gravel path to the front door and around the side of the house looked like a couple of bullocks had been playing on it, with much of the stone scattered across the grass. Crude lettering in red was sprayed on my front door saying "IRA shit". God was in a smiting frenzy.

I moved with caution as I crept around the house. I stopped in horror when I looked down the garden.

Vegetable tops lay scattered, scythed down by a stick or a weapon of some sort. Drills of potatoes had been kicked, throwing earth and plants aside. A row of gooseberry bushes had been slashed. The garden bench between the apple trees, so beloved by Cyril, was upturned with one of the legs pulled off. Some branches had been torn off the yew tree by the gate and stacked in a pile as if someone was about to start a fire. The gateway to the pasture was empty apart from Blazing Bolt, who was looking apologetic as he stood in the gap where the gate used to be.

Gristle and Card came quickly after I phoned them.

'Wanton destruction,' I said, as we looked down the garden.

'Destruction is never wanton,' Card said. 'There is always a message from the destroyer or about the destroyer.'

'Why do you think this is directed at you?' Gristle asked

I waved my arm over the garden. 'Who else lives here?'

'You go around with us and some people don't like us,' Gristle answered.

'Not us, you,' Card added.

'What about the message on the front door? None of you are connected with the IRA,' I answered.

'That's *your* weak spot and you could be seen as *our* weak spot,' Card said. 'They get at you, they get at us.'

'They could have gone for you as our weak spot,' I said. 'They could have sprayed "Bum Boy" on your front door.'

'Why do you keep saying "they"?' Gristle asked.

'Because there are two of them.'

'Assuming this was done by the two soldiers,' Card

said. 'They threatened only to kill you. Why waste time kicking over your garden? It doesn't fit.'

'I remember old Bertie Boscoe years ago when I was just past being a lad,' Gristle said. 'He used to breed and race pigeons. The finest flock anywhere in the county. Someone broke into his loft and wrung the neck of every one of his birds. Left Bertie a broken man. The ten years in jail meant nothing after that.'

'Why did he do ten years?' I asked.

'Bertie found out who did it and killed him. Walked into the police station and confessed before they found the body. The bloke killed the birds because he knew it would hurt Bertie badly.'

'What's that got to do with my garden?' I asked.

'I'm just saying, it has to be someone local who knows what the garden means to you. The soldiers don't know that. This might have been done to break you, or to provoke you into doing murder. That way they would get rid of you. I think it is a warning.'

'Now *you're* saying "they",' Card said.

'Exactly,' Gristle said in one of his typical enigmatic statements. 'More than one, when you look at the state of this garden.'

'You don't think it was the two soldiers?' I asked him.

'I agree with Card. They'd kill you, not kick over your garden.'

'You got any paint?' Card asked. 'I'll cover up that graffiti on your front door.'

'We can get started on the garden,' Gristle added. 'Can't let them think they are winning. They don't know they are already a few steps ahead.'

I shook my head as I worked out who Gristle meant. 'I can't see any of the CPPP getting their hands dirty with this kind of attack.'

'I agree,' Card said. 'But, what about the sons of Bill the butcher?'

'In that case,' Gristle said, 'we know who we are dealing with. They can't be allowed to kill you. That's best left to the soldiers.'

'What a cheery thought,' I said.

'What I mean is, with the soldiers you know they will do it properly and you can defend yourself. Those three idiots are unpredictable and could catch you unawares.'

'So what do you propose we do?' Card asked him.

'I know one or two chaps who owe me and who can't stand the brothers. They will keep an eye on them and warn us if something is going to kick off.'

'Whatever,' Card said. 'As long as it gets them off our backs. We need space to manoeuvre right now.'

I thought old Bernie Boscoe had made the right choice in taking the law into his own hands. The judge should have let him off with a few hours' community service.

'Our next step is to get you squared away with the smugglers,' Gristle said. 'That will need a lot of personal influence, if you are to get out of that alive.'

Kitchen Meeting with MI5 Handler

Tuesday 12th May 2015 – Hawthorn Moon

The sound of the curtains being yanked back woke me. That and the noise from the two large men in my bedroom. The soldiers I knew as Big and Small Hillside were invading me again.

Big Hillside prodded me. 'Get up, you lazy sod. It's 0530 hours. You country lads should be out herding cows and ploughing fields.'

I moaned at the thought of another bad session with these two. 'Leave me alone. You can't walk into someone's hou—'

The bedclothes were whipped off me.

Big Hillside stood over me looking at my pyjamas. 'Where did you get that gear? An antique shop? You look like a dirty old man in them.'

First Cyril, now this thug was disparaging my night gear.

'What d'you want?' I asked.

Big Hillside pulled me off the bed. 'The boss wants a word. Downstairs. Hurry up. Put on something decent. You can't go down wearing those things.'

I pulled on a dressing gown that had been hanging on the side of the wardrobe.

'That's as old as your pyjamas,' Little Hillside sniggered. 'Suits you, gramps.'

I glared at the silly sod. 'I didn't know you two had a boss. Means someone with more intelligence. Bet he wasn't hard to find.'

Big Hillside pushed me towards the stairs. 'Shut up or you'll get my boot up your arse.'

Their boss was sitting at the table facing me as I was pushed into the kitchen. He was a narrow-shouldered man with slicked-back black hair and two small eyes that had been made in the same place that made plastic eyes for teddy bears.

'My name is Lawson, *Mr* Lawson. You know my colleagues Kevin and George. Think of them as your angels, guardian or avenging is up to you and how you act.'

Even with proper names, they still reminded me of two hillsides.

'I'll make a cup of tea.'

'Sit down,' he said.

I shuffled to the chair across the table from him as he continued. 'I am in charge of you. I own you. You will do what I tell you, when I tell you, in the manner in which I tell you to do it.'

He glanced down at a page in front of him. 'What are you calling yourself these days? Never mind, I will call you Little Worm, your call sign – on our hook, as bait, under our total control, to be disposed of if you don't catch what we want.'

'Are you the mouth or the small brain cell behind these thugs?'

He flicked his eyes to the one standing to the right of me. 'Kevin,' he said.

A blow to the side of my head knocked me sprawling on the floor. I lay there, unable to focus, feeling nauseous. My head was registering sensations it was not designed to deal with at 5.30 in the morning. The ticking of the clock was the only sound as they waited for me to get up and sit back on the chair.

Lawson waited until I gave him my full attention again. 'You and your kind are of no consequence to me. You are the purgative we have to work with. You flush out the shit I dispose of. I don't like you. I resent using you or being associated with you. I tolerate you as long as you collect the information I want. I will not put up with your lip, your arrogance, or your smart-arsed attitude. Kevin will be happy to kick you back in line any time you need reminding of that.'

I stared at him. There was no sign of emotion on his face. His hands were clasped in front of him on the table but he wasn't leaning forward. He seemed to be indifferent to any response from me to what he was saying.

He poked at the piece of paper on the table in front of him. 'Your main purpose in life is to collect the information I tell you to collect. I will snuff you out if you fail, or if you step out of line, or if you are no longer any use to me. My two colleagues would be more than happy to eliminate you right now. They lost comrades and friends to the likes of you. Your kind come in all shapes, colours and backgrounds. You are all the same to me, whether you are white, black or yellow, wear funny headgear or soft hats, pray to weirdo gods and speak with an Irish or a Middle East accent. All of you pollute the world. I will wipe you off the arse of the world. In the meantime, be grateful I let you live for a little while, but know your place, shut your mouth and listen to your orders.' He paused to glare at me. He was trying to show he thought little of me. His ploy was working.

I sat very still without saying a word. I had nothing to say and he had told me to shut up.

'You know this man.' It wasn't a question. He pushed a photograph across the table to me.

I nodded. It was the Commander.

'What do you know about him?'

I shrugged. 'The same as everyone in the village. He was in the Navy, captain of a nuclear sub.'

'Carrying nuclear warheads,' Lawson interrupted.

I nodded to show my agreement.

'What does he do now?' Lawson asked.

'Retired.'

His eyebrows twitched a little. Maybe he was irritated with me. He wanted more than that. 'He goes to the pub on a Sunday night. Five of us meet up for a pint. The rest of the week he does very little. I think he gives the odd lecture at a submarine college, or wherever it is they train blokes to drive the things. He goes away from time to time to do that.'

He pushed another photograph across to me. It was Bottle Blonde. 'What does she do?'

'Anything you ask her to do, as long as you pay her. You want me to set it up for you?' I asked, forgetting his warning.

His eyes flicked to Kevin. I finished on the floor again. It took me longer to get up this time.

'Well?' he asked. 'The woman?'

'She and her husband own a string of sex parlours across the Midlands.'

'Why is she setting up business with Commander Buryman-Claymore?'

'He can't stand her,' I said.

'So why is he setting up in business with her?'

'I don't know.'

Lawson sat back in the chair, his eyes boring into me. 'Find out.'

'He's retired. He can do anything he wants, can't he? What's it to do with you?'

My head was very sore this time when I managed to climb back onto my chair. I decided to take Lawson's advice and keep my remarks to myself. Kevin seemed to be punching harder each time, or maybe my head was becoming softer.

Lawson waited until my eyes could focus again. 'I don't like former captains of nuclear subs mixing in the sex world. He knows too much and could be compromised through sex. Dig around and tell me what is going on.' He took back the photograph of the Commander. 'There is another little job for you. You will infiltrate the new political party in the area, that independent one getting all the publicity. A friend of yours is big in it.'

I raised my eyes in a question. 'None of my friends have joined a political party.'

'Your butcher friend,' Lawson said.

'Not a friend,' I said.

'You meet up with him and his associates.'

I didn't answer. The less he knew about my activities with the CPPP, the better it would be.

'Find ways to discredit him and the party he belongs to. As a sign of my goodwill towards you and in recognition of your co-operation I can give you a sliver of information you could use.'

I liked the 'sign of goodwill'. It showed he was sarcastic as well as vicious.

'Your friend the butcher was in trouble with the Food Standards Agency. His organic butcher's shop was selling horsemeat imported from Eastern Europe. On top of that, his halal and kosher meat wasn't what the label said.'

'He wasn't named in the horsemeat row,' I said.

'No, he wasn't. He did a deal with the FSA to tip off the Excise about smugglers in the area and tell them when the next contraband delivery was to take place. In return there was to be no mention of selling disguised horsemeat in his shops. I understand you deal with the same smugglers. You do lead a risky life.' His mouth twisted a smidgen in what could have been a sarcastic smile.

Again, I stayed silent. Lawson knew too much about

what was going on in the area. I wasn't going to add to what he knew.

'An informer is not the image your butcher friend should take into the political arena where they are all supposedly squeaky-clean. A word from you in the right place could damage the image of his party and derail his political ambitions. Your smuggler friends would be unhappy to find your butcher friend was behind their losses.'

He was being cynical as well as being sarcastic. I was playing dumb.

'Your main interest to us is still to do with your youthful misdemeanours in Northern Ireland where you were a naughty boy delivering bombs.'

'I never delivered bombs.'

'Bomb-making equipment,' he said. 'It is the same thing. You killed those people just as much as the bomb maker. You will testify in court when we are ready to use you. In the meantime, you will stay hidden in this dump of a place and work for me.'

He hadn't mentioned the delivery of *that gun* to Derry. They had me only on the bomb-making materials. He must have picked up some response in my eyes. 'Don't try anything stupid like hiding or running away. I'd hand you over to the IRA without a thought. They feel strongly about people like you deserting them, especially if I added you are an informer as well. On the other hand, it would be interesting to see how the Protestant paramilitaries would deal with a bomber who killed so many of their people. Come to that, Kevin and George here would welcome half an hour with you in payment for their friends killed in the line of duty by scum like you.'

I risked another blow to the head but I had to be sure of something. 'Did you and your men wreck my garden?'

He tilted his head slightly to one side as if he was searching for hidden meaning in the question, or as if he was looking for a touch of insolence that deserved another punch to the head.

'Why would we do that?'

'To give me a message, or threaten me.'

He looked from Kevin to George as if he was sharing a joke. 'Do we look like people who kick over gardens? We might kill you, or put you in jail for a long time, or send you abroad for interrogation and treatment, or hand you to the IRA. Where does kicking over a garden rank in that list?'

He searched in his pocket and then slid a mobile across the table to me. 'Any time that rings you will answer it immediately. If there is someone with you, say, "I don't want to make a PPI claim," and redial within five minutes when you are alone. You will be called from a different number each time so it is pointless trying to ring us other than using redial. You will update us on your progress each time you are called. Should you fail to answer, we will know you have broken your agreement with us. You will be punished, severely. Think of it as a telecom ASBO.'

He stood up and, without another word, walked out of the kitchen, George opening the door for him. Kevin followed behind, but as he passed the worktop, he reached out and swept everything onto the floor. 'Oh dear,' he said, with a grin, 'my arm just happened to make contact. I hope none of this was valuable.' He ground the broken fragments into the floor with the heel of his boot. 'Bye, Little Worm. See you around.'

The front door slammed behind them, leaving me alone with the silence in the house and the eddying and pulsing currents in the air marking their passage. What was it about me that made me such a popular choice as a spy by the nasty people I had met recently? The difference this time was that *Mr* Lawson didn't know my secret information. That would have been pure dynamite in his hands, and I knew how to deal with requests to be a spy. *Mr* Lawson might be scarier than the CPPP but the likes of him could operate only because they lived under stones. Lift the stone and they lost their power. I headed to the phone. I needed Gristle to help me fight back and to tie up some loose ends.

The Smuggler Chief
Wednesday 13th May 2015 – Hawthorn Moon

'Let me do the talking.'

I turned towards Gristle. 'I know him too.'

'You were a client. I am a fellow entrepreneur and a long-time friend. He is less likely to shoot you if I do the talking.'

'I didn't betray him,' I protested.

'He has still to be convinced of that. He only agreed to see you without shooting you as a special favour to me. He lost a lot of money and his reputation was damaged by that raid.'

'I almost walked into the middle of it,' I said.

'Which is why you are a prime suspect because you got away.'

Gristle halted his battered Range Rover at the gateway into the farmyard, even though there was no gate. Two Alsatian dogs stood facing us as if on the other side of an invisible line.

'He'll come out in a moment, his shotgun broken open over his left arm and he'll say he's going to hunt for foxes. Politely refuse if he invites you to join him. You might suffer from an accidental discharge of his weapon in the woods. An invite into the house will be ok if he tells the dogs to sit. If I'm invited with you, relax, he won't shoot you in front of me. We go back too far.'

We sat watching the farmhouse door. The dogs stood watching us.

'Nice dogs,' I said, feeling nervous at the coming meeting.

'To look at. Cross the line into that yard without his say-so and they'll tear you apart,' Gristle said.

The farmhouse door opened and Miles Herfman

213

stepped out into the yard with his shotgun broken open over his left arm. He pretended surprise when he saw Gristle's Rover. 'Gristle,' he called. 'Fancy you calling in.' He walked down the yard towards us, clicking his fingers at the dogs as he passed, telling them "Sit". 'Who's with you? Ah, your Irish friend. I'm just off to shoot some foxes.' He paused and looked at Gristle, who shook his head slightly. 'But maybe the pair of you would like a cup of tea. The foxes will wait till later.'

'It's ok,' Gristle said to me. 'Climb out slowly and keep your hands out from your sides so he can see you're not carrying anything.'

'What would I be fecking carrying?' I whispered.

'Just do what I tell you,' he hissed back. 'He is still tetchy and won't take any chances.'

The farmhouse kitchen was big and roomy. A solid table in the middle of the room and four worn chairs said this was a room well used over the years. 'Take a seat,' Herfman said, pulling out a chair for Gristle before lifting a cover on the Aga and pulling a kettle onto the plate.

'How's Jenny?' Gristle asked.

'Still at her mother's. She was a bit upset by the incident we had a little while ago. A woman shouldn't have to put up with that in her own house. Says she doesn't feel safe here any more. Hard to understand, but that's women for you.'

'Tell me if I can do anything to help her,' Gristle said. 'Sometimes it takes a friend from outside to reassure the women and put things right.'

'Thank you. I appreciate that. I'll ask her if it will help.' He sat at the table and stared at me. 'Personally, I would prefer to find the bastard who set us up and deal with him. Right the balance, know what I mean?'

I nodded. I knew exactly what he meant.

'We came to talk about that,' Gristle said. 'Can't leave things out of balance. GG here has some information I thought you would want to hear. He has a vested interest, of course, so you have to make up your own mind about what he has to say. After all, his business suffered as well as yours and he was almost caught by your unwelcome visitors.'

'I know. We have been wondering how he was so close, because he was the next one due in, but somehow managed to skip off.'

I noticed he had switched from "I" to "We". I had been the topic of a debate with no one there to argue my side.

'I know who tipped off the Excise,' I blurted out.

Herfman pulled a face.

'Don't use that name in this house,' Gristle told me. 'Sorry about that, Miles. He doesn't know the rules. Although, having had lots of rough encounters with the bastards over the years, he should know better.'

Herfman glared at me. 'Who?' The type of question I liked, simple and direct.

I glanced at Gristle, as if asking for his approval. Gristle said, 'He is a bit uneasy about telling on anyone, even if it is well deserved, as in this case. That should be a point in his favour.'

Herfman nodded agreement with Gristle. Once again he asked simply, 'Who?'

'Bill the butcher.'

Herfman sat back in his chair and fixed his eyes on me. He pursed his lips, giving a lot of attention to the statement I had just made. He was thinking before he committed himself to any questions or statements. He looked across to his shotgun he had carefully placed on the worktop just inside the door. 'How do you know?'

'He has a source,' Gristle told him.

'What source?'

'He can't say because his life is in danger already. You can take my word that what he is saying is the truth. I will swear to it. You have known me since we were lads, Miles. Have you ever known me to lie to you or let you down? Remember the times I helped you with your boys, sometimes when nobody else would turn out on your side for them. This bloke here risked his life for me, and other than you, not many would do that. I owe him. You can trust him like you trust me.'

We sat in silence while Herfman thought through what he had heard. He seemed to be weighing up his options.

'Bill is a slimy git, but why would he shop us?'

I told him the story of the horsemeat trouble with the FSA, how he had got off because of his deal to shop the smugglers to the Excise, being careful not to use that word in the house. I gave him all the details I knew when he quizzed me about the story as he checked to make sure it stood up to scrutiny. When he was satisfied, he stood up and made the tea. 'Or would you like something stronger?' he asked. Both of us shook our heads.

There was silence as he poured three mugs of tea and sat down again, pushing milk and sugar across the table to us.

'There's a bit more,' Gristle added.

'Always is with you, Gristle,' Herfman said.

'The butcher is out to get me, him and his mates in the village,' Gristle said.

'I always said we should have shot that lot years ago. What are they up to this time?'

'Making out I am a paedophile,' Gristle said, lifting his mug to hide his mouth as he said it.

Herfman looked at him for a minute and burst out laughing. 'You. A paedophile? You could be called lots of things, Gristle, but not that.'

'It's what they were going to have me done for,' Gristle said, 'and if it hadn't been for this Irish git here they would have me in prison by now. He saved me and it put him in danger of being killed.'

'By that crowd in the village?'

'No. By some other nasty chaps they know. As well as that, they have robbed Card of his invention, you know that app thing I told you about, and they had Cyril locked up in a mental asylum until this fella here came up with an idea to rescue him.'

That wasn't entirely accurate but I needed all the boosts I could find to stop this man on the other side of the table putting me in a crate on the back of a lorry heading for Estonia.

Herfman had put his serious face back in place as he thought further about what he had heard. 'Any suggestions about what we should do?'

He was back on the "we" again but this time I think he was including Gristle and me in whatever group he had in mind. He looked towards his gun lying on the worktop.

I shook my head. 'Any accident or any disappearance will bring the unmentionables down on us again. They will suspect anyone who was connected with the incident if the butcher is dealt with around here.'

'They'd be bloody right too,' Herfman said.

'Hear him out,' Gristle urged.

'What I was thinking,' I said, 'obviously working under your control, we should not do anything to him.'

He stared at me and then smiled in a way that did not seem friendly. 'Not do anything? Is that a suggestion?'

'I didn't say that. I said *we* don't do anything.'

'Do you have a tooth fairy in mind who will do it for us?'

'Let me put it this way,' I said, taking it slowly because I wanted the final suggestion to be his. 'Do you know he sells halal and kosher meat?'

'Of course I know. He makes a fortune selling it around the Midlands. We get a number of Muslim drivers from Eastern Europe calling in here. They buy loads of it off him to take back home.'

'Suppose it wasn't genuine halal or kosher.'

'They'd be pissed off and...' He sat looking from me to Gristle as all the possibilities opened up in his mind. 'Fucking hell!' he said. 'Some of them lads take their religion very, very seriously.'

'Nothing like a bit of religion to bring out the murder in people,' Gristle added.

'Whatever they decided would have nothing to do with us. None of us need go near him,' I concluded.

Herfman looked at Gristle but nodded his head in my direction. 'Devious bastard, isn't he?'

Gristle smiled. We were home safe and dry. 'You don't know the half of it,' he said. 'You could put your life in his hands, except he talks to ghosts and the fairies at the end of his garden.'

'I don't talk to fairies,' I protested.

'What do you think?' Gristle asked Herfman.

'I think we let the fuss die down about the raid, pretend we are putting it down to experience, pay the fines and tip the wink to a few of the drivers about the halal and kosher stuff. Leave it to them to do whatever they think is necessary. He might even find himself on free trip to Eastern Europe on one of the lorries.'

'Appropriate for a would-be politician intent on stopping immigration,' I said. 'Let him see what it is like to be an unwelcome illegal immigrant.'

'He won't see much from the inside of a crate,'

Herfman said. 'What's all this to do with immigration?'

'Ignore him,' Gristle said. 'You should hear the way he addles my head when I take him anywhere. I should put him in a crate and dump him back where he comes from.' He looked around the kitchen. 'Any chance we might move on from the tea to something stronger, now that we have finished our business?'

Conference by the Fire
Wednesday 20th May 2015 – Heather Moon

It was like old times, except it wasn't a Sunday night and the fire wasn't lit. Basher had greeted us with more than his usual suspicious look as he subtly enquired, 'What are you lot up to, coming in here mid week?' The buying of beer and an order of sandwiches eased his concerns about our visit. We had serious business to conduct without Basher's interference. Winning over the Commander to our plans was our main purpose.

Card opened the proceedings in a calm way once the sandwiches and beer were on the table in front of us. 'GG is spying for MI5,' he told the Commander. We carried on eating as if Card was announcing nothing more important than the price of milk going up again. The Commander stopped as he lifted his sandwich to his mouth and gave me a puzzled look. 'Why did they ask *you*?'

'He's in great demand as a spy,' Gristle said, adding complexity rather than clarity to the situation. 'Spymasters everywhere want to sign him up. He's a natural. He watched all the Bond movies. Knows everything about spying.'

The Commander put his sandwich back on his plate, wiped his hands on the paper napkin and looked around the group as if checking he was among real people and not still in bed in the middle of a dream. This was a man who had been trained to press a button sending a missile thousands of miles to obliterate millions and render major parts of the globe uninhabitable. His only sign of being surprised was a slight cough as he cleared his throat. 'When did this happen?'

'Day before yesterday,' I said, in between bites of my sandwich. 'Bloke called *Mr* Lawson. We have to say the

Mr part like that if we are talking about our handler.'

The Commander picked up his sandwich, clearly in control again. 'I thought you had to be secret if you were a spy.'

I nodded.

'So why tell us?' he asked.

'He thought we should know he is spying on *us*,' Card said.

'Well, to be accurate,' Cyril said, 'he is spying on *you*, Commander. We told him it was fair to tell you. In case you might want to keep stuff hidden from MI5. We all do, don't we?' The idea that MI5 would be interested in Cyril and his activities was stretching credulity a bit but the Commander didn't notice. Why would he pick up on a silly exaggeration when he had been told he was under investigation and by a spy in his own camp?

'He didn't volunteer, which is something in his favour,' Gristle said. 'They threatened to kill him if he tells anyone he is a spy. He is taking a bit of a risk by warning you. We thought that was nice of him.'

The scourge of the Russian Navy in the Barents Sea sat still, his mind exercised as he made sense of what he was hearing. His rigorous training as a ruthless hunter-killer submarine captain ready to annihilate the world reasserted itself. 'What information do they want? How will you get it to them? Why are you telling me? They threatened to kill you if you break cover.'

'He's fed up with skulking around all the time,' Card said.

'Wants to come in from the cold,' Cyril added, 'like that spy fella.'

'Phil Kimby,' Gristle added.

'The other way round,' Card told him.

'Kimby Phil? You sure?'

221

'Never mind,' Card said. 'The point is, he needs to finish with MI5 because the IRA want him to spy for them, as do all the other groups in Northern Ireland and he fancies going home, or even to Spain where the Basque separatists want him to work for them. The weather out there is good.'

'And the Russians and the Yanks,' Gristle added.

'And some in the village,' Cyril said, on cue.

'But he really wants to go home,' Card concluded.

The madness around him was taxing the Commander's trained missile-launching brain. Like any man losing his grip on reality, he grasped at the nearest straw. 'Some in the village?'

Card nodded. 'Worse than the Yanks and the Russians,' Gristle said.

'They leave MI5 in the halfpenny place,' Cyril added.

'It's you the village gang are after,' Card said.

'For what?'

'What you are up to with Bottle Blonde?' Cyril said, in a tone of voice that left no room for doubt.

'We told nobody what I am doing with Marylyn,' the Commander said.

'Is that really her name?' Gristle asked.

'Careful what you say in front of him,' Card said, nodding towards me. 'He doesn't know what the two of you are doing, which is why he is spying on you.'

'We're setting up a business together, if you must know,' the Commander protested. 'The business will have three parts. There will be a sex therapy clinic, a deep litter chicken farm and a special therapy unit for ex-service men and women traumatised by conflict,' the Commander said. 'I will be the chief exec. My service background will be useful in running the place and winning MOD contracts.'

'Espionage cover,' I said.

'Honey trap,' Card added.

'A place to lure and bribe the gullible and the powerful into selling their souls to the enemy and to the forces of evil,' Cyril said.

I thought he was going a bit far now. Time to get the conversation back to a semblance of reasonableness. 'You didn't get approval from the gang in the village and you haven't arranged to pay them a cut of what you make,' I said.

'Why should I bother with them?' the Commander asked.

'Because they will tell your secret to everyone and blacken your name if you don't play ball,' I said.

'What secret?'

'The *real* reason you left the Navy.'

An innocent man will always flounder when faced with an accusation he knows is untrue. Indeed, it would not cross his mind to consider refuting it because the accusation is so ridiculous. After a few moments and some face pulling and swallowing, he said, 'I retired. That's why I left.'

'Not what them lot in the village believe and it's them lot put MI5 on to you and they are making GG spy on you. They said you are a traitor to your country after what you did in the Navy, and Bottle Blonde is your contact and handler.' Card sat back waiting for the next question that had to come. None of us had relished telling the lie we were about to tell the Commander so we had tossed a coin to see who would give the made-up answer to the question he had to ask.

'Why did they say I left the Navy?'

Gristle wiped his hands on the knees of his trousers before looking up at the Commander. 'You dived your sub when some of your men were still on deck picking up wounded SAS chaps. You were afraid you might be attacked. The seven men on deck drowned. Their bodies were never recovered. You were drummed out for being a coward.'

Total silence around a table in a pub is a rare event. This silence was not only rare, it was unnerving. Personal anguish is never pleasant to behold. We were looking at a man who was holed below the waterline by our remarks but we needed his help and he had to be warned about MI5. We thought we could justify combining both considerations. Looking at the anger on his face made me think we might have gone too far. He stirred himself, coming back to the current moment, years of trained responses taking control of his mind muscles.

'Do you believe any of this?'

'No,' we answered in unison. Cyril being a priest and used to going on about things, added, 'Not a single word, suggestion or hint of such a thing. Totally outrageous, uncalled for and wrong.'

Card glared at him, hinting he should shut up.

'What will you tell MI5?' the Commander asked me.

'That it is all lies made up by jealous people who are out to get you in spite of your outstanding service record. I'll spin them yarns until we find a way of silencing the gang in the village. It won't stop them spreading lies about you in the area.'

'Smoke without fire and all that stuff,' Card said.

'When they put that story out your new venture will be dead in the water before you even open,' Gristle said. 'You know the way rumours work.'

'We're in the same boat,' Cyril added, continuing the run of seafaring metaphors. 'They are tarring us with the same false rumour brush.'

'Only we intend to put a shot across their bows,' Card

said.

'Then sink them,' Gristle added.

I hoped that was the end of their run of sea comparisons. Then the Commander started it up again. 'You want me to come on board with you. Is that it?'

'Fight under the same flag…'

'Blockade and destroy them…'

'Attack them before they leave harbour…'

I had to stop it. 'We need your help,' I said, bringing them all back to reality.

'Doing what?' he asked me.

'Setting them up. Deploying your strategic brain. Making use of your attention to detail without losing sight of the overall picture.' I paused for a moment before giving him the real reasons we needed his help. 'Oh, we were also wondering if you could see a way to persuade Bottle… er… Marylyn to assist us.'

'What do you want her to do?' he asked.

Cyril's eyes lit up at the range of answers he would have liked to give. I cut him off before he started.

'We need to investigate two women who are in their group. Enquiries by a woman would be so much more subtle and could go unnoticed.' I was about to add something about Bottle's Blonde renown for sensitivity, delicacy and ability to blend into the background but thought that would be pushing my luck.

The Commander reflected for a moment before telling me, 'I think I could persuade her to do that. It is in her interest to stop those people doing damage to her business plans.'

'Not just her business plans,' Cyril said, 'there is her personal reputation as well. The village gang make out that she performs in her sex and massage parlours, that for a few quid she will strip naked, let you pour warm oil all over her body and let you swing—'

'I didn't hear them saying that,' Gristle said, without realising that this was Cyril indulging in one of his fantasy moments.

'Not exactly in those words, but you can imagine it and hear them going on about it, can't you?' Cyril groaned at the image he was creating.

I sighed and glared at Cyril, who was seeing it all in his mind. 'Cyril, let's keep on target here.' His hankering after the delights of Bottle's Blonde body would have to be curbed or sublimated. Maybe we could persuade him to take up free-fall parachuting as a way of taking his mind off her. Then I remembered what had happened at the small airport near Warwick when they had their Open Day and a woman pilot had showed Cyril the sights from the back seat of her biplane. Parachutes would not do the trick.

'When will you be ready to implement your plans?' the Commander asked.

'Reconnaissance already done,' Card said.

'Opening stages initiated,' I added. The Commander liked that type of talk.

'Behind enemy lines already,' Gristle said.

'Ready to stuff the buggers,' Cyril concluded.

'We need to block their right flank, and that is where your help will be invaluable. We will swing the victory once you and Marylyn turn that flank and hamper any retaliation.'

The Commander nodded. 'I will contact Marylyn and get her to slip into her role. She is good at going deep and feeling her way round until she gets hold of what she wants.'

Cyril groaned at the images the words were creating.

'Give me a day or two. Maybe she should be part of the meeting next time,' the Commander said.

I thought that was a step too far, but considering the way we had bamboozled the Commander into helping us, I thought the least we could do was to go with his request and make such a sacrifice. I looked at the others.

Card grimaced and nodded.

Gristle frowned but said, 'Fine by me.'

Cyril was sitting with the grin they could have used as the model for the Cheshire Cat in that film.

'Fine with us, Commander,' I said. 'We will look forward to meeting up with her again.' The whole meeting had been built around a lie. Why not finish it with one?

I walked down the lane with Cyril after we had left the pub. 'Why do you always bring sex into it?' I asked him.

'Not always,' he said. 'Only in certain situations, like when I think about women and stuff to do with them.'

'All the time, then?' I suggested.

'Not as much as I used to,' he said. 'Twenty years ago it was on my mind more or less all the time. Not like that any more. Now I have to figure out if my knees will cope and will there be a cup of tea around afterwards.'

'Do the women complain?'

'No. They are very kind. They are quite imaginative and can get on with things much more than they used to do. I like it now that I am done onto rather than having to do to others. Like a new twist on an old Gospel saying.'

He saw my puzzled look. 'GG, you need to read your bible a bit more, but not before you make me a cup of tea and let me sit in your garden on this lovely afternoon. I need to tie up a few loose ends and you are the only person who can help me.'

I laughed at him. 'I'm happy to tie you up if you can cope with me doing it instead of one of your belles.'

He didn't smile back at me. 'We need to take stock and have more than one string to our bow. This whole business could still go wrong and leave people hurt. I don't want to be responsible for that because we were sloppy and didn't plan properly.'

'No fear of that,' I said. 'We hold all the cards. Nothing can go wrong.'

I should have remembered what my Nan used to warn about God unexpectedly smiting the unwary with great smites of his powerful and ever-loving hand. But even in the presence of a holy man of the cloth, the thought never crossed my mind. I would live to regret that slip. Hindsight is so harsh in its judgements.

Looking Back

Wednesday 3rd June 2015 – Heather Moon

We do not grow wise with age. Ageing just makes it harder to speak. People think slowness in speech shows wisdom, when in fact it shows a failure of mind, mouth and meaning to line up quickly.

As we age we became more outspoken, or more difficult to live with, or more set in our ways, or more obdurate in our opinions in the face of unassailable reasoning, or more skilful in twisting everything to suit our dogma regardless of facts. The operative word each time is the word 'more'. We don't change; we become more of what we always were.

Gristle grew more determined as his birthdays whizzed by. Card, on the other hand, became more fastidious about details and about probity. The Commander developed a new sharpness in the way he issued commands. Cyril went deeper and further in searching for a link with the power of the cosmos and for a way to walk with the increasing number of inter-world spirits who were populating his life. Me? I still didn't learn fast enough. I put up my defences more slowly.

Over the weeks that followed the recruitment of the Commander and his 'associate', Bottle Blonde, the positive surge of energy in the group lifted us to new heights of derring-do. Or, you might say, we grew overconfident and careless. We were riding high on the wild black stallion called pride. We should have been wiser but wisdom has little to do with ageing.

Cactus, the estate agent, was the first of the enemy to be brought low. Pulled over by the police for having a faulty brake light, driving erratically out of the golf club late at night, stopping across a halt line at a T-junction, he

229

refused to be breathalysed at the scene. Calling the officer a "Billy goat" and urinating in the back of the police car hindered any hope he had of appealing to their gentler nature when they reached the police station. Calling the policeman a "Billy goat" was a novel term of abuse. In other circumstances and in other times, it would have been ignored. However, the police are so sensitive these days about being called names that it is dangerous to address them in any words other than 'Certainly, officer, you are correct. I am in the wrong in whatever way you say. I stand corrected.'

The subsequent search of Cactus's car threw up a treasure store of stolen goods, to the delight of the police, who had stopped Cactus on our tip-off but now claimed their success was down to astute detective work on their part. Being a bigger fool than we had given him credit for, Cactus stored in his car the individual mementoes he took from his illegal visits to houses he had sold. Along with his trophies was a box of door keys that opened the locks of houses across the area. The possession of the keys led to a further charge being added to his crime sheet, that of going equipped to commit a burglary, or whatever posh phrase they use to stitch up someone in such cases.

A small team of uniformed officers was set up to assist the detective in charge of the case and was given great publicity across the media, orchestrated by the chief constable, delighted to have good news for a change. This team returned the keys and stolen items, which the owners had assumed had been lost into the pockets of the removal men who had carted them to their new houses.

Competition to be part of the 'returning items team' was intense. Visits to superior-type homes where they were served with superior-type cake and freshly ground coffee were preferable to intervening in drunken brawls, chasing shoplifters who knew their rights, escorting drunks puking and talking nonsense, breaking up domestics and sitting through bum-numbing stakeouts behind the butcher's shop watching for illegal activities down the side of the pub across the road. Cactus and the pleasure and promotions caused by sorting out his car went down in the annals of the local police.

We ticked off our first victory against the CPPP.

Bottle Blonde proved her worth early on, in spite of our reservations about allowing her to join our team meetings. Working closely with the Commander – we were still not sure how close that was – she unmasked Philomena Luge, the forthright upholder of the community's morals and a staunch proselytiser for the local church of Jehovah. Bottle, or Marylyn as the Commander insisted we now call her, identified Philomena as a regular visitor to one of Skinny Slug's Eastern Delight Sex Therapy Massage Houses.

That particular house offered a speciality catering for women only who sought entertainment with either male or female 'therapists', or both, singly, or at the same time. Her pseudonym at the Eastern Delight House was Katie Krakatoa. We thought it best not to explore the significance of the name chosen by Philomena. Skinny Slug, aka Bertram, as the Commander instructed us to call him, provided photos of Philomena, alias Katie, in several acts of seemingly pleasurable pursuits if one ignored the anguished look on her face. Cyril, being an expert on such activities, said the anguished look came from the concentration demanded by the contortions and in no way lessened the pleasure she would experience on completion.

I asked why Skinny took and kept photos showing such intimate and personal acts, imagining his actions might be construed as an invasion of personal privacy. Bottle looked surprised at my innocence. 'Insurance,' she said without any further explanation.

'Is that professional indemnity or contents insurance?' I asked.

'Personal protection,' the Commander said.

'A potential future income stream,' Bottle Marylyn added, with a tone that suggested there was no more information to be gained through asking stupid questions.

I translated her answer to mean blackmail. We did the same by sending these photographs to Philomena's church, to the local papers and the national redtops. We had rejected the proposal to post the photos on every lamppost and tree in the high street on the grounds that they might be seen by the young, who would be corrupted by them, and by the elderly, who would be upset that they were no longer able to reach such heights of sexual excess. I reminded myself of what Philomena had done by having Cyril locked up in the mad house for crazy and perverted priests. That made me feel comfortable with what we were doing.

Philomena left the village within a day of being summoned to a meeting for prayer and reconciliation with the elders, or whoever ran the Jehovah's church. Forgiveness was not extended to a sister captured in raptures of delight, especially when 'captured' seemed to be the operative word that described what was happening in the photos they spread on the table in front of her. Philomena told the taxi driver who took her to the airport that she was taking an overdue holiday to visit her widowed sister who had joined a nunnery in Anchorage, Alaska. She wasn't to know that the long arm of Apple Corporation would reach out to her there, or indeed anywhere she might choose to go. At that time, she didn't know Apple Corporation would soon be interested in everything she did.

The downfall of the much-detested postmistress, Olivia Cenhelm, should have taken longer because of the complexity of our plot against her. By involving the law, we had laid ourselves open to the time wasting that goes with gathering secure evidence.

Basher's reputation among his former colleagues was boosted as the initiator of the enquiry that led to Mrs Cenhelm's exposure as a fraudster and robber of the Royal Mail. No one minded the charge of robbing the Royal Mail following the takeover by a French woman who then sold it to a crowd of money manipulators. Locals did object to their mail being interfered with and items being taken out of envelopes without permission. That came out only after the investigation was literally sparked by the doings at the post office in the middle of the village.

The real investigation was supposed to be into her involvement in an unsolved biker gang murder from many years ago. That enquiry was tangled up with other investigations, but even so, Basher took a lot of credit for uncovering and removing what had been a thorn in the side of the CID for many years.

Afterwards, Basher explained to us that biker loyalties lasted many years after their gangs had been disbanded, an occurrence that was both regular and frequent and brought about by long sentences in prison, severe disablement, death, or a combination of all three. CID enquiries, Basher told us, had stirred up the mud in the bottom of that stagnant cesspool where remnants of the original bikers, who had suffered the untimely death of their leader, still lived. With their questions and suggestions the officers of the law roused the loyalty and bloodlust of the remaining gang members by taunting them that the lure that had baited the trap that killed their leader had been the sexual overtures of one Hammerhead Lusty Momma, now known as Mrs Olivia Cenhelm.

One-Finger Frisbee and Cyd Smallpox Sullivan, the only members of the gang alive and still at large, took it upon themselves to bypass the incidentals of evidence gathering before they passed sentence and executed judgement on Hammerhead Momma. Their firebombing of the post office was not the outcome we had anticipated.

The resulting transfer of the licence back to the Patel family who had held it for many years was greeted with great delight in the village. The CID investigation into the accusations against Mrs Cenhelm opened up so many serious breaches of the law that Hammerhead Lusty Momma was barred from applying for licences ever again. The prospect of a long jail sentence because of these frauds, along with the possibility of a guilty verdict on aiding and abetting a murder, led her to plea bargain her way out of a long sentence. In return, she coughed up to involvement with biker gangs in scores of illicit activities across the West Midlands area. Naming names as she did led to her being given protection and a permanent move to a part of the country where no one would find her because it was highly unlikely anyone would ever go there. But Apple Corporation would have no problem tracking her to her small outhouse on a farm in the Welsh mountains. Apple Corporation prides itself on having a more effective system for finding people than the FBI, the CIA or MI5 and MI6 mixed together, even when the fugitive hides in the depths of Wales.

Basher basked in the glory of his achievement. Having exhausted his pub regulars with detailed accounts of his key role in unmasking the network of biker gangs, drug dealers, pornographers, paedophile rings, Russian spies and gold bullion hijackers, he started talking about the possibility of setting up his own private detective agency. Subtle piss-taking from us led him to consider upgrading his ambitions and establishing himself as a consultant to the new breed of CID officers who were so obsessed with evidence gathering that they were in danger of losing the art of planting evidence and jumping to conclusions. There was even talk at one point that he might be offered his old post. A quick reminder of why he had had to leave so suddenly persuaded the chief constable that such a reinstatement might not be in the best interest of a force already beset by corruption and brutality scandals, never mind what it would do to the justice system. Basher unleashed from any semblance of restraint on his unbashful nature was almost too much to bear. We considered moving our meetings to another pub. Events overtook us and halted any planned moves.

The black stallion called pride was about to buck us off.

Gristle's School Gang

Tuesday 9th June 2015 – Heather Moon

'That kid Scutler is a right one,' Gristle told us. 'Sharp as a pin. Keeps to the job in hand and manages the other kids really well. They like working with him. He could be a real handful if he put his mind to it. God help his teachers in the senior school in September if they rub him up the wrong way.'

'Did Arthur the paedo pursuer suspect anything?' I asked.

'Not a sausage. He walked into it. He asked to meet the kids you had named.'

'I can just imagine him doing his usual Mr High-and-Mighty act,' Card added.

Gristle nodded. 'He did. First off, he spoke to all the kids in an assembly. Scutler mimicked him perfectly. That kid has some great talents. The paedo killer bleated on to the whole school about danger stranger—'

'The other way around; stranger danger,' Card interrupted. Ofsted bods have to correct every little mistake. It's part of their training.

'Whatever,' Gristle answered. 'Then he wanted a session alone with the senior class, the class I spoke to. He told the teacher to leave so he could have some private time with the kids.'

'He isn't allowed to do that,' Card interrupted.

'Maybe they changed it since you were a Grand Inquisitor,' I said.

'Will you two let me get on?' Gristle asked.

Card snorted at being corrected. I shrugged my shoulders as a sign for Gristle to continue.

'He started pontificating to the class about the danger of paedophiles. He asked about recent visitors and if the kids noticed anything unusual, or if the visitors said anything that was out of the ordinary. The kids played along, like I had told them, telling him about the strange man from a few weeks ago. Me.' He smiled at us as if waiting for approval.

'We know it was you,' I said. 'There aren't that many strange blokes around.'

Gristle frowned at me as he worked out if I was taking a liberty.

'Paedo Arthur then asked what I had said and what happened. He wanted to know if the strange man, me, took them into the toilets.'

'He isn't allowed to ask questions like that,' Card said. 'He was seriously out of order. He should have known better than to question them, if he was properly trained. His first duty was to go to the named person for safeguarding if he had suspicions.' He paused. 'Even if those suspicions were false and had been planted in his mind.'

I looked at Gristle and raised my eyebrows. 'Ignore Mr Ofsted genius. Carry on with the story.'

'As he talked, the kids took photographs of him. A shy, puny kid called Gurgle Methison-Blockheimer was the kid in charge of the recording and he took the photos using his iPhone. Watch out if he is around because he works magic with recordings and photos. He has a pair of eyes that never stop moving, taking in everything around him. He looks like a meerkat on guard duty. You'll hear him before you see him because of his irritating habit of clearing his throat, constantly. He knocks around the village with Scutler and the other kids. Apparently, he is the best tree and drainpipe climber they have.'

'Gristle, get on with the main story,' I urged him.

'I'm getting there. You are so impatient sometimes.'

I could only sigh out loud as a way of expressing my

irritation with him.

'Anyway,' Gristle continued, 'when the paedo man… incidentally, the kids now call him the Paedo Pedalo and–'

'Gristle!' we both said at once.

'Ok, ok. When he told them how to recognise a paedophile, one of the kids asked would he pretend to be a paedophile and talk the way they would. That way they would recognise if one came near them.'

'How old did you say these kids are?' I asked.

'Eleven going on twelve.'

'Did he do it?' Card asked.

Gristle nodded. 'I told you he fell for it hook, line and sinker.'

'And all this is recorded on that other kid's iPhone?' I asked.

'And has since been edited,' Gristle finished.

'You said about photographs,' Card prompted him.

'The kid called Gurgle photographed him in the classroom and he didn't notice a thing. Scutler mentioned the strange man, me again, taking them into the toilets and asked Paedo Pedalo if he could help them recognise what a paedo might do in there and they would be able to tell him if the strange man, me, had done any of those things.'

'Don't tell me he agreed?' Card asked.

'Why would he not?'

Card put his head in his hands and shook his head. 'I don't believe it.'

'They have photos of him looking over the toilet stall doors and kneeling down looking under them like a paedophile would do. Then he gets one of the kids to stand in front of a urinal and he goes over and puts his hand on the kid's shoulder and whispers something in his ear. Another kid is standing to the side in one of the photos looking at the pair with horror on his face as Pedalo looks towards the genital area of the kid he is touching on the shoulder. The other kids mutter about how useful this is but they make sure never to speak over Paedo Pedalo so you can hear his voice clearly on the recording they made.'

'And these kids are only eleven?' I said.

'They all will be by the end of August when they go to the big school,' Gristle told me.

The three of us were sitting on the bench in my back garden. None of us spoke at that point as we went over the details Gristle had given us about the school visit trap. I found it hard to accept that kids that young could be so duplicitous, until I thought, at least they aren't hiding weapons and smuggling bomb parts as I was doing when I was their age.

I looked towards the yew tree and out to the pasture on the other side of the hedge. 'Cyril loves sitting here,' I said. 'Is he off on one of his adventures?' Card and Gristle stared off into the distance, ignoring my question, so I knew I was not supposed to dig any further. 'You lot are worse than MI5,' I said, 'with your secrecy and your sudden goings and comings'. They continued ignoring me. 'Cyril says that the inter-world spirits come across that pasture, in through my gate and into my yew tree,' I said apropos of nothing.

'According to Cyril, they are harmless poor things,' Gristle said.

'Why do ghosts have to use your gate to get to the yew tree? Ghosts should be able to come straight through the hedge,' Card said in his typical doubting-Thomas attitude.

'Your problem, Card, is you don't believe in anything you can't count, measure or weigh,' I said.

'I don't have a problem with that,' he answered.

We slipped into our silent mode again for a while.

I broke the silence. It was my garden. 'Where are you

up to now, Gristle?'

'Gurgle and Scutler have worked on the recording to make sure there is no kid's voice on it. They have doctored the photos on a Photoshop gadget so you can't see the face of any kid. What they have left is a brilliant performance of a paedophile, caught in the act, standing close behind and touching the shoulder of a kid who seems to be weeing in a toilet, with another kid looking on in horror. In other photos, he is climbing over toilet doors and standing in what is clearly a classroom with his arms around boys reaching towards their genitals. They will post the results on YouTube. Then all hell will break loose.'

'Will they be able to trace the camera and the computer used?'

'Gurgle reported his iPhone stolen and he dumped it in a cesspit once the photos were uploaded onto a computer.'

'Whose computer?' I asked

'The school library,' Gristle said with a smile. 'These kids think of everything.'

'You know what will happen next, don't you?' Card asked.

Gristle nodded a 'yes'.

'The police will be all over the school once they track down which one it is.'

'The name of the school is clear in the background in one of the photos,' Gristle said.

Card continued, 'The teacher will be suspended, the kids will be interviewed, they will have an unannounced inspection from Ofsted that will tear apart the governors, the management and all their policies and interrogate mercilessly all responsible post holders.'

'You forgot to mention what will happen to our friend Arthur Stockleman, the outstanding member of the Children's Safeguarding Board member and well-known blackmailer, bully, liar, cheat and self-appointed guardian of the morals, practices and tidiness of the village,' I said, in case anyone lost sight of why we were doing this.

'Goes without saying,' Gristle answered. 'He will be arrested. He will spend a long time explaining away the damning spoken and video evidence of his performance. He will never serve on any public body again and will always have allegations hanging over him – smoke without fire and all that. I might feel some sympathy only for the fact he intended to do all that to me and he intended to rob Card and threatened you. He did something bad to Scutler's family and ruined their lives, which is why the kid was so keen on doing him over.'

'And he doesn't know Apple will be heading his way when the police have finished with him,' Card said.

'The kids will be interrogated by the police,' I said.

'I know,' Gristle answered. 'They have it all worked out. Their story is that they were traumatised and were afraid to seek help in case they got into trouble. They will ask for counselling. It seems the county has a lot of private counsellors on their books, mostly relatives of office staff at County Hall, who need the cash. The sessions with the counsellors will keep them off school until the holiday and then they will leave.'

We were covered in silence once more until I brought the meeting to a close. 'The frightening thing is that they could just as easily do this to someone who is innocent.'

'I know,' Gristle said, 'but you would have to annoy them first.'

'And they are only eleven years old.'

'They have a great future in front of them if they are properly managed,' Gristle said as a final word.

The Final Blows

Thursday 11th June 2015 – Heather Moon

'I received an official letter from Apple this morning confirming they have instigated legal proceedings against the CPPP for violation of copyright. Apple will settle out of court for ten million plus the withdrawal of the app from the market. If they go to court Apple will sue for the highest sum possible and will start by asking for 50 million dollars.'

We tried to imagine that amount of money and, more satisfyingly, we dwelt on the panic that would grip each of the gang when they were informed of the lawsuit against them. Two of them were on bail, one had left the country for Alaska and two had yet to have their punishment visited upon them. None of them was beyond the reach of the mighty Apple Corporation or their person-finding software.

'Are you implicated in any way?' Gristle asked Card.

He shook his head. 'The legal ownership of the app and its software lies in the hands of the CPPP in equal parts. They insisted that I put that in writing. I volunteered to Apple that the original version of the app was designed by me. The naughty bits were added after I had handed over ownership to the gang. The Apple people were impressed by my software and they are keen to take up any other ideas I might have.'

'How will you explain the naughty software?' Cyril asked him. 'None of those five idiots could write it.'

'One of the butcher's sons has a software repair and design business. The piece of pirated software will turn up on one of his machines when the investigation starts. One other benefit is that Apple will pay a reward for the information I gave them when the lawsuit is settled.'

'How much?' Gristle asked him.

'Ten thousand pounds.'

'They will be ruined,' Gristle said. 'Just what they planned to do to me and what they had started doing by robbing Card.' He gave a loud sigh. 'You know, I think I am starting to believe there is a God.'

'God had little to do with this,' Card said. 'We did it.'

'Don't be too hasty to shove God out of it,' Cyril chipped in.

'He didn't write the software, so why should he get the credit?' Card asked.

'Can we leave religion out of this?' I asked. I felt uneasy going on like this as if we had done it all ourselves, which of course we had when I looked at it objectively. It paid to cover your bets when so many people like Cyril suggested God had a finger in lots of pies. It didn't detract from our success to give God a little nod of recognition, just in case he was there, listening to us and waiting his chances to give us a slap around the ear as my grandmother always warned. If he wasn't there, then there was no harm done. 'Next step?' I asked.

'They will receive the letter from Apple in a few days,' Card said. 'Gristle then tells his young lads to post the video and recording of Arthur the Paedo on YouTube. Final step will be the butcher being taken care of when the next shipment comes in from Eastern Europe.'

'In the next week or so,' I said.

'All set then,' Gristle said. 'Then we can relax with the job nearly done.'

I didn't pick up on what he meant by "nearly done" until later. Had I known at the time I would have tried to stop them, or I would have gone on the run and to certain death, as Cyril never tired of telling me.

The video of Arthur acting as paedophile in the local

school hit YouTube and took off in what was regarded as one of the fastest growing viral phenomena known. By the following day, Arthur was under arrest. He was said to be beyond words when the police took him away in handcuffs in front of his neighbours. The police had to act within the constraints of the law and took him into custody according to protocol for such occasions. They resisted the temptation to rough handling and kicking for which they were renowned because of the many witnesses there. The crowd outside Arthur's house was not bothered by such niceties of protocol and showed little respect for the delicacy of Arthur's feelings. Police reinforcements took their time battling through the crowd, who were exacting revenge on Arthur. Under the protection of riot shields and protective armoury, they escorted Arthur to an even more hostile reception in the cells in the local nick.

The arson attack on Arthur's house that night was put down to high spirits on the part of the younger element of the community. Those not inclined to blame the young for every misdeed saw the pyre as an outpouring of disgust by those parents who had children in the school. Those in the know attributed the conflagration and the badly parked cars blocking the access by the fire engines to the vengeance of Arthur's neighbours, who had put up with his interference and domineering manner for many years.

In Triumph

Sunday 14th June 2015 – Heather Moon

At our specially convened meeting in the pub on Sunday evening, we sat in front of our non-fire to celebrate a mighty victory for the cause of right. Bottle Blonde and Skinny Slug sat among us beaming with delight at their promotion to such highly regarded company. Card told us his new 'friend' James had moved in with him and would be joining us at the pub from the following Sunday. Even Basher made an effort to be welcoming and hearty. He didn't quite pull off the hearty part but we did acknowledge he made an effort to celebrate our victory.

Card tried to insist we had taken the law into our own hands and what we had done was not the most outstanding example of civic responsibility. He was talked down, with the final shot in the argument coming from the Commander, who reminded us that in warfare it was the military still on the battlefield, or, in the terms he preferred, still afloat with navigable ships, who were declared the victors. The accusation of criminality was never levelled against the victor, he said, only against the loser. With the battle won, only the victor had a say in accounting for what happened. Who were we to argue against the weight and logic of history and the conviction and dogmatic tone of the Commander in full sail?

We were the winners. Right had triumphed.

The Road Accident

Sunday 14th June 2015 – Heather Moon

I don't usually spend much time lying in ditches so I was confused when I regained consciousness stretched out in one.

I had left the pub with Card at the end of our celebratory meeting, walking towards his house, which was on my way home. I heard the car coming. Expecting it to slow down as it passed us on the narrow road, I stepped onto the grass verge. Card followed me but stayed on the edge of the road, still talking, with his back to the oncoming car, or van, or whatever it was. I saw it swerve at the last minute, catching him so that he was thrown, hitting me and sending us tumbling and rolling in a tangle of bodies. I heard the car doors open and feet running towards us. Hands pulled at me, dragging me out from under Card. I tried to tell them to take care of Card, who hadn't moved or cried out. I was punched in the face. The shock of the blow was as bad as the pain. More blows to my head and face and kicks to my chest and lower body sent waves of pain through me until I lost consciousness.

I came round, confused about where I was. I realised I had ended up in a ditch after the beating. I remember thinking how lucky I was that the weather had been dry. Images of Card flying through the air came back to me. The sounds and suffering of being battered and kicked shot into my mind, explaining the pain pulsing through my body. My chest felt like it had caved in. I could not move my left arm. The men had attacked me savagely. What had they done to Card?

I inched my way up the side of the ditch to where Card was lying on his back on the edge of the road. I shook his shoulder and called his name. There was no answer, no movement from him. I tried to work out how far I was from the pub and how far from Card's house. Which would be nearer to go for help?

I don't know if I crawled, staggered or walked back to the pub, or how long it took me. Basher bellowed at me as he unlocked the door. My hammering on the door had dragged him out of bed, he told me later. I fell into the pub muttering about Card being dead on the road. Basher left me lying on the floor of the pub while he ran down the road to see if I was telling the truth. He came back out of breath, and only after he had called the ambulance and the police did he tend to me, dragging me over to our bench near the fireplace. Leaving me propped up, he ran out of the pub to return to look after Card as he waited for the ambulance to arrive. As I watched him run out, I thought, why don't you light the fire for me? I passed out after that and was told later they found me lying in front of the fire my hand holding on to the open grate. Cyril interpreted that as a sign that I was reaching for the fire of life, determined to make a new start from the ashes of my life. I said I had passed out and didn't remember grabbing at the fire. Cyril said it was a good job it had not been lit.

I woke up next in a better place than the ditch or the pub floor. It was a bright room, but a very cold one. I was lying on top of a flat, hard bed with only a sheet covering me, efficient-looking nurses circled around, a young man in a green gown and a funny hat was giving orders, using words I didn't understand. Maybe he was one of those foreign doctors I had read about. I wondered why he was dressed in a green gown but didn't have the strength to ask him. I wanted something for the pain. I mumbled to the nurse, telling her exactly what I wanted but she must have been foreign too because she ignored my request. She stroked my hand and told me everything would be sorted out, all in perfect English, so why didn't she understand me asking for painkillers? Words were so difficult to get out of my mouth. There was no answer to my questions about Card. Maybe she didn't know him.

Every time my eyes closed, even for a minute, and opened again there were different people around me. At some point, they changed the look of the room, turning it into a darkened, quiet room, apart from the humming of machines pumping something, or was it a computer I could hear? In the end, I gave up trying to talk and let the sleep sweep over me. It was such a peaceful feeling, such a soft, floating, painless, warm sensation that I let go and floated away. Maybe heaven was like this.

I woke in hell.

Pain searched out every part of my body that had not been ripped a minute before. It was like a piercing pain was playing hide and seek with a tearing pain in every new part of my body that could be found. My chest was wrapped in bandages for some reason and my left arm was anchored by a heavy weight. I was unable to move my tongue around my mouth because someone had drained away all the saliva, leaving a woolly surface behind. My lips felt like two thick rubber strips that wouldn't come together. I was doomed to remain speechless.

I opened my eyes to see an angel from heaven looking at me. She wiped a piece of wet cotton across my lips and inside my mouth. I understood then what it was like to be rescued after wandering lost in the desert for days without water. The angel smiled at me. 'I'm nurse Bradshaw. I'll just pop and tell them you are awake. Don't go away. I'll only be a minute.'

Go away? The only place I wanted to go was back deep into the pain-free softness and comfort I had left before waking in the bowels of hell, where pain seemed to be the order of the day.

Women in different shades of blue uniforms appeared, lifting some bits of me, poking at other bits, shaking tubes hanging from steel rods, tapping dials and talking shorthand that only nurses understand.

The one with the darkest blue uniform spoke. 'Hello, I'm Sister Caruthers. I'm in charge of the unit. How are you feeling?

'Gerws, glich an drin cul don?' I sighed through puffed-up dead lips, but she didn't give me the glass of water I asked for.

'Good,' she said. 'You had a bit of an accident. Do you remember what happened?'

'groloh sculty carblome suckle?' I managed to squeeze out.

'Yes, it is bound to hurt and it will hurt for a while, but we will give you something to control the pain. We don't leave patients in pain.'

I expected that, but she had totally ignored my question about Card. I wondered if he was dead. I tried again, enunciating the words more precisely this time, 'gro-loh scul-ty car-blome suckle?'

'You relax. You are in good hands. Nurse Bradshaw is looking after you. She will get you anything you want. When you are better we will allow you to have visitors.' She led out the troupe of nurses who had prodded and lifted anything that could be moved.

It was clear that the sister in charge could not understand English spoken to her, having ignored everything I said, even though she could speak fluent English in return. Maybe they trained nurses from overseas in spoken English but didn't train them in listening English. I lifted my good hand and passed it in front of my face to check it still belonged to me. The fingers were sore like they had been trapped in something. The foreign nurse from heaven was sitting beside my bed. I touched her arm and then pointed to my mouth.

'Do you want a drink?' she asked, once again in perfect English.

'Aghala plesso,' I said, as slowly as I could so that she could translate what I was saying into her own language. I had never realised before that moment how blessed is the taste and the feel of water flowing over a dried mouth that had seemed as cracked and drained as a reservoir after a two-year drought. My mouth started working again. What a miracle that a little water could work such magic.

She laid my head back on the pillow and put the beaker with the childproof top on the cupboard beside my bed.

'Thank you, nurse,' I said, spreading out my words. My words sounded different now I had drunk the water.

'You're welcome,' she said.

I was amazed that after such a little time under my guidance and because I spoke slowly, she was beginning to understand spoken English. I smiled at her but stopped quickly as the torture associated with a smile found a few places on my face not yet torn by pain. I drifted off, congratulating myself on my expertise as a teacher of listening English. Given time, I might train all the doctors and nurses in the hospital before I left.

The Visitation

Monday 15th June – Heather Moon

When I next woke, the room was in darkness, apart from a soft light from the corridor. Two figures were sitting, one on each side of my bed. Both of them were dressed in black suits and wearing clerical collars. They looked like priests.

'Did you kill the angel from heaven?' I said.

'What angel?' one of them answered.

When I opened my eyes again, the two men were still sitting there looking at me.

'Am I dead, or am I dying?' I asked. 'I didn't ask for a priest.'

'Be quiet, you daft thing. It's me, Cyril, and that's Gristle.'

I was sure then that I had died and was in some part of the other world where spirits dressed up and pretended to be someone else.

'Go away,' I protested, 'I'm not ready to go through the gate yet.' And I closed my eyes, wishing the apparitions would be gone when I woke up next.

'Delirious,' one of them muttered.

'More like his usual mad self,' the other said.

I opened my eyes to peep at them. The pair was still there. They looked like Cyril and Gristle, but they were dressed like priests. Maybe my accident was worse than the doctors thought. 'Put on the light,' I said. 'Let me see you properly.' They would disappear if they were ghosts.

One of them walked to the door, closed it and turned on the light. Once my eyes adjusted, I stared at them. Jesus, I thought, I am delirious, the pair of them look like Cyril and Gristle.

The smaller one who looked like a wild gnome stood

over me. 'Look, it's me, Gristle,' he said, stretching out his hand to touch me.

I stared at him. 'You look like Gristle, but why are you wearing a priest's outfit? That one can't be Cyril. He doesn't dress up like a priest.'

The one who reminded me of Cyril said, 'It is me, Cyril. We had to dress up. It was the only way we could get in to see you. We told them we were your parish clergy and were worried about losing your soul.'

I stared at him, wondering how to get my brain back under control instead of wandering off on these excursions into wild imagination. 'If that one is Gristle, where did he get the clerical gear?'

'Off my former curate,' the Cyril lookalike said. 'The fella left it behind when he ran away last week.'

'How long have I been here? What day of the week is it?'

'It's nearly Tuesday,' the gnome-like one said. 'You were knocked down on Sunday night. That'll teach you not to drink and walk.'

An image flashed through my mind. 'Where is Card? How is he? Is he alive? He was dead the last time I saw him. The van hit him.'

'He's alive,' Cyril said. 'He was badly bashed around but he'll be ok. He'll walk with a limp for a long time. They broke both his legs. You got off light.'

If I got off light, I thought, poor Card must be in a bad way. 'What have I got?' I asked.

'A bit of a fractured arm, badly bruised ribs, multiple cuts and bruises and concussion,' Gristle said.

'How do you know what I have?' I asked him.

'Because, smarty-pants, I chatted up the nurse on the way in. He,' and he nodded at Cyril, 'wanted to do the chatting up but I told him to hold his lust in check because we hadn't time to let him go messing with the nurses.'

'You speak for yourself,' Cyril answered. 'How do you know how much time I need for what I had in mind?'

Oh God, I thought, this is real. Listening to these two convinced me I was over any concussion and back in reality. 'I want to go home,' I said.

'You can't,' Gristle answered. 'The nurse said the doctor has to clear you to go home and he won't be back before the morning.'

'Suppose I took bad in the night, could they get him back to cure me?'

'Don't be stupid,' Cyril said. 'You aren't allowed to take a bad turn during the night. If you feel death coming on, hold on till the morning and the doctor can take a look when he comes in.'

'Did you see who it was?' Gristle asked.

I shook my head.

'You said just now it was a van,' Cyril said. 'Did you mean a van?'

'Almost sure,' I answered. I thought hard for a moment. 'I am sure. One of those small vans, like the little delivery vans you see around. It was white. I'm sure of that.'

Gristle looked across at Cyril before saying, 'It was a narrow piece of road where it happened, a well-known accident spot.'

'What are you on about?' I said. 'I saw it coming. He swerved into us. He did it on purpose. Card had his back to him, but I saw it as clearly as anything. It was no accident. The van hit Card first, then me. He landed on top of me and the blokes dragged me from under him, started on me and threw me in the ditch.'

The two of them were quiet for a moment. 'Don't suppose you saw their faces,' Gristle said.

I shook my head again. 'All took place too quickly,' I said. 'I do remember there was a strong smell of pig shit off them.'

Gristle and Cyril looked at each other again as if this confirmed something they already knew that they were not telling me.

'Were they after you or Card?' Cyril asked.

'Me, I suppose. Must be something to do with them soldiers.'

'Maybe not this time,' Gristle said. 'It looks like after they threw you in the ditch they drove the van over Card's legs. They wouldn't have done that if they were after you.'

'Over his legs? God above!' I said.

'Aye,' Cyril said. 'He will walk with a limp for the rest of his life. These bastards are pure evil. They deserve everything they are going to get.'

'Do you know who they are?' I asked him.

'Not with enough evidence to make it stick in a court of law,' Cyril said.

'Good job we're not going to a court of law, isn't it?' Gristle added.

The Release

Tuesday 16ᵗʰ June 2015 – Heather Moon

The doctors said they would release me into the supervision of a responsible adult. Card was the nearest to that type of adult but he was being kept in the hospital while the doctors continued to pin his legs together. For some strange reason, the medics thought Cyril was responsible enough just because he showed up in his clerical gear to collect me, driven by Gerard in one of Gristle's Bentleys. I departed the hospital in style, but under false pretences.

Gristle told me later that the decision to board me for a few days at the rectory was because Cyril lost the toss when they decided my fate. Gerard said that wasn't true. He told me I ended up with Cyril, because Gristle was away sorting out some business or other. Nobody would tell me where he was, or what was going on. I was getting more and more irritated at being left out of discussions about my future. Cyril said it was for my own good. It was not the slightest bit reassuring to know my well-being was in the sure hands of one who was pilloried as a paedophile and of another recently kidnapped out of the diocesan mental hospital for mad and pervert priests. Who better to decide what was good for me?

Cyril persuaded me to sit with him in the graveyard behind his house after dinner on the first evening of my release. My aches and pains still tore at me if I turned or moved without thinking through what I was about to do. I was happy to sit still in a peaceful setting.

'It's quiet here,' I said, without thinking how obvious a statement that was.

He nodded in agreement.

'You do this a lot, this sitting out here?' I asked him.

'Most nights.'

'Busy time of the day for them, is it?' I asked half-jokingly. I should have known better.

'No busier than any other part of the day,' he said. 'They move around in their own time frame.'

It was my turn to nod without saying anything.

'I am more relaxed at this time of the evening, and that makes me more receptive to them. They know that, so they wait until I am ready. See for yourself, you know how to look.'

I shook my head. 'Not tonight. I have enough bother with my ribs and arm and all the other bits of me without making myself cross-eyed as well.'

He raised his hand a little and waved gently in the direction of a new headstone. 'Old Mrs Hennessy,' he whispered. 'She hasn't settled since the day they put her there. Family affairs are still up in the air following her death. That sort of thing causes a lot of anguish to the dead. They blame themselves for not sorting everything before they passed over. As if their children's greed was down to them.'

I looked at the yew tree at the other side of the graveyard. 'Is there one of the cosmos gates over there?' I asked, content to cover ground I knew something about from previous conversations.

'No,' he said. 'We don't have a gateway to the other place up here. The nearest one is at the other end of the village. It's part of the hedge around the car park.'

'Why is it down there if the graveyard is up here?'

'The work house was down that end of the village. The lane is still called Cold Comfort Lane where it used to be. They buried the poor in unmarked mass graves out the back of the place. The rich were buried up here next to the church. They paid to build the church because they felt they should be buried here without the poor being planted alongside them. There are many more poor people than rich ones so it makes sense that the gate to the energy of the cosmos should be down there where they were buried. Years ago they pulled down the work house, covered the burial site and turned it into a car park.'

'That was a bit rough on the ones buried there.'

'Could have been worse,' Cyril said. 'Often the graveyards for the poor were sold to a farmer who would dig up the bones and pound them down to use as fertilizer.'

'You now bury the dead poor among the dead rich up here,' I said.

'The dead didn't mind. The objections came from the living. Dying has that effect on people. Gives them a more balanced perspective.'

Cyril's front door bell rang, its echoing chimes reaching us on his back patio where we were sitting.

'Stay here,' he said. 'I'm not expecting anyone. I'll do a quick check and let you know who it is.'

A few minutes later he came out the back door. 'Some chap wants a chat. Crisis of faith, or conscience, or something. It'll take about half an hour. I couldn't turn him away. D'you mind being by yourself for a little while?'

I swept my good hand towards the graves laid out in a perfect garden setting in front of me. 'Course I don't mind. How could I be lonely with all this lot to keep me company? If Mrs Hennessy pops up for a chat I will reassure her none of the problems were down to her.'

'Don't upset her, whatever you do,' he said, hurrying back into the house.

I settled back in the reclining garden chair ready to enjoy the late sunshine, the smell of the evening blossoms and to watch the laborious wing beats of crows heading home.

Mr Lawson and Small Hillside walked around the side of the rectory to spoil my evening. I struggled to remember that this hillside was called Kevin. He grinned at me, not in a friendly way. *Mr* Lawson didn't smile or show any pleasure at meeting me in such delightful surroundings. He was probably trained never to let any sign of happiness cross his face. Even the successful extraction of information from a battered and physically wrecked prisoner leaves his type po-faced, wondering where the next bout of torture and torment will take him.

Small Hillside yanked the back of my recliner so that I was jerked forward into an upright sitting position. *Mr* Lawson stood in front of me.

'You didn't answer your phone when I rang,' he said.

'I was in hospital.'

'You answer when I ring unless you are dead.'

'Someone stole the phone,' I said.

'You will reimburse the tax payer.'

'I was unconscious.'

'That's your own fault.'

'Did you send those assassins after me and Card?' I asked.

'No.'

'You could be lying. You do that a lot.'

Small Hillside standing behind me slapped me across the head with an open hand that was almost as painful as one of his punches. 'D'you mind not doing that?' I shouted at him. This pair was pissing me off. Apart from shouting at them there was nothing I could do to stop them.

I tried again. 'Why did you try to kill us? I thought I was supposed to be spying for you.'

'If we set out to kill you, we will succeed. Spying is too grand a word for what you are doing. You gather scraps of information. What have you found out about the Navy traitor?'

'He isn't a traitor.'

'You don't decide that. What did you find out?'

I thought through what was safe to tell him. 'He is working with a partner to set up a home for servicemen and women who had bad times in conflicts abroad. Does that sound traitorous to you?'

'What else?'

'There is a rumour, but only a rumour, that a wing will be set aside for sex therapy treatments, mainly for members of MI5 who have lost the balls to do anything without gangs of thugs to back them up when beating innocent—'

I should have known better than to irritate him. I saw him give the slight nod just before the blow across the side of the head made me dizzy.

'Again,' he said to me.

'He intends to build a wing for sex therapy treatment.'

'For international patients?'

I shrugged my shoulders. 'As far as I can gather, it is to be the meeting point to pass information to the enemy while they are all enjoying sexual bliss of the highest quality. Lots of Eastern Europeans girls...' I paused for a moment, '...and boys for those that way inclined.' He didn't pick up on the implication, or maybe he intended to batter me over more substantial issues.

'What else?' *Mr* Lawson asked, staring at me with his lifeless eyes.

I was stuck. He wanted more information than the lies I had made up.

'Chickens,' I said, in desperation.

'What about them?'

'Thousands of them,' I said, as I worked out a story that might be plausible enough to get rid of them for the moment. 'He is building industrial-sized chicken sheds, deep litter sheds, mass production on a mega-industrial scale, hundreds of thousands of eggs, broiler hens, bottom-of-the-range chickens for supermarkets, cooked, frozen, raw, disguised as turkey pieces and the rubbish used to bulk up mincemeat and hide the taste of horsemeat in burgers.'

Mr Lawson frowned. I think that is what he was doing if I was interpreting the twitch of his left eyebrow correctly.

I hurried on before he could think of a question. Confusing detail was now called for. 'He intends to generate funds from the chicken farm to support the sex therapy, using nerve-damaged soldiers as a plausible cover. Bodies of his enemies will decompose quickly if they are buried in the chicken shit. Add in money laundering, importing drugs stuffed inside chicken carcasses, people smuggling in the chicken lorries bringing in slave workers and sex workers, plus good cover to travel and meet enemies of the state.' I waited to see if he was biting. I went for broke with the T-card. 'I think he is planning a terrorist attack.'

The tiny but swift tilt of his head told me I had hit pay dirt.

He pursed his lips and took a few breaths before he asked, 'What sort of attack?'

'No details available, not yet,' I said, as sincerely as I could manage. 'I mean, you're the expert, but if it was me, I would be looking at spreading wholesale salmonella through chickens sold in every supermarket in any given town. Or what would happen on the RAF fighter bases all down the east coast if all the pilots were struck down with food poisoning? How many chickens do troops stationed abroad buy from English suppliers? Every curry house, every KFC and McDonald's would be a source of death and illness. The economy would be wrecked, the poultry industry would be in tatters and half the country would be unable to get treatment because of overcrowding in hospitals. The streets would run with blood, people would be unable to find food or get treatment. Where would it stop? On top of that, who checks the lorries carrying thousands of chickens heading into London? A dirty bomb on one of those lorries would wreck the seat of government. If you ask me, the whole plot hangs together too well. They have the means of wreaking havoc on the country, with the foreign contacts to fund them, on premises above suspicion where right now they could be making a dirty bomb, under the direction of a man who captained a nuclear sub with warheads at his fingertips and all under the banner of doing great work for our fallen heroes in foreign wars.'

I wondered had I gone too far. I shut up and waited.

Mr Lawson reached into his inside pocket and took out a mobile phone. 'Don't lose this one. I want more details next time I phone you. I want the information soon, or you will be heading back to Northern Ireland and I don't care how they deal with you when they get you there. You will never get to trial, but your punishment in whatever form will be made to look kosher.'

'I need a few days, so take your time before you phone,' I said. 'I have more to do than wait on your phone calls and root around for information for arrogant bastards like you. I'm the one taking all the risks while you swan around enjoying yourself. I have a life to live that doesn't revolve around you, even if you think you are the biggest prick in the dormitory.' Sometimes you realise you have said the wrong thing as the words are leaving your mouth, too late to pull them back and too pointed to be rescued by a quick apology. *Mr* Lawson paused as he was turning away and nodded to Small Hillside. The punch to the side of my head was well delivered, with venom. I was still lying on the ground when Cyril found me.

'Mrs Hennessy prove too rough for you?' he asked, as he helped me back into the reclining chair.

I groaned and said nothing.

'Your "friends" knew you were here,' he said. 'The one who wanted to talk to me about his faith was a decoy. Judging by his size and the idiotic way he talked, I guess he was one of your soldier friends. Seems to me we need to move you on again before anyone else finds out you are here. Gristle will know where to take you.'

The Bidford Dog
Wednesday 17th June 2015 – Heather Moon

'Where are we going and why are we using one of the Bentleys?' I asked.

Gristle turned around in the front passenger seat and grinned at us. 'Flaunting my wealth before the eyes of the CPPP, rubbing their noses in it, irritating the hell out of them, taunting them by showing what they failed to get their hands on.'

'Don't go too far,' I warned him.

'I went too far with that lot years ago by staying alive and by not buckling under their pressure to sell them everything. If it wasn't for me they would control the whole village by now. Anyway, four of them are off the scene.'

'They can be dangerous still.'

'All in hand,' Gristle said, turning to check the road ahead.

'Where are we headed?' I asked him.

'To the river, at Bidford. It's a nice day. I thought Cyril could do with plenty of fresh air and sunshine after his holiday in the diocesan mental asylum and you need to wave your injured arm around and let the river air into your lungs.'

Cyril grunted without saying anything.

'Will this monster of a car be able to cross the narrow bridge over the river?' I asked him.

'When Gerard is driving, this car will go anywhere he wants it to go,' Gristle said, smiling at the driver. 'Will the bridge give us any trouble, Gerard?' he asked.

'We've been over that bridge many times,' Gerard said, without taking his eyes off the road. 'Sometimes when the picnic area is flooded we park on this side and walk across.'

I sat, lounging beside Cyril, thinking of Card Index, who ought to have been with us. The comfort and the absence of ankle-deep litter made a change from riding in Gristle's battered Range Rover. This was a style of travel I could grow used to without any effort.

We drove the next few miles in silence. Approaching the village of Bidford, Gerard asked Gristle, 'Do you want to pick up Sebastian?'

'I think so. That way you can get out and walk around while we talk,' Gristle said.

The traffic light controlling movement onto the bridge was on red. Gristle climbed out and walked away before it was our turn to cross the bridge.

'Who is Sebastian?' I asked Gerard.

'A valuable friend to have around when things might be dodgy,' Gerard answered as he turned into the picnic area by the river and parked in the shade of the trees.

'I love this place,' I said, stretching my back as we stepped out of the car. 'The river, the smell of the flowers and the sound of the ducks makes me feel at home. When I die, lay my body on a small boat, launch me from here and send me floating down the river.'

'That's your ancestral Viking blood coming through,' Cyril said. 'Shall we set fire to the boat?'

I smiled at him, 'Naw, might upset the fishermen to have a blazing boat drifting past, not to mention the Council getting uptight about incinerated bodies floating around without permission and without paying crematorium fees.'

Cyril stood on the bank looking down the river. 'Actually, this would be a good place to leave your body. There is a gateway down the river that way, like the one in your yew tree. It is well used by many heading back into the energy of the cosmos. The travellers use the path along the edge of the riverbank here so you would feel at home.'

'Here comes Gristle,' Gerard said.

I could see Gristle's head and shoulders above the bridge wall, moving in fits and starts as if he was resisting being moved. When he cleared the bridge we could see the problem. He was being pulled along by one of the strongest-looking dogs I had ever seen.

Seeing my surprise, Gerard said, 'That's Sebastian. Gristle likes to take him out when we come down here.'

It was debatable if Gristle was doing the taking out or the other way round, judging by his struggle to manage the dog.

'Whose dog is it?' I asked, looking at Gerard.

'Gristle's.'

'Where does it live?' I said.

'He lodges it with a lady who lives around the corner from the Bridge Hotel.'

'Is the lady *young*, and is she a *good friend* of Gristle?' Cyril asked, already sussing out what was going on.

Gerard hesitated for a moment. 'Young-ish. Yes, a friend.'

'Close friend?' Cyril asked.

Gerard turned away to gaze at the river.

'Apart from the dog's young-*ish* landlady, why does Gristle keep such a massive dog down here?' I asked.

Gerard rubbed his jaw and pursed his lips so I knew he was not going to tell me the whole truth. 'Sometimes, you know how it is, with people being nosy and you want to do something in private, a dog is handy to stop busybodies getting too close. They take one look at Sebastian and they don't want to know.'

'Would it be private things Gristle is doing with the dog's landlady, or private doings on the river?' Cyril asked.

Gerard shrugged and pulled a face. He was uncomfortable with all the questions about his boss.

'It's ok, Gerard,' I said, 'his secrets are well known to us.' But not this one, I thought, so I couldn't help fishing some more. I smiled to myself at my little pun. 'I suppose it is to do with the barges he meets,' I guessed.

Gerard nodded.

Handy, I thought. Barges moving up and down the river, many holiday lets mixed in with long-term river folk, a foolproof way to move 'certain goods' without being noticed by plod or the Excise. Raids would be difficult when the barge was in the middle of the river. Approaches to moorings were along narrow paths easily guarded with early-warning lookouts. Privacy guaranteed. Police speedboats not allowed. As a way of transporting illegal goods the river was more secure than any motorway. My smuggler friends would benefit from the advantages of the inland waterways.

Gristle staggered and stumbled across to us behind his dog. 'Whoa up, Seb,' he shouted. 'Stay, you stupid thing. Ease up or you'll have me in the river.'

Gerard raised his hand towards the dog. 'Stand,' he said quietly. The dog sat on his haunches, his eyes fixed on Gerard.

'I can never remember which word works with him,' Gristle complained.

At a distance the dog had seemed big. Up close he was *very* big and very fearsome looking. His brown eyes were fixed on Gerard since he had last spoken to him. The broad jaws and round thick-looking skull gave the dog the appearance of a monstrous chewing machine capable of eating through branches or limbs. The bundles of muscles bunched across his shoulders told you this was not a dog to be outrun and not one to mess with.

'He's a cross between a Rhodesian Ridgeback and maybe a Rottweiler, but a gentle one,' Gristle said. 'He wants to be friends with you,' he said, looking at me.

'Why me?'

'He wants you to like him.'

'When did he tell you that?' I asked.

'I can tell,' Gristle said. 'Believe me, it is better to be his friend than to be against him.'

That, I could believe, but it was not a telling argument for making friends with a dog this fierce looking. I couldn't create any images of me running around a park throwing sticks, or favourite dog toys, for him to fetch. More than likely, if I threw a stick he would come back with a live child, or the branch of a tree in his mouth. 'I'm happy to look at him from a distance,' I said, stepping back.

Gerard brought the dog to stand directly in front of me. 'Friend,' he said, pointing at me. Looking at me, Gerard said, 'Look him in the eye, put your hand near his nose and let him smell you. Let him lick your hand when I say "friend" again.'

'I'd rather you didn't say anything…'

'Friend,' Gerard said with emphasis to the dog. 'Your eye and hand,' he said to me.

I looked the dog in the eye and inched my hand towards his mouth with the same lack of enthusiasm I would have felt if I were reaching out to stick my hand in the fire or grab the blade of a growling chainsaw.

The dog stared at me. I thought he was deciding which part of me to eat first. He sniffed my hand, looked around at Gerard, who again mouthed 'friend'. The dog turned his head and licked my hand. I must have tasted better than I looked because the dog moved and stood beside me without tearing any bits off my body.

'There you go,' Gristle said, 'a friend for life.'

'What about him?' I asked, nodding towards Cyril.

'His need isn't as great as yours,' Gristle said.

'What need?'

'You never know,' he answered. 'We all need a little help now and then.'

I stared at Cyril, looking for help but he pretended to be fascinated by the sights and sounds of the river.

'You need a couple of basic commands for him,' Gerard said. 'Keep to single words, say them quietly without fuss and let him do his business according to what you tell him.'

'Such as?' I asked.

'Say "come" and he will reach you wherever you are and whatever is happening. "Leave" tells him you want him to stand down from guarding you and to leave you alone. The word "stand", as you saw, puts him under your total control and he will guard you till death if he has to.'

'His or mine?' I asked with a stupid grin to ease the tension I was feeling.

For a minute, Gerard looked puzzled. 'His, of course,' he said. 'I hope you are taking this seriously.'

'Of course,' I muttered. Why wouldn't I when I had just been adopted as a friend by a killer dog?

'He will stop anyone attacking you, but most people will look at him and clear off. However, if his looks don't do the trick, you say "down" and point at the person threatening you.'

I swallowed before asking the next question. 'Is that his order to kill?'

Gristle shook his head. 'He isn't trained to kill. Not that he would shy off killing if you were being attacked.'

'It's good to know he won't kill without a good reason,' I said, still with a shaking feeling in my legs.

'What does the word "down" make him do?'

'Probably bite off an arm or a leg,' Gerard answered. 'We never got that far with him, except in training.'

'Do you say *bite* or bite *off*?' I wondered aloud.

'*Off*,' Gristle said. 'It would be as difficult for him to manage a tiny bite as it would be for a heavyweight boxing champion to give you a mild hard uppercut. He'll take the whole lot off in one bite.'

'Does he definitely know I am his friend?' I asked. 'Have you convinced him of that? I would hate there to be any misunderstanding between us.' It was best to clear up these issues when you were as nervous as I was.

'He knows who you are now,' Gerard said. 'You have a friend for life whenever you need to call on him. He will never do anything wrong to you.'

'How many friends does he have?' I asked, looking for something to say that would cover up my nervousness.

'Me, Gerard, the kind lady who looks after him for me and a few other special people,' Gristle said.

'Does he not make friends easily,' I said, still anxious over this friendship arrangement.

'Only when we tell him,' Gerard told me. 'He is only a dog so he can't cope with too many friends. I'll take him with me now to guard the car while you two are talking. The kids round here love playing with Sebastian, but his main job is to keep the nutters away from the Bentley. I don't spend all my time polishing it for the pointy-heads down here to start pawing it and dribbling on it.'

Gerard called Sebastian to him after I was told to say "leave". I walked across to the picnic table where Cyril was sitting.

'You and the dog looked the ideal couple,' Cyril said as we joined him.

'So at home in each other's company,' Gristle added.

'Feck off, the pair of you,' I answered. 'I almost wet myself when he sniffed at my hand. I could see my arm disappearing down his throat while he decided which piece of me to eat next.'

'You'll be fine when you get used to him,' Gristle said. 'Just think of him as your piece of insurance.'

'Against what?'

'Against *whom*,' Cyril corrected me.

'All right, against whom?'

'You never know,' Gristle answered. 'Could be anyone, anywhere. Best to be prepared.'

'Do you lot know something I don't know?'

'How could we?' Cyril asked. 'You are always a step ahead of us.'

I knew then that they were lying and I was in trouble.

'Tell me now, or I will call over Sebastian and set him on you.'

'Don't even joke about doing that,' Gristle said. 'Let's say we want to give you extra protection in case those soldier fellas or the IRA lot come after you.'

'And what if they turn up at the house? Do I ask them to wait while I phone Gerard and ask him to drive down here and fetch Sebastian back to my house to eat them alive?'

The pair of them sat there looking as guilty as a kid with chocolate on his mouth denying he even knew the bar had been hidden in the red jar at the back of the bottom cupboard.

'You'd better tell him,' Cyril said. 'You know how difficult he is when he doesn't know something. He will nag the life out of us until we give up the will to live.'

'I don't nag. I am not difficult to be around, except when those who should be my friends are being secretive and stupid.'

Gristle stood up. 'Come on, come with me,' he said. 'I want you to meet someone.'

'Who? Where are we going?'

'I told you he would start nagging,' Cyril said. 'Do you want me to wait here?'

'Best if you stay here,' Gristle answered. 'Fewer security checks if it is only him and me.'

'What security checks?' I asked.

'Just go,' Cyril said. 'Leave me to the ducks without your nagging getting in the way.'

We walked along the riverbank path, Gristle leading the way while I moaned about the secrecy and daftness that was going on. He stopped by a large tree that was doing its best not to topple into the river. 'See over there,' he said, pointing to the far bank. 'See that dead tree covered with all the ivy? That's one of those gate things that Cyril goes on about.'

'Do you believe in his spirits?' I asked.

'Only when Cyril wants me to believe.' He looked around for a moment like he was searching for something, or was listening for a particular sound. 'It's ok, we can go on now.'

'What's ok?'

He ignored my question.

'Tell me what this is about, or I am not going any further.'

He stared at me and sighed. 'Cyril was right. You can be a pain in the arse. This is about your plan B.'

I couldn't help feeling puzzled. 'I didn't know I had a plan A.'

'See smarty-pants, you don't know everything.'

'What is plan A?'

'Nothing to do with me. That's Cyril's job. Ask him.'

We walked on in silence.

'There you are,' he said pointing along the river. 'There is the heart of your plan B, you and Sebastian of course. We're heading to that barge.' We were looking at a moored green and black narrowboat picked out with gold lines and intricate lettering in blue. 'That's it. *Pequod II*.' We stopped beside the boat. 'Ahab,' he called out. 'Ok to come aboard, you silly old bugger?'

'*Ahab*?' I said, 'And the boat is named *Pequod*? Are you telling me—?'

'Best not ask at the moment,' he said, hushing me into silence as a squat, broad-shouldered man with a black beard appeared on deck. Fortunately, he had both legs or I would have been worried about my sanity, or the sanity of those around me.

The bearded one screwed his eyes against the sun, staring at me. 'Are you the stupid one who risked his life for that load of shite there?'

'I wouldn't put it in those words exactly,' I said, surprised at his greeting.

'He's the one,' Gristle interrupted.

'Come aboard my boat,' he said, 'and let me shake your hand. It is a pleasure to meet you. There aren't many silly enough to stand up for that daft one, so that puts you in a select, but very small, group of idiots.'

'Can we go below ships, or whatever you call it?' Gristle asked, 'or do you want us to die here on the riverbank listening to you blowing all this hot air? You are as bad as this fella with all your blathering. He can blame being Irish. You don't have any excuse.'

Ahab lifted his right arm in the air and then lowered it to scratch his head. 'Come aboard, me hearties, and join me in my humble home.'

I looked around to spot whoever he had signalled but could see no one, only a pair of water hens scudding across the river and expanding ripples where a fish touched the surface. Maybe there had been a movement by the old tree covered in ivy, but I couldn't be sure.

Captain Ahab indeed! Stranger things had happened. Not too long ago I had started believing in spirits and wondering if men had walked on the moon. I had just been officially adopted as a friend by a killer dog. Maybe I should check the river for Moby Dick. Naw, I thought, that is stretching my imagination too far. I would soon learn I had not stretched it far enough. Moby Dick didn't have to be a whale.

'When do you want him to come aboard?' Ahab asked Gristle.

Gristle looked at me before answering, like he was judging how willing I would be to go ahead with whatever he was about to say. 'I suggest as soon as possible, like later this evening. He has been hiding at the rectory since he left hospital and we can't leave him there any longer and we certainly can't allow him home by himself. Too many people looking for him since he was sprung from hospital.'

'Are you going away soon?' Ahab asked.

'Tomorrow. It's all set up for a meeting on Friday. We'll come back on Saturday. We could stay the next day in case there are any complications, or if further proof is needed.'

'Would anyone mind if "he" had a say in what is being planned here?' I asked. 'In case "he" might have an opinion.'

'Your opinion doesn't come into it,' Ahab said. 'As I understand it, you have a simple choice. Either we help you to stay alive, or you can choose to be dead.'

'That sums it up well,' Gristle said, before I could make an answer. 'We'll collect a few things for him and bring him down here after dark, or would you prefer us to

273

deliver him to Evesham?'

'Both too public,' Ahab told him, again ignoring me. 'You know that little landing stage at Offenham?' Gristle nodded. 'Bring him there. Come in your old Range Rover. That tart's car with the cloth roof will stand out. Is the dog coming?'

Gristle nodded. 'He stays with GG from now on. If I can deliver them both this evening then I can head off tomorrow with an easy mind.'

'Where are you heading?' I asked him.

'To Northern Ireland to see old friends of yours and sort out this mess one way or another.'

Cruising on the River

Saturday 20th June 2015 – Oak Moon

Years working smugglers' trails had taught me to be patient. I could sit still for hours outwaiting those set on trapping me. A ground-nesting bird sitting on its clutch without moving when the hunter drew near had nothing on me. The secret was in focusing the mind. I could hold one thought, or one image, letting it take up the whole of my mind, inducing a sense of total relaxation. That one thought let me be still for long periods of time.

For the few days Cyril and Gristle were away, my mind was not focusing for me. I paced up and down. Not that there is much scope for pacing on a narrowboat. Thoughts rushed through my mind like the river cascading over a weir.

We had passed a few of those as we headed up the river towards Stratford. Ahab involved me in the working of the boat, but for long periods of time there was nothing to do but sit and watch the world go by, slowly. Occasionally Ahab would order me to sit below in the cabin with the curtains drawn across the windows. When I complained that the cabin was too small and was like a cell he told me the next size down was a coffin and I was lucky to have a cell.

Most of those days were taken up with trips to Stratford or Evesham and back to the mooring by Bidford. A number of times we had pulled into the riverbank where Ahab talked quietly to cyclists or walkers. The passing of envelopes usually concluded the conversations before we moved off again. Being sensitive to the demands of doing business quietly and in a confidential manner, I did not ask questions and went below decks to avoid being a witness.

We picked up Ahab's son where the canal marked the

boundary of a golf course above Bidford late on the Friday evening. 'My John,' Ahab announced, as the tall and broadly built young man stepped down into the cockpit of the boat. My hand disappeared inside a large hand when he greeted me. He didn't say anything but stood there shaking my hand, staring at me.

'He doesn't speak,' Ahab said. 'You have to face him if you talk with him, so he can see your lips. His hearing and his speech let him down since he was a baby.'

'Pleased to meet you, John,' I said, hoping I would find my hand that was still hidden inside his grip.

He smiled and nodded at me before releasing me. He put his large knapsack on the deck and turned to face his father.

'Put them below in the cabin,' Ahab said, indicating the knapsack.

John nodded and handed over an envelope.

Ahab tore it open and read the note. 'How long ago?' he asked.

John made a circular movement with one of his hands.

'Did she take the call herself?'

John nodded.

Ahab handed him back the note. 'Destroy that now and put your stuff away. We may not need it, but best be careful.'

John bent his body and struggled through the door into the cabin of the narrowboat.

'That was a message from our friends on pilgrimage in Ireland,' he said, smiling at me. 'They have made contact with the high priest and negotiated a way forward so that we can all worship in peace in our own church.'

I frowned at him.

'That's what the message said. John's missus took the call and wrote it down as our travelling friend with the clerical collar dictated.' Realising I still had not got the message, he added, 'It looks like the trip was a success and you are almost off the hook.'

'You mean the…' I paused, remembering his warning earlier that voices carried a long way over water, '…will the dogs of war be called off?'

'Looks like it,' he said. 'The pilgrims will be back tomorrow afternoon. They will explain it all then. In the meantime, keep out of sight so that the hierarchy of the other church can contact their wandering priests and tell them to return to the monastery without taking you with them as a sacrifice.'

I could see the hand of Cyril in all this hidden message stuff. He would be enjoying the cloak-and-dagger messages and piling on the church imagery.

'I suppose I should go to my cell for a bout of meditation,' I said, getting into the swing of the language.

'If you like,' Ahab said. 'John and me are about to meditate with a few beers. But you please yourself.'

'On second thoughts,' I said, 'I'll join you in the beer. I can sit in my cell another time.' I felt good to be free at last. It looked like all my troubles were nearly behind me. I folded my arms on the chin-high cowling of the cabin and rested my chin on my forearms and watched the banks of the river slide by as the narrowboat putted its sedate way along, brushing against weeds and easing swans and ducks out of its way. For the first time in many years, I could relax and be at peace with the world. I wondered if Ahab had something a bit stronger than beer. I wanted to celebrate big time.

Gristle arrived at the moorings in one of his Bentleys on the Saturday evening and started his usual abusive conversations with Ahab. John came out of the cabin to greet Gristle by hugging him and lifting him off his feet and pretending to drop him overboard, to Gristle's delight. Sebastian stood beside me on the cockpit watching the arrival of Gristle, waiting his turn to be recognised. When John released him, Gristle bent down and hugged Sebastian, setting the dog off on a tail-wagging exercise of mammoth proportions. Then it was my turn.

'You still here?' Gristle asked. He turned to Ahab. 'I told you to get rid of this one overboard by the weir. I want my five pound back that I paid you.' Then he grabbed me in a fierce bear hug. 'You stupid sod,' he said slapping my back. 'All those years and you never told us.'

'You did it?' I said, when he let me go and I caught my breath.

He was smiling broadly, still holding me by the arms. 'Yep,' he said. 'Cyril sends his apologies but you know what he is like about preparing his Sunday sermon on a Saturday evening. He will be down tomorrow and we will celebrate in style.'

'How did you pull it off?' I asked.

'Charm, intelligence, astuteness, being clever and because I am the smartest person you know.' Behind him the passenger door of his Bentley opened. Gristle half turned and said, 'And she was a great help.'

I stared at the woman who had climbed out of the car. She was the most stunningly beautiful woman I had ever seen. Her hair, her eyes, the way she stood, exuded beauty and power at the same time. She was dressed in what I could only imagine must be top-quality clothes. Sebastian stood quivering, waiting to be unleashed, representing how I felt as I stared at her. She raised her hand slightly and Sebastian bounded off the narrowboat and danced around her, full of delight as she bent down and hugged him. If she greeted her friends in the same way, I would sign up to be a close friend.

Gristle grinned at me standing with my mouth open. 'I think you know Magella.'

I shook my head. I would never forget if I had seen this woman before.

'That's Aggie, Bert's missus,' Gristle said. 'Don't tell me you have forgotten her already.' He grinned at me as he watched my brain come to terms with the stunning vision in front of me and the memory I had of the hag with the fag and the patch over one eye at Bert's Bestest Butties mobile café. He turned to Ahab. 'Do you slip something in his food to shut him up? Be worth a fortune whatever it is.'

Ahab smiled at me. 'I locked him below most of the time. I got more chat out of John than out of this fella. Evening, Magella,' he called to the vision now playing with Sebastian on the towpath. 'You're looking fit, if you don't mind me saying.'

'Thank you, Ahab,' she said, in what I could only describe as a quiet and calm voice that found its way into every cell in my brain leaving me tingling. ''Tis well you're carrying yourself.' She waved to John, who was gazing at her. 'Hello, John,' she said, giving him the type of smile that would melt the bones of wild men. He waved at her in a way that suggested it was normal for him to be in the presence of outstanding beauty.

Gristle nudged me. 'You coming, or are you intending to stand rooted there for the night. Magella and me are going for a meal and a drink. Ahab and John have a bit of business to do. You might as well come with us and leave them in peace. We can talk you through what has happened.' He stepped off the barge and stopped beside the woman. 'He's not used to women, as you can see. Could you help him put his jaws back in contact with each other before his mouth opens any more? At his age, he is liable to dribble, not a pleasing sight.'

She smiled at me, provoking a reaction I was at a loss to describe except it left me unable to move. 'Are you coming?' she said, reaching out her hand to me as if she wanted to help me off the boat.

'Ah,' I gurgled.

'Hi,' she said. 'It is such a delight to meet you properly. I have heard so much about you. I am looking forward to getting to know you better.'

'Ah,' I gurgled again. What else was there to say? How could I even begin to find words to say something sensible and meaningful? What was wrong with using a simple word to capture all the delight and sensations that went with being fully alive with a beautiful woman holding on to me? Babies speak like that all the time and get away with it. I stumbled towards Gristle's car feeling the heat of her hand where she held my arm. She could have dragged me by my bad arm and kicked my bruised ribs and I would have made no protest.

'I'll sit in the back,' she said, when we reached the car. 'Give you more room if you sit in the front. Sebastian can come in the back with me.'

I watched her climb in and fasten her seat belt. Gristle closed the door for her and turned to me. 'Get in the car, you silly old sod, and stop being so dumb-looking. She's only a woman.' Then he paused for a moment and frowned. 'Well, maybe the most beautiful and sensuous woman you have met, or are ever likely to meet. Get over it and stop looking so stupid.'

We drove in silence down lanes and back roads just wide enough for a car. When I say in silence, I mean I said nothing; my mouth was struggling to make contact with my brain, which was in turmoil at being in the same car as the most beautiful woman I had ever seen. My silence didn't stop Gristle blathering on aimlessly, telling me every detail of his flight to and from Belfast.

'Did you hear me?' a voice said, as Gristle shoved my shoulder.

'What?' I said, the longest word I had said in almost half an hour.

'We're heading to *The Why Not* in Astwood Bank. Are you ok with that?'

I nodded. 'Aye. They do the best Guinness for miles around.'

'Plenty of privacy there if we use the gardens out the back. With a bit of luck I'll bump into one of the Davis lads running the steam engine rally and do a bit of business.'

The pub fell silent, with everyone staring at Magella leading the monstrous dog and the two oldies as we bought our drinks and made our way through to the garden outside the dining area. We found a table towards the end of the lawn. Gristle went off with our food orders, leaving me alone with Magella. By now, my voice and brain were in contact again, almost.

'Did you go with him?' I asked, nodding towards where Gristle had gone through the door into the pub.

'Yes, just the three of us. Gristle had made contact the time you were in hospital. He wore a very smart suit for the trip. Dearest Cyril wore his full religious outfit, his Anglican one,' she hastened to add, so she obviously knew about his druid outfits. 'A clerical collar still carries some weight over there. He made the arrangements for the meeting.'

'Why did they drag you along?'

She smiled at me. 'I'm like you,' she said. 'I have connections over there still. I was able to vouch for the two of them and to help ease their meeting with the top men.

Kind of go-between, I suppose.'

'How could…?' I stopped puzzled.

'I am originally from Donegal. My family were always involved in… well, the sort of group you used to belong to. They still know people and are respected by individuals who are now important and in very high positions.'

'You don't sound Irish. You don't look Irish,' I said, gazing at her brown eyes, jet-black hair and a touch of darkness on her skin.

'I would have been Spanish if the Armada had gone home a different way,' she said with a smile. Her constant smile kept me feeling warm and friendly towards the whole world. 'Those shipwrecked sailors left behind marks of themselves, like the Vikings in Waterford and Dublin or the Jews and Huguenots in Cork.'

Gristle came back carrying our drinks. 'Twenty-minute wait for the food,' he said as he sat down. 'You two getting on ok? He's not annoying you, is he?' he asked Magella. 'There's a high hedge down at the end of the garden and I'll throw him over it if you want me to.'

'Stop tormenting him,' she said. 'Tell him what he wants to know.'

'Before I get to that,' he said, after taking a sip out of his pint, 'did you hear the news about last night?'

'What news?' I asked.

'Couple of lads I know in the pub were telling me there was a bit of kerfuffle last night not far from Hillers Cross. Barry, the eldest son of our friend Bill the butcher, had an unfortunate accident and shot himself in the ankle and then in the kneecap on his other foot.'

'Shot himself? *Twice?*' I asked.

'So he said when the police turned up. It appears two different guns were used but poor Barry couldn't find either of them when the police asked for them. He blamed thieves, saying they must have taken the guns when he was unconscious.'

'Bill won't be happy about that,' I said.

'That's the other strange thing. Bill was seen being helped into the back of a lorry not far from where Barry had his accident. Hasn't been seen since. You didn't have anything to do with it, did you?'

'I was with Ahab all night,' I protested.

'It'll be the Muslim lads you told me about,' Magella said. 'I keep telling them not to be so uptight about religion. Look where it got us in Northern Ireland.'

'Maybe if they had Cyril's version of religion adding the druids to their other beliefs they would get a better grip on life,' Gristle said. He saw me looking at him impatiently.

'Ok,' he said, 'I can tell you officially, you are off the hook. We saw the top men. Once we explained everything, they thought you should be given an assurance that nothing would happen as a result of your activities all those years ago. They had found out about your man the shooter on Bloody Sunday and had dealt with him a few years ago. Officials had blamed the IRA for the Bloody Sunday shooting, but all they could do was swear they had no guns that day.'

'Why didn't they turn over the one who fired the shots?'

'He went down fighting when they went to take him. They had no witnesses and could only repeat their story, which was true as far as they were concerned. They discussed bringing you out now as a witness but decided it would only stir up too many problems. They would prefer to silence you for good in case the other side got to you. We assured him that in your old age you are most forgetful and it would not be worth killing you. Magella swung it for you, reminding them there were other bits of information people would dredge up if anything happened to you.'

'What about the MI5 lads and the two soldiers?' I asked.

'The blokes we spoke to have enough pull with the English government. Those soldier lads of yours have been called off. You will not be contacted again.'

I breathed easily, not realising I had been holding my breath.

'Magella asked them for one of those letter things, one of those freedom from prosecution letters they gave out in secret so you can forget about your thumbprint on the paper on the bomb.' He looked at his watch. 'Anyway, by now that piece of evidence will have been lost.'

'I can't tell you how grateful I am,' I started saying. 'It is like the whole of my life has been turned around and I can live freely again.'

Magella frowned at Gristle, who looked down at the table.

'What?' I asked.

She smiled at me, which made the next piece of information easier to accept when she said it. 'They wanted assurances that you will never reveal what you know about the gun and that you will never give up the name of the person you gave it to. If you did, you would destroy the whole peace process and put people at each other's throats again.'

'You can tell them I promise,' I said.

'They want assurances, not just promises,' Gristle said.

I looked from one to the other, puzzled why they were faltering over this.

Magella took a deep breath before answering. 'You must never go back to Ireland again.'

'I can manage that,' I said, with a grin. 'I've been out

of it so long now it would be hard to find my way around if I went back.'

Gristle sighed. 'They want you to change your name and leave this country. They can't afford you to be caught by the other side.'

'Leave here? Leave England? This is where my life is,' I protested. 'I can hide here. No one will find me.'

'Someone found you,' Magella said. 'Others will do so.'

'Where could I go? I don't know anyone in France or Germany. Holland is too flat, any other place is very cold and as for—'

'South America,' Gristle cut in. 'They will arrange for you to go to South America.'

'Actually, Brazil,' Magella said quietly.

'That's where the fecking runaway bishops and priests run to when they are caught with their pants down, or their hands in the till, or on someone's arse,' I protested.

We sat in silence for a moment.

'They will set you up with papers, some money to start with, a place to stay and people who will help…'

'Like fecking prison guards, you mean.'

'Easy on, GG, hear us out. We got the best deal we could. The other option was to let them kill you,' Gristle said. 'These guys mean business. They don't fiddle around.'

'Tell me,' I snorted.

'Once you are established, you can go anywhere you like,' Magella said.

'Anywhere in Brazil you mean,' I muttered.

'It's a big place,' Gristle said.

'Most of it is fecking jungle,' I said.

'Think of all them beaches, the women, the football.'

'At my age? How will I learn to speak Spanish?'

'Portuguese,' Gristle said unhelpfully.

'You'll be alive,' Magella said.

'And free,' Gristle added. 'With enough to live on without having to worry about working. Enjoy your retirement.'

'Like the fecking gorilla locked up in the zoo,' I said.

Magella lifted an envelope out of her handbag. 'That's your freedom from prosecution letter. A sizeable deposit will be made into your bank account, followed by a top-up every month. You will be given an airline ticket in the next few days.'

I picked up the envelope. 'This is what my life is worth, is it?'

'No,' Magella said. 'That is the price these people are willing to pay for your silence. In their eyes, your life is worth nothing.'

'Why don't they just kill me and have done with it?' I asked. 'Far cheaper all round.'

Gristle drummed his fingers on the table. 'Listen, you stubborn old sod, this woman put her neck on the line. We took a huge risk. The dangerous people are holding back. You have the chance to live a few more years, in comfort and without the threat of being killed. Magella told them much more would come out if you were killed. We made it clear that several copies of your statements existed and if anything happened to you, at least one of those copies would be released. Stop arsing around and recognise you have got a brilliant deal. A better deal than you had this time last week when mad people tried to kill you and the soldier lads were waiting to pick up the pieces. Getting you out of the country keeps you out of the hands of the other side and guarantees them that nothing will disrupt what they have going now.'

I sat back in the chair and let all the information

muddle its way around my head. So many angles, so many options, so many thoughts and feelings, and not all of them making sense or fitting together.

They sat waiting for me to talk. 'I like it around here,' I said quietly. 'I know people. The shops are handy. I drink in the pub. I even told Cyril what to feed me after I die.'

'They have called off the MI5 mob to give you a bit of space. You have the freedom letter as a sign of their good will,' Gristle said. 'They want your answer on Monday. What more is there to think about?'

'That is the day after tomorrow,' I protested.

'How much time do you want?' Gristle asked. 'What could happen tomorrow to make you change your mind?'

The Butcher Boys

Sunday 21st June 2015 – Oak Moon

I didn't sleep well on the barge that Saturday night. Confused images of smugglers and inter-world spirits and running men with guns tumbled through my mind, turning the night into a battlefield. Several times my grandfather Big Ter stood on the edge of the action calling out to me. Each time I tried to go to him, hands grabbed my feet, pulling me towards a fire, or to a swamp in the middle of a jungle.

Ahab's phone ringing didn't wake me, I was already half awake, dozing in the early-morning sunlight filtering through the thin curtains. I heard him grunt a few times before rolling out of his bed, waking his son John, who had returned to us late the previous night. The noise of the ropes being cast off and the engine starting told me we were in a hurry as we headed away from the mooring. The abruptness of the start stirred an alarm in my mind, adding to the dreams and images that had been trampling through my troubled sleep.

Ahab was at the helm, steering the barge out into the middle of the river. John was standing at the prow with a club in his hands, his eyes scanning both sides of the river, Sebastian standing guard beside him as we moved along at what seemed to me to be an unusual turn of speed for the old boat. 'Morning, Ahab. We seem to be in a rush. Everything all right?'

'Nothing for you to worry about. Just some business I have to do.'

'Can I help?'

'Everything is under control. Get yourself below decks and stay out of sight.'

'Who was the phone call from?'

'Why don't you make us some tea and a bit of toast,' he suggested. 'We can have a proper breakfast later.'

'Where are we headed?'

'Down river. We'll stop beyond Pershore. I'm meeting someone there. Be a good place to have breakfast.'

He turned his attention to the river and to steering the barge, leaving me little choice but to go below and make the tea and toast.

It was late in the morning when Ahab stopped and moored the boat.

'Where are we?' I asked, poking my head out of the cabin door.

He looked down at me from his seat by the tiller. 'Just above Eckington, not far from Tewkesbury. You can come out.'

I stood on the deck and looked around. John was still in the prow of the boat with Sebastian but seemed more relaxed, although he still carried the club in his hands. The sound of the traffic on the M5 came faintly across the fields. The fishing pitches along the riverbank were full.

I looked around for some reason why we should stop here. I was still wondering why we had made such a speedy and early start to the journey. I was supposed to signal my agreement to my exile in Brazil the next day and I ought to have been at home in my house instead of all the way down here.

A familiar battered old Range Rover pulled up in the small car park on the riverbank. Gristle, Cyril and the Commander climbed out and hurried towards us. This had not been part of any plan that I knew about. 'What are you lot doing here?' I asked, in greeting them.

'Couldn't get enough of your ugly face last night,' Gristle answered.

'How are you?' Cyril said.

'Fine, now that you and that mad fella there saved my bacon. I owe you for that. Maybe not as much as you might want considering you are dumping me in Brazil.'

'You're welcome,' he answered. 'Best not say the name of the place too often, in case anyone is listening.'

'You have any food?' Gristle asked.

'There's a café over there,' Ahab said. 'Tell me what you want and I'll get it for you. GG, you make the tea. John can keep watch and make sure everything is peaceful.'

I looked at him, wondering what he was going on about, but he ignored my raised eyebrows. The Commander had walked along the bank examining every inch of the barge before standing to the side and saying, 'Permission to come aboard?'

'Stop pissing about,' Gristle told him.

Ahab poked him hard in the ribs. 'Shut up, you. Permission granted. Come aboard, Captain.'

The Commander stepped smartly onto the cockpit as if he did it every day. He saluted the flag flying from the stern and then Ahab. 'Tight ship you keep, sir,' the Commander said.

'Thank you, Captain. I appreciate that coming from a seafaring man such as yourself.' He turned to glower at the three of us. 'Good to see someone has manners and keeps to protocol.'

We sat in the cockpit eating our hot bacon and egg sandwiches chatting about people and things happening in the country. There was no hint as to why we were there, or why we had to have a meeting, because that is what our getting together was starting to look like.

'Right,' said Ahab when we had all finished eating, 'time for a bit of business. I suggest we go below. More privacy.' He tapped John on the shoulder so that he turned and faced his father. 'Stay out here and keep watch. Knock on the door if you see anything out of the ordinary, anything at all. Ok with that?'

John nodded and smiled.

We squeezed around the table in the cabin, the Commander at the head seeming to swell in an environment in which he was at home. Submariners must delight in confined spaces that make the rest of us scream with claustrophobia. He took deep breaths, filling his lungs as if he was searching for a smell of something. His eyes darted around the cabin taking in every detail, or maybe he was looking for the torpedo tubes, or the missiles we could launch to wipe out Gloucester or Tewkesbury.

'Crew, come to order,' he said. He was definitely back in the zone. Next he would be issuing orders to splice the mainsail, or clear the fo'c's'le, or all hands on deck, or whatever they shouted when they were about to blow China off the face of the planet with a shower of nuclear missiles.

I sat back and smiled to myself at allowing such humorous thoughts to cross my mind.

'Bad news first,' the Commander said, looking directly at me as he said it. 'Your house was firebombed early this morning. We have every reason to suspect that it was done by an enemy and was meant to be a personal and fatal attack. Fortunately you were not on the premises.'

The early-morning phone call, the speed of our departure from Bidford, Ahab confining me below decks for most of the journey, the warning from Big Ter in my dreams during the night, all now fitted together.

The confusion in my mind tied my tongue for a moment. 'Who... what time... are you sure? I thought...' Then I took control of myself. 'Gristle, you told me last night the bad guys had called off MI5 and the soldier boys.

Why did this happen? Is it a warning, or a message, or a last fling at killing me?'

'None of those,' Cyril said. 'We called our sources as soon as we heard the news. They were as surprised as we were and very annoyed that their orders might have been challenged. They phoned back a little while ago and swore it was none of their people. MI5 and the two soldiers had been called off. They told us that this is a local dispute.'

'The butcher boys,' Gristle added. 'As soon as we heard about the fire, we suspected it was them and we had to get you away from Bidford and Offenham in case they tracked you there. They probably blame you for what happened to their brother Barry and to their father because you are well known for your connections with the smugglers.'

'Was it the smugglers who shot Barry?' I asked.

Gristle frowned at me. 'Who do you think did it? Barry didn't shoot himself through the ankle, throw away the gun, find another one and shoot himself in the knee and then lose that gun too. I know you didn't do it because you were surprised when I told you about it and Ahab swore you were with him all the previous night when Barry was shot.'

'The tactic now is concealment,' the Commander announced. He would say that, having spent most of his working life concealed under miles of ocean waiting for the other side to move so he could kill them. I had had enough of concealment all my life and was about to start another bout of it, this time in fecking Brazil on the other side of the world.

'I need to get my passport and my clothes,' I said. 'I have to say goodbye to people, make sure Blazing will be looked after, claim any rebate on my gas or electricity bill. What about my Council Tax? That will owe me something.

Johnson in the paper shop will have to cancel my papers and magazines. I need a bit more time to get myself organised before gallivanting off to the bottom of the world. You lot seem to think this is a game of hide and seek with me playing the part of the one in hiding.'

The four of them sat staring at me, letting me vent my irritation without any interruptions from them. It was most unlike them to give me the floor this long, even if my case was a valid one.

'There is one other thing you need to know,' Cyril said, pausing as if he didn't want to tell me the next piece of news. Gristle nodded encouragement to him.

'Around the time your house was firebombed, Card's house was done as well.'

I shook my head and blew out my breath, 'Jesus, those butcher brothers were right busy. Not the most neighbourly way to be going on at that hour of a Sunday morning. Good job Card was still in hospital. Two houses at the same time. Feck me, but that was some going. Still, only houses, eh?'

Gristle answered me. 'Card's friend James was in the house. They tied him to the bed. He died in the fire.'

We sat in silence.

I don't know what I do with my body when I hear savage news. Maybe my mouth drops open, my hands rest on my lap, my eyes stare off into the distance, my hearing closes down apart from allowing one normal noise like the ticking of a clock to get through and my lungs slow down so that I breathe easily. My mind, on the other hand, goes into its pragmatic mode. 'We need to tell Card.'

'Did that before we came down here,' Cyril said.

'He won't be safe in that hospital.'

'We told the police and they have a guard on him,' the Commander replied.

'Where will Card go when he gets out?'

293

'He will stay with me,' Gristle told me.

'What will he do about James?'

'I'll bury him and take care of his spirit,' Cyril answered.

'Where are the murdering bastards now?'

'Looking for you,' Ahab said.

'Which is why you have to stay in hiding until your passage abroad is organised,' the Commander said, breaking the silence that followed Ahab's statement.

'How can I go if I have no passport?' I asked, turning back to my predicament.

'You will leave on a light plane out of Staverton airport near Gloucester; land in France; go by road over the Pyrenees; board a train to Portugal; take a flight to Brazil. You will pick up your new passport, new identity, clothes and background information that will be your cover story.'

'What if it goes wrong?' I asked.

'It won't,' Gristle said, with assurance. 'It is a well-tested route used by the IRA when they had to move out individuals too hot to keep at home in Ireland, except they by-passed Gloucester.'

Ahab took over. 'We will sail down to Gloucester docks to hide while we wait for the signal for you to go.' He turned to Gristle. 'How long will he have to wait?'

'We will confirm the agreement with the top man tomorrow. It will take a few days to put everything in place. We could be looking at take-off on Thursday, Friday at the latest.'

'You still ok with all this, GG?' Cyril asked me.

'Do I have a choice?'

'Good,' Ahab said. 'All we have to do is keep you out of sight for a few days. Gloucester docks will be the last place anyone will think of looking for you. We are on the last leg; home and dry.'

Near-Death Experience

Monday 22nd June 2015 – Oak Moon

The journey to Gloucester docks took the rest of Sunday. Ahab and John were on deck all the time on lookout. I was confined below deck. When I pointed out to Ahab that he had said no one would think of looking for me in this part of the country, he frowned and told me he was taking double care, after what had happened to James. Sebastian sat on the cockpit deck with Ahab, except when John took him onto the towpath for a run. I gave up trying to go with them after my second attempt was blocked by a stubborn Ahab.

We were moored in Gloucester docks when my phone rang. Not my ordinary phone, but the one my MI5 handler had given me. I let it ring for a while. He should not be phoning me. He had been called off. Maybe he was ringing to assure me it was all over, or to say goodbye, or to apologise. I answered the phone. 'What do you want?'

There was silence, except for the breathing at the other end.

'Who's there?' I asked. 'You can't call this number. It is a private number.'

'I'll get you, you bastard.'

'I think you have a wrong number,' I answered.

'I know whose number I have. You think you are smart getting us called off. One day I will catch up with you and you will pay for all those you murdered.'

It sounded like one of the hillside-shaped soldiers, although I couldn't be sure which it was. I would put a bet it would be the small surly one who liked kicking and hitting people.

'Sod off, you sad bastard,' I said. I could afford to be cocky. I was miles away from him and he didn't know where I was. 'You've been called off, so on your bike and find some little boys to attack.'

The breathing at the other end grew louder. 'When you die, it will be slow, painful and full of tearing flesh and breaking bones, all yours. I will make sure that every word you ever said comes back to haunt you. I will watch and mock as I slowly cut you into pieces.'

'Oh my goodness, I am so struck with fear at your terrifying words. Who will save me from such a ravening beast as yourself?' I said. 'Listen, arsehole. You have a personality disorder problem. You should see a psych. Too much of that funny dust on your brain from your time killing innocent people in foreign countries. You can get medicine for it now. Do that, or go suck one of your hand grenades with the pin out. Don't phone me again, or your boss will hear about it and he will practise penalty kicks on you until his leg wears out.'

'You can't hide from us,' he shouted.

I switched off the phone and dropped it through the porthole into the dark waters of the dock. I didn't need that lot phoning me and that was the best way to say goodbye to my contact with them. I wondered why he had said 'us' at the end. Was the other hillside shape annoyed too? It didn't matter. I was safely hidden and would be leaving the country in the next few days.

The strong smell of pipe tobacco woke me; a warning from my grandfather. I checked the clock, almost five o'clock in the morning. I strained to listen for any sound that might have disturbed me. Water lapped against the side of the narrowboat. A fox coughed and the echo across the water drew a response from another fox. The narrowboat was quiet. John had left with Sebastian late in the evening to take some exercise and to go for a drink. I had not heard them come back. I looked towards Ahab's bed. It was empty. I waited to hear him come back from the toilet.

A rope creaked as the narrowboat tugged against its mooring. Possibly the tide was pulling at the boat. Only, there should not be a wave movement in a dock. Someone had rocked the boat by standing on its edge and was stepping down into the cockpit, very quietly. Ahab had probably been for a walk for a breath of fresh air. I lifted a corner of the curtain to check if John was with him; his bed was empty too.

Ahab was lying spread-eagled on the dockside, his face turned towards the narrowboat. His eyes were closed. It wasn't John who was now standing on the cockpit deck gently trying the handle of the door.

I scrambled out of the bed and picked up the small club Ahab had given me to protect myself with, 'in case of piracy', he had joked when he had given it to me. I crouched in the corner beside the steps from the cockpit deck, my club ready to protect myself against whoever came down.

The door opened slowly, a foot appeared, feeling for the top step. I knew from the way I climbed into the cabin that the next move would be the appearance of the other leg. After that the intruder would bend to lower his head enough to guide him as he held onto the upper edge of the door frame to manage his descent. Once the head came through the door he would spot me and my surprise would be lost.

I pushed my club behind the two knees that now stood on the top step and pulled hard on the club, hooking the intruder off balance, tumbling him onto the cabin. I had landed several blows on his shoulders and arms when I was attacked from behind with a blow to the head that knocked me senseless. Sod it, there are two of them, I thought, as the blackness swept over me.

I opened my eyes and blinked like you do after being knocked unconscious. The pain would follow close behind. I knew the sick feeling in my stomach would go away if I kept still. I am not an expert on regaining consciousness but recently it had happened a few times too many. Someone stamping on my damaged ribs was a new addition to the list of conditions that went with this abuse of the human body. Groaning was permitted because no one paid any attention to you when you moaned in pain.

'Wake up, old man. Open your eyes for us.'

I opened one eye and turned my head towards the voice. It was one of the butcher's sons. A simple burglar would have suited me fine. The other brother must be behind me waiting for me to turn towards him. I didn't disappoint him.

He grinned at me. 'Surprise, surprise. You thought we would never find you down here. Silly old granddad, thinking such daft thoughts.'

He was sitting on the bench at the side of the cabin and he bent over me. He could do that because I was lying on the floor between them. He held my club in his hands and waved it towards my face. 'My little brother here is all in favour of bashing in your face, hanging you by the neck using piano wire and then dropping you in the dock with large stones tied around your feet. But then you did whack him with your little club. Not a nice way to welcome old friends. What do you think, granddad? What would you do?'

'I thought you were burglars. If it is down to me, I'll make a cup of tea and forget the whole business.'

He pursued his lips. 'Nope. I think not.' He pressed the end of the club against my patched-up ribs. 'What would you suggest, little brother?' he asked, ignoring my cries as

I tried to squirm from under the end of the club that was creating havoc with my damaged ribs.

His brother stamped on my injured arm. 'I'm going off all that blood that sprays around when we kill someone. It messes up my clothes. I think we should strangle him, or maybe start the engine and hang him over the back and let the propeller chop him to bits.'

'Bad for the engine,' said the club-wielding brother. 'I was thinking we might take this boat since no one seems to own it. Vandals could come along and wreck it if we abandoned it. I know, why not hold him over the side, head down and wait for him to drown?'

'Too easy,' the other one said.

'But clean, and at his age it won't take too long.'

'What about the old fella outside?' the stamping brother asked.

'Take him with us. Dump him in the river when we reach deeper water.' He turned his attention back to me. 'Your soldier friend sends his regards. He would love to be here but his boss would disapprove. However, him and his mates want their phone back. Seems they have to pay for it if you lose it. All the paperwork gets on his nerves.'

That was how they found me, I thought; bloody phone-tracking system.

'Where is it, granddad?' the club-wielder asked.

'It fell in the dock.'

'Ah, what a shame.' He paused. 'Tell you what; we'll tell your soldier friends that the phone jumped into the dock when you were not looking. You were so upset you dived in to fish it out, but somehow you were tangled up in something down there and couldn't find the phone before you unfortunately drowned. How's that sound to you?'

I closed my eyes in resignation. One time I might have retaliated but there were two of them, they had youth, strength and a club on their side and I was lying at their feet with one of them almost standing on me. 'Whatever you want,' I muttered.

They pulled me to my feet. The club-wielder led the way onto the deck. 'Tie his feet with that rope there,' he said. 'We can dangle him over the side without having to hold onto his smelly feet. Tie his hands behind his back. When he drowns we will take off the ropes and let him float away.'

'Just one more thing,' the stamping brother added.

'What's that?'

'I owe him this for attacking me,' he said, punching me hard in the side of the head so that I fell to the deck, my sense of balance shot to hell. 'Easier to tie his feet together now.'

I was conscious enough to realise they didn't lower me gently into the water. They threw me overboard. I wriggled like a fish at the end of a line as I twisted, looking for the way to the surface. I was pulled up, feet first, my head just clearing the water when I thought my lungs were about to burst from holding my breath.

They leaned over the side of the barge. 'Any sign of the phone?' one of them asked. 'See any pirate's treasure down there?' Laughing, they lowered me again. This time the strain on my lungs was acute. Hauling me up, they let me swing against the side of the barge, doing nothing to protect my bruised ribs. The next dip under would be my last.

I didn't pay attention to the noise that burst around me. My proximity to death was a distraction. All I heard was a snarl, a thud, a cry of pain and then I couldn't hear anything because I was under the water, struggling to hold on to my last bit of breath. I ignored the loud splash in the water close to me, as you do when you are drowning. My feet were being pulled towards the surface again, but this time the pulling continued until I was dragged roughly across the rail and dumped on the cockpit deck of the narrowboat. I suspected I had been rescued when I saw Ahab's son John untying me from the ropes. There again, I might have been imagining things and had woken up on the other side looking for the nearest gateway to the power of the cosmos. Sebastian licked my face. I was convinced I had been rescued.

'What kept you?' I spluttered, as if I had been expecting them all along.

John gave me the thumbs-up sign before vaulting off the narrowboat. He returned, supporting his father, who was struggling to stand upright. I pulled myself across the deck to sit with my back against the rail, my feet stretched out in front of me. John plonked his father on the seat by the tiller and smiled broadly at the pair of us. Sebastian sat up in front of me, looking pleased with himself.

Seeing the state of Ahab with his crossed eyes, bleeding from a head wound and unable to stand upright, and feeling the pain running roughshod over most parts of my body, I could only think how good it was to be alive. I grunted, managing to draw a look from one of Ahab's eyes as his other one tried to focus on the same spot. 'We should give up this lark and let the youngsters get on with it,' I said to him.

He nodded and fell off the seat to lie in a heap on the floor.

We managed to take Ahab below deck. I held the door open while John carried his dad. John cleaned and bandaged his father's head and covered him to let him sleep. Back on the cockpit deck again, I noticed one of the butcher brothers lying very still in the corner. 'What happened to him?' I asked John, making sure I was facing him when I asked the question. Through a series of gestures, actions and grunts he told me, I think, that Sebastian had taken out this one, leaping at him, knocking him unconscious as he fell backward smashing his head against the rail. John had a particularly good sound effect to describe the smacking of a head against the rail. The rather savage bite on this brother's arm that had torn off a large flap of skin and broken the bone bore testimony to the power of Sebastian's jaws when he got hold of someone.

I pointed to the body floating in the dock. John indicated himself and pantomimed punching someone and sending them tumbling backwards, catching the back of his legs against the rails and falling into the water. I flopped down on the seat by the tiller and thought the sooner I was out of this mess, the better. One body in the water drowned, another on the deck not long off joining his brother to judge by the state of him. I looked at my watch. It wasn't even six o'clock in the morning. What a way to start the day.

John hooked the body of the drowned man and I helped lift him on board by uttering encouraging words to John. He carried away the one with the fractured skull and the broken arm and laid him in a doorway where he would be found once the shops opened. We headed out into the Severn. I called the emergency services and told them we had seen an injured man on the docks as we had jogged around the quay. When they asked for information I tapped the phone complaining I was losing signal. Having been tracked once with phones, I threw the handset overboard. I could always ask for another when I was on my travels.

Once out on the Severn, we helped the drowned man carry on with his drowning by placing him carefully overboard, making sure the propeller did not catch him. I remembered the brothers saying that a body caught in the propellers caused damage to the engine. John was trying to explain to me why he had been late rescuing us but I wasn't familiar with the gestures and pantomimes he played out. I told him to wait until his father came round. In the meantime, I took Ahab's phone to make several phone calls to bring the rest of the group up to speed with the early-morning events, now safely concluded. Hopefully, I could be on my way within the next day or two, they had said. So soon, I thought. I shouldn't be still running at this time of my life.

For some reason, I remembered a bit of a poem I had learned in school about nine rows of peas, or was it beans? I didn't know if they grow peas or beans in rows in Brazil. I know they have nuts, footballers and women who walk to the sea at Ipanema. I know also it is big enough place to lose a body without anyone knowing what happened so that no blame kicks back on the ones who ordered the killing. That was assuming the light aircraft didn't disappear into the sea on the way to France. I would be happier growing beans or peas where I was.

The Final Run

Tuesday 23rd June 2015 – Oak Moon

We hid out at an overgrown mooring on the Severn for the rest of Monday. Ahab had woken mid morning with a terrible headache and a terrific hunger. We fed him and told him what had happened. He wouldn't rest easy until he checked out his barge to make sure there was no damage to it. Dead and dying bodies, bruises, cuts and severe near drowning of the living were minor considerations compared to his anxiety about his barge. He busied himself with it for the rest of the day.

The call came through on Tuesday that I was to make my way to Staverton airfield the following afternoon where a light plane would waft me away on the wings of fortune to a new and exciting adventure. That was how Cyril described it. I felt I was a kamikaze pilot waiting to take off on his final flight, except for me there was no glory in it.

Ahab guarded me all day. Maybe he felt guilty that he had let me down when the brothers almost killed me. A few times he tried chatting but gave up in the face of my silences or dismissive grunts.

That evening John went off again, this time leaving Sebastian on guard. Seeing the questions in my eyes as we watched John going off, Ahab said, 'It's his missus. He can't bear being away from her for too long. She follows him if ever we are away overnight and she stays somewhere close by. He always sees her for a few hours before coming back. That's where he went the other night. I told him to go because you were safe with me.' He tried to smile, and then he looked away from me. 'I got that wrong, didn't I?'

I cooked a simple meal and we sat on the cockpit deck watching the river and the birds. The silence grew long.

'I'd miss all this if I had to go,' Ahab said. 'A place becomes part of your life. This boat and the river are in me. I can't be more than a few miles from them.'

I had nothing to say.

He looked at me as if he was trying to see inside my mind. 'I suppose, at our age we have to ask what more is there to do? How do we balance up a few years in a place we love against a few extra years in a place we don't know?'

I squinted at him. 'What do you mean?'

'Well,' he said, 'it seems to me that everyone is telling you to do what suits them. Nobody is asking you what you want. There should be a law that everyone gets what they really want, at least once in their life.'

'There is a law like that,' I said, 'it is called the law of being true to yourself. My grandfather used to say you had to do what you thought was right, no matter what others said. That takes real courage and he saw some terrible things before he died.'

'Where did he die?' Ahab asked.

'In his own bed, with his family around him.'

'That's a good way to go.'

I nodded. A line of geese swung over the river in perfect order before dropping gracefully into the water. 'They make it look so easy, don't they?' I commented.

'It is, if you are born to it, or if you decide that is what you will do.'

I smiled at him. 'If it was only that easy.'

'What is not easy about deciding what you really want?' he asked me. He went into the cabin and on his return he handed me a small wooden box. 'Take that. If you are still here in the morning, give it back. If not, think of it as a loan. I'm off to bed. Good night, and good luck.'

I sat alone on the deck and opened the box. Inside were

six tightly rolled bundles of fifty-pound notes.

It was close to midnight before a lorry stopped to give me a lift. Having a ferocious-looking big dog walking with me dissuaded most drivers from stopping.

'Where you heading?' the lorry driver asked when we were settled in his cab.

'Heading home. An old chap once told me that following the sun would always get me home.'

'Not much sun this hour of the night.'

'It was going this way the last time I saw it.'

'Sound man he was, that old chap. My name is Huw,' the driver said.

'Welsh are you?' I asked.

'Celt yourself?' he countered.

I nodded agreement.

'Big dog you have.'

'Big *soft* dog,' I said. 'I tried to leave him but he kept following me.'

'I love dogs. Good company. What's his name?'

I thought for a moment. 'Lazarus.'

'Like the chap in the Gospel?'

'The very one,' I told him.

He grinned across at me. 'Come back from the dead did he, your dog?'

'No. He brought *me* back from the dead. We're heading off to a new life, to make good use of my resurrection.'

'You're as barmy as my nan,' he laughed. 'You'd get on with her. She comes out with all sorts of daft sayings.'

'Nans are prone to that,' I agreed.

We drove in silence, rolling through the night as we crossed the bridge into Wales. 'Where does your nan live?'

'Oh, miles from anywhere. Up the Valley Road, then

further up beyond the houses and when you think you have reached the top of the world, you have to go on further still. Even then, it is hard to find her. It's what she wants. She likes it there but she still wants to change the world. You can't do it from up here, I keep telling her, but she won't leave the place. Said she once tried to change the world but the world didn't want to be changed. She retreated up there with her dog, her spirits, to live in her forest and its flowers. She has all the peace and privacy she wants.'

'Her spirits?'

'Oh aye. Great place for the gathering of the dead before they pass over, or something like that. They wander all over the place up there, according to her. Busy as Swansea on a Saturday night, she says.'

'And nobody disturbs her?'

He laughed. 'No one could find her. If they did, they wouldn't stay long. All that quietness and living off the land would drive them mad. Probably, the dog would eat them for breakfast if they upset her.'

'How often do you go up?'

'Me? Every four or five weeks, just to make sure she is ok. Nothing wrong with her, mind you. She is fitter than me and healthier than most people I know. She says she will live for ever.'

'I bet she will, one way or another. I'd love to meet your nan,' I said.

'If it is meant to be, you will,' he said. 'Next time I see her, I'll tell her I gave you and Lazarus a lift. Mind you, she probably knows that already. She is unnerving when she reads the cards and tells us things that will happen. If you are in her cards then you will be up there one day, like it or not.'

'You might be right,' I said. 'My grandfather used to say every man has a great woman waiting for him. I never found mine.' Sebastian stirred on the floor beside me and seemed to sigh. 'I don't need a commentary from you, mister,' I said, rubbing his head.

'What's your name?' Huw asked.

'D'you have a thing about names?'

'You're in my lorry,' he said.

'Fair enough,' I answered. 'My friends call me Green Goalie. GG for short.'

'Why Green Goalie?' he asked.

'I once tried to save Ireland from scoring an own goal,' I said. 'But now I'm saving myself with a new start. I think I know how a phoenix feels when it steps out of the ashes. Where is this Valley Road you talked about?'

———————

About The Author

Ted Dunphy was born in Ireland and hit the emigrant trail at an early age when his family moved to England. He grew up and has worked in England most of his life.

He believes that small moves big and that memories are built from the tales of individuals. Without them, there is no history, no story and no meaning.

Schooled to distrust happy endings, he believes in the power of humour to upstage the stark surprises of life. His black humour is a consequence of his Celtic ancestry, his upbringing on Merseyside and his delight in tickling the underbelly of life.

In this, his second book, he draws on the characters, places and events he has lived through. Once again he is interested in the way ordinary people make when they are forced into unusual situations.

His first book, *Rowing Down the World to Auckland,* established him as a writer who combines humour with an acute observation of characters and social situations. The dark humour in his writing shines through again as he presents his characters and their efforts to be respected.

Don't Poke the Fire